# INTO THE LAND OF SHADOWS

Historical Western Romance

KRISTY MCCAFFREY

### Historical Western Romance

The Wren

The Dove

The Sparrow

The Blackbird

The Bluebird

The Songbird (Novella)

Echo of the Plains (Short Story)

The Starling

The Canary

The Nighthawk

The Swan

The Falcon

Rosemary

Alice: Bride of Rhode Island

The Crow Brothers Collection

The West: A Romance Collection

### Contemporary Western Romance

Blue Sage

The Peppermint Tree

A Mirthful Wish

***Contemporary Adventure Romance***

Deep Blue

Cold Horizon

Ancient Winds

### *Praise for Into The Land Of Shadows*

"*Into the Land of Shadows* is a must read. Kristy McCaffrey tells a story that is engaging and edge-of-the-seat gripping. Her vivid descriptions and great cast of characters, with exceptional dialogue, bring this story to life."
   ~ Cherokee, Coffee Time Romance & More

"…a haunting story with suspense, passion, and excellent character building."
   ~ Jane Bowers, Romance Reviews Today

"With a vividly painted background, engaging and compelling characters and pages that just fly by, *Into The Land Of Shadows* is a superb read for any western or historical romance lover."
   ~ Wendy, Romance Junkies

"The author's descriptions of the Arizona desert and the Indians who inhabit it are beautiful. You almost feel as if you are there. There are surprises, an element of the paranormal, which is done exceptionally well, and romance. If you love Westerns, then don't miss this one."
   ~ Linda Tonis, Paranormal Romance Guild

"…as if 'Romancing The Stone' and 'The Good, the Bad and the Ugly' and 'Dances With Wolves' got together and had a kid." ~ Armenia, Reading Alley Reviewer

"…pure entertainment—a good old-fashioned western, a romance and an adventure with a tiny bit of comedy and a good twist of paranormal thrown in. I loved it!" ~ Barnes and Noble Reviewer

Into the Land of Shadows

First edition published by Prairie Rose Publications, 2013.

Second edition published by K. McCaffrey LLC, 2021.

Cover Design: Earthly Charms – earthlycharms.com

Editor First Edition: Cheryl Pierson – prairierosepublications.com

Author Photo: Katy McCaffrey – instagram.com/katymccaffreyphoto

E-book ISBN-13: 978-1-952801-05-1

Print ISBN-13: 978-1-952801-06-8

kmccaffrey.com

kristy@kmccaffrey.com

*For my daughter Kate—*
*creative, confident, and a stubborn Irish lass in her own right.*

*And for Chaco, wolf-dog and inspiration for Bart.*
*Although he no longer walks the earth, he continues to live in the hearts of those*
*who loved him.*

# Chapter One

---

*Northern Arizona Territory*
*May 1893*

"Smells like trouble, Whiskey."

Ethan Barstow reined in his horse and the mare shook her head. From the cover of a band of pine trees, he had a clear view of a glade just below their hillside lunch break. A light breeze caressed the yellow tufts of grass and a startled coyote ran for cover in the distance.

Whiskey snorted and flattened her golden-brown ears as Ethan adjusted the brim of his hat and waited.

The distant sound of hoof beats became audible and a head bobbed into sight over the crest of the open countryside. A torso soon appeared, and then a donkey, toting the whole package and doing its best to move quickly.

Ethan frowned. It was a woman. She wore a hat with a string cinched tight to her chin. Her bouncing upper body was covered with a dark blouse and brown hair flowed behind her. She would have been a vision to behold if she hadn't been moving up and down in the saddle like a woodpecker attacking a virgin tree.

The woman's head whipped around to look behind her and Ethan followed her line of sight. Three men on horseback materialized.

"Not a fair chase," Ethan murmured.

The men drew their guns and Ethan's instincts took over—he slid his rifle from its scabbard. With a smooth motion he lined up the sight and shot one of the men's hats from his head. The man ducked and frantically looked for the shooter.

Whiskey shifted. "Easy."

One of the men, mustached, aimed his gun at the woman so Ethan shot it from his hand. The man immediately cradled his fingers and yelled something at his companions. In a flash, the other two began shooting wildly at the woman. Out of the corner of his eye, Ethan saw her fall to the ground with a thud. As the riders continued toward her, Ethan shot one man in the leg and another in the shoulder. More yelling, and they suddenly changed course, veering away from Ethan's lookout and disappearing over the hill. The gray-colored donkey had continued to run and was now out of sight.

Knowing he might not have much time before they returned, he kicked Whiskey in the side and proceeded to the motionless body of the woman. He hoped they hadn't gotten her.

Whiskey halted her long stride in a cloud of dust when they were upon the woman's body. Ethan slid from the saddle, put the rifle back in its holder, and pulled his gun instead. The woman groaned as he scanned the surrounding countryside.

Ethan kneeled beside her and pushed the hat from her face. "Are you hurt?" he asked.

Her hand came to her forehead and she moaned. "I see stars." She opened her eyes and looked straight at him.

Blue eyes. Long lashes. Rosy lips that made him lose his train of thought.

Mentally shaking himself, he glanced down the length of her. The dark blue riding skirt bunched around her knees, revealing ivory pantaloons. Further down her boot-clad feet were laced up to just below her shins. Thankfully, he saw no sign of blood on her person.

"Can you stand?" he asked. "The men chasing you could return any minute."

"Yes," she replied. "I'm fine, really." She pushed herself to a sitting position.

Ethan took her elbow and helped her to her feet, holding more tightly when she swayed. She felt petite in his hands but hardly frail.

"Head to the woods," he said with a nod toward his rest stop for lunch.

As she moved hastily for the cover of the trees, Ethan whistled sharply to his horse. Whiskey turned and followed. Ethan walked backward as he scanned the meadow and the sloping hill beyond, his gun cocked and ready at his side. Cooler air greeted them in the shade of the pine trees as Ethan urged them further back until they came to his second horse, Brandy, loaded with supplies.

"You sure you're all right?" he asked as he holstered his gun and adjusted his hat. She was looking at him again, and damn if it didn't make him fidgety.

"Yes. Thank you for your help." The woman glanced in the direction of the clearing.

The tip of her nose was reddened from the sun and her long, loose hair flowed around her in endless waves, making her appear just a bit wild. Why hadn't she bothered to put it up like most women? Ethan tried to look away but couldn't. "Why were those men chasing you?" he asked.

Her gaze swung back to his. She hesitated then planted hands on her hips. "Well, first of all," she said, clearly about to defend herself, "I did take their donkey, but they'd had the gall to steal my horse first. I don't think it was entirely wrong of me."

"You didn't think they'd come after you?"

She bit her lower lip. "Well, I hadn't planned on that. Or that donkeys are so slow."

"Are you traveling with someone? I'd be happy to backtrack your trail and get you to your group."

"Um, no, that's all right." She rubbed her forehead again. "Actually, I'm heading north," she added then sighed. "And the donkey has all my gear."

"I might be able to catch him."

"Really? I'd greatly appreciate the help. My name is Kate Kinsella." She extended her hand.

In a rush, Ethan's cursory fascination with her came crashing down around him. *Kate Kinsella.* The name of Charley's fiancée. He'd learned three days prior in Flagstaff that Charley had left town abruptly—heading north—and that his betrothed was hot on his heels. No coincidence here. And if the engagement didn't put her in off-limits territory then Ethan's history with Charley did.

He grasped her hand. "Ethan Barstow."

She froze. "What?"

Releasing her, he wondered why she appeared so stunned, her lips parted, eyes wide, and her complexion suddenly gone pale.

"I'm Charley's brother," he added.

She stepped back, and Ethan had the distinct impression she was about to run from him.

---

KATE WONDERED how far she'd get on foot before the man standing a few feet away caught her and did God-knew-what.

*Ethan Barstow.*

Of all her bad luck. She had never met the man, but Charley's recollections of his brother filled her head. *Liar. Swindler. Killer.*

"You must be Charley's fiancée," he said, watching her closely, his gaze dark.

Swell. He knew who she was.

She nodded, deciding now wasn't the time to share the truth about her and Charley's relationship.

Instinct told her she needed to ditch Mister Barstow, but losing the donkey was a bit of a problem. Maybe she could find the animal herself on foot. But what if the three buffoons who'd stolen her horse were still out there?

"I arrived in Flagstaff three days ago looking for Charley," Mister Barstow said. "I was told he'd left town unexpectedly, so I've been trailing him. I take it you don't know where he is, either?"

She cleared her throat. "No, I don't."

"Is there some reason why he wouldn't tell you where he was going?"

*Well, it's not me, but Agnes he didn't tell.* It was far too complicated to explain, least of all to this man, so she uttered, "We've had a bit of a misunderstanding."

"Yeah, Charley and I've had a bit of a misunderstanding as well," Mister Barstow said quietly, almost to himself.

Kate plastered the biggest smile she could onto her face. "I think I'll just go look for that donkey myself. I really don't want to be a bother to you."

She moved past the man who was a dead ringer for Charley, possessing the same angular cheek bones and long nose, the same dark hair, the same lean build as her fiancé. Her fiancé! What a ridiculous mess that was. There had been a time, far back in the beginning of her acquaintance with Charley, when she'd found him attractive and fun. It had been short-lived, especially once Agnes entered the picture. Now, she was face-to-face with a man much like Charley, but while his eyes had been green and his demeanor inviting, Ethan's eyes were blue, almost gray, like a lake frozen over. There were other differences, as well, and none of them flattered Mister Barstow. He was a man who had killed other men, and Kate knew she would never find anything appealing in that.

"Hang on a minute," he said. His hand wrapped around her forearm to stop her—a large, warm hand. "I don't suppose you have any idea who I am since Charley and I haven't spoken in over five years, but I came to Flagstaff to hopefully put the past in the past. I came to see if Charley and I could bury our differences. The least I can do is to help you find him, especially since we'll be kin one day."

She made the mistake of looking into his eyes. Up close, she could see flecks of gold buried within the blue, and a few wrinkles in the skin around the edges of his eyes. It must be her imagination that he seemed the slightest bit more friendly. Charley had charm and it would seem his brother did as well, although Kate sensed it wasn't without shadows.

*A killer of men would undoubtedly have many shadows to keep him company.*

She couldn't think of how to reply. The last thing she wanted was company, and least of all this man's company. She'd find her damned fiancé herself. "Yes, it would make sense to look together." *So much for thinking fast on her feet.* Her brother, Owen, had always said she was a little slow off the mark. It would seem he was right.

"You can ride Brandy." Mister Barstow released her arm. He moved to his other horse and began untying the bags of supplies he'd brought with him. He moved the largest satchel to his horse and tied several knots swiftly to anchor it in place.

Kate chewed her lip. She could just make a run for it. The only after-effect of her fall from the donkey was a splitting headache—her legs were perfectly fine. But Ethan Barstow would probably chase her down. And then, he'd wonder what was wrong with her. And then, maybe he'd just shoot her in the back if he decided she wasn't worth the trouble.

The image horrified her. Perhaps she should at least be civil to the man, to ward off her immediate murder. An opportunity for escape would surely present itself.

She had a plan. This was good. Her plan was to make small talk with Charley's brother, then run for her life when she got the chance. It was probably beneficial to wait until they had located the donkey since it was unlikely they'd find the three criminals who'd stolen her horse.

Mister Barstow stood before her. "Miss Kinsella?"

"What? Did you say something?"

"Brandy has an easy disposition. I don't think you'll have any problems with her."

"Thank you. You're very kind." *Kind! A killer who was kind.* Kate moved to the horse with a light-brown hide and a darker mane and tail. The animal really was quite magnificent-looking and an almost exact copy of the other horse. Kate swung into the saddle. "What's your horse's name?"

"Whiskey," he answered, deftly mounting the animal.

*Whiskey and Brandy.* Great, the man was a killer and possibly a drunk to boot. But the image of Mister Barstow unable to hold his liquor didn't fit neatly into the small slot she'd allocated for him in her mind.

"They're mother and daughter," he added. The horses began to move through the woods. "I've raised both of them since they were foals. They dislike being apart."

Kate couldn't relate. It had been quite some time since she'd last seen her own ma. After her ma had remarried when Kate was nine years old—just one year after her pa had been killed—Kate had never felt entirely at home again. By the time she was seventeen, the itch to strike out on her own was too much and she'd jumped at the opportunity to stay with the Finley's in Flagstaff. That Mr. and Mrs. Finley had known her pa only made her newfound independence sweeter. She loved hearing stories of a father she felt she had hardly known.

"How long have you and Charley been engaged?" Mister Barstow asked, as they broke out of the forest.

Kate squinted from the bright sunlight, the sun still shining strong although midday had come and gone. She tugged at the brim of her hat as she mentally calculated the length of the engagement in her head since it wasn't something she often thought about. "Three weeks," she answered.

Her horse moved beside the other one, and Kate's leg brushed against Mister Barstow. She tried to move Brandy just a few feet to the right, but the young mare resisted.

The man laughed, the sound startling Kate. It made him sound almost normal. "I forgot to mention that Brandy tends to stick close to Whiskey, physically close. I've never tried to break the habit."

"Wonderful," she muttered. She kicked Brandy's side and pulled to the right on the reins. Nothing. She did it again, harder. Still nothing. *Brandy, you sure are stubborn. You're never gonna grow up if you stay tied to your mama's apron strings.* Kate knew that firsthand. She'd not only left her mama, but she'd cut those strings with an ax.

After several more tries, Kate conceded defeat with the horse and tried her best to ignore the close proximity of the man beside her, despite the fact that their legs kept touching. But it wasn't a problem, she told herself. It wasn't as if she found Ethan Barstow attractive. In fact, once she hog-tied Charley and dumped him on Agnes's doorstep, she'd be glad to never hear the name *Barstow* again.

"How'd you and Charley meet?"

Kate frowned. He didn't seem in any hurry to find her donkey. "I help a woman, Mrs. Finley, run a boarding house. When Charley came to town, he boarded with us."

"How long have you and Charley known each other?"

Again, Kate had to mentally force herself to remember. "Let's see, about five months I think." When she glanced at him, she was surprised to see him looking at her with nothing short of censure on his face.

"What?" she asked. "Is there something wrong with that amount of time?"

"It seems awfully short to decide to marry."

He was right, but she didn't think it wise to agree with him on this.

She pasted a half-smile on her face and turned away. "I guess when you know, you know." That was vague. She scanned the surroundings. A pair of eagles caught a downdraft above them and began to circle in lazy spirals. "And why are you looking for Charley?"

"I guess I shouldn't be surprised he hasn't mentioned me."

*Oh, he's mentioned you.* She remembered clearly the few pointed times when Charley had talked about his family. He'd been deep in a bottle of whiskey each time and the pain and bitterness when he'd spoken of the brother who had a mean streak and had stolen everything from him after the disappearance—and likely death—of their pa had made Kate realize that the unhappiness she'd felt while with her ma and stepfather didn't compare to what other people had gone through.

"We haven't spoken in over five years," Mister Barstow continued. "I think it's been long enough, so I came to Flagstaff to try and work out our differences. But then, I learned he'd skipped town. Any idea why?"

Kate shook her head. According to Agnes, Charley didn't know about the baby she carried, so he hadn't left because of that, at least not directly.

"When do you think we'll find the donkey?" she asked, hoping to change the subject.

"We've been following its trail." He pointed out the flattened grass to their left.

"We have?" She thought he'd forgotten all about the search.

"Shouldn't be far now. I'm sure he was spooked by the gunfire."

"Did you shoot any of those men chasing me?"

"I hit two of them."

"Oh." His casual tone made her remember his reputation of having killed other men. But he'd also most likely saved her life.

"Whereabouts are you from, Mister Barstow?" she asked cheerfully, striving to hide her doubts and downright nervousness.

"I've a spread in Colorado."

"Really?" When did a desperado have time to put down roots? Charley had never spoken about this aspect of his brother.

"You look surprised."

"Well, you just don't seem like the settling-down kind of man," she replied quickly.

"A man's got to live somewhere. And by the way, you can call me Ethan."

She smiled, but she was confused. The man was quite pleasant to talk to. As she often did when she watched the night sky, she tried to connect the stars into a pattern, a picture that made sense. But connecting Ethan's individual stars didn't make a consistent picture, or at least one that made sense to her.

"Didn't Charley ever speak of his past?" he asked. "About where he grew up?"

Kate shook her head. It probably did seem odd that she didn't know much about Charley's family beyond what he'd said of his older brother, but then she hadn't been the girl Charley was sweet on.

"We grew up outside Trinidad," Ethan added.

"I lived in Trinidad for a time," Kate replied. "When I was a girl." She wondered that she and Charley had never spoken about this shared location.

Suddenly the terrain dropped away, and Kate spied the donkey off in the distance, head down. He'd finally stopped to eat.

Ethan pushed Whiskey into a gallop and Brandy soon followed, not wanting to be left behind. When they reached the donkey, the animal lifted his head and watched them while continuing to chew his meal. Kate dismounted, and after a quick survey, was relieved to see that all her gear was intact.

"How did those fellas steal your horse?" Ethan asked.

"Last night, while I was asleep."

"You're lucky they didn't do more than that."

"I suppose you're right," she agreed.

"It wasn't the smartest thing to go after them."

Ethan Barstow was lecturing her on the smartest thing to do? No doubt he would have simply killed all three of them and been done with it, for no other reason than to take their belongings. But he'd had the opportunity and didn't.

"How'd you find them?" he asked. "You were on foot, weren't you?"

"Yes. For some reason I awakened shortly after they'd completed the crime." And it was an odd reason because Kate normally slept like a log. Her mother had always complained that waking Kate was like shaking a dead person back to life. "I found them not far from my own camp. When they all went to sleep, I sneaked in and stole the donkey."

"Why not your own horse?"

"I was a little nervous," she admitted, "and good ol' Pick—that's my horse—was on the far side of their encampment. I didn't think I could get there without getting caught. Then I practically tripped over the donkey. I needed something to ride and those imbeciles certainly got the better end of the deal. Who would've thought they loved this guy so much," she said and stroked the donkey's neck. He brayed and showed his teeth, causing Kate to jump back.

*Come on, show some gratitude. You're better off with me.*

"Well," Ethan said, lifting his hat and scanning the sky, "you can ride Brandy and we'll shift the gear to him."

Kate rubbed the side of her nose. "I do appreciate all your help, but it's not necessary for you to accompany me."

"You're gonna go lookin' for Charley by yourself?"

She cleared her throat. "Well, yes, that's my intention. Actually, if you'd like to head home, I could tell Charley you're looking for him." She started to dig around in one of her saddlebags. "I have a pencil and paper in here somewhere. You could write down your address and I'll be sure to give it to Charley."

"If it's all the same to you, Miss Kinsella, I plan to continue my search. And seein' how we're both lookin' for the same thing, it only makes sense we travel together. We'll be related soon enough, and I wouldn't feel right if anything happened to you. It might be safer if we traveled together."

Kate felt slightly queasy. Having a known killer as a companion didn't seem safer to her. She'd rather take her chances with men like the ones who'd stolen her horse. As she stopped rummaging for the paper, she gave Ethan a nod and a hopefully sincere smile. She should've been an actress since she seemed to enjoy pretending so much.

"I suppose you're right," she said. But her mind raced to possible alternatives. She would have to devise a plan to escape and nightfall would be the most obvious time.

"We best keep moving," Ethan said. "Wouldn't want your new buddies to catch up with us." He proceeded to rearrange the gear so the donkey carried most of it.

Once they were mounted and on their way, Brandy moved close to Whiskey, and Kate tried once again to get the horse away from her mother and the tall man who rode with such ease and confidence.

Kate clamped down her frustration as her leg bumped Ethan's, but the constant touching didn't seem to concern him. Perhaps she should jump into his lap—it might be better than continuing to struggle with Brandy for the rest of the afternoon.

She refused to delve any deeper as to why that thought had merit. Tonight, she'd slip from camp and be well on her way before Ethan was more the wiser.

She'd find Charley, tell him Agnes carried his child and that he needed to return to her side as soon as possible, and that his brother—the killer—needed to speak with him. Once those tasks were accomplished, she'd be free of this charade once and for all.

## Chapter Two

E than placed another pine branch on the already crackling fire, the embers pulsating with an orange glow. The heat felt good against the cool night air, and the wind rustling through the trees made him homesick for Colorado.

He glanced across the fire at Miss Kinsella and wondered what made her homesick. She'd never said he could call her Kate. It shouldn't bother him, but it did.

Her nose was still buried in a book she'd dug out of her belongings earlier, and while he couldn't say she was exactly rude to him, he also couldn't say she was overly cordial, either. And for the life of him, he wasn't certain how to handle the situation.

He thought to ask her about Charley, but hesitated. He'd like to hear more about his brother, but a bit of gossip bandied around while he'd been in Flagstaff stopped him. An older woman at one of the mercantiles had shared the fact that Charley had left a broken heart or two before he'd abruptly left town. The fact his brother romanced more than his fair share of women didn't surprise Ethan—they had always come to Charley easily—but that he'd left a woman like Kate Kinsella behind *did* bother him.

Ethan would be the first to admit he didn't have a horse's sense when it came to women, but it seemed wise at this point in his acquaintance with Miss Kinsella to speak about something other than his wayward brother.

"What are you reading?" he asked. He rested an arm on a bent knee and poked a stray twig into the fire.

She looked up at him. "Astronomy."

He smiled. "So you like to watch the stars. I guess that would make you a romantic."

He noticed her frown. He'd never met a woman who disliked sharing her interests and opinions so much. Most of the women he'd known had always given him an earful.

"I've never really thought of myself as that type of woman," she replied as she placed her ribbon bookmark decorated with tiny hearts onto the page she'd been reading. She set the book aside.

*She's not Charley's type.* But he hadn't seen Charley in over five years, so he could hardly claim to know his brother anymore, let alone the type of woman he would commit to marry.

"How long have you been in Flagstaff?" he asked.

"A little over two years." She watched the flames crackling between them.

Ethan watched *her*. She'd braided and pinned her long hair at the nape of her neck, revealing a perfectly shaped oval face that reflected shadows from the fire. Long lashes concealed round eyes, and her nose sloped gently toward her lips, the lower portion fuller than the top. When she'd smiled earlier—although it had appeared forced to him—her face had taken on an entirely different aspect. She had an appeal to her, and Ethan was beginning to think she had no idea of it.

"Do you have family in town?"

"No," she answered. "My mama still lives in New Mexico."

"What about your pa?"

"He was killed when I was a child." She unpinned the hair behind her then pulled the long braid across her shoulder and began fiddling with the ends. Ethan noticed it wasn't as dark brown as he'd first thought; the firelight caught shiny glimpses of lighter strands.

"I'm sorry," he said. "How'd it happen?"

"An accident, I was told."

"How old were you?"

"Eight or nine, I think."

"So you grew up in New Mexico?"

She shook her head. "I grew up everywhere. My pa worked for the railroad, he designed them. So we went wherever his next job was. Then my mama remarried, and my stepfather dragged us into the middle of Apache country."

"I take it you didn't like it."

She thought for a moment. "No, I *did* like it. But for some reason, getting out seemed mighty important to me."

"Sounds like you wanna go back."

She chewed on her lip and finally looked at him. "I haven't been home in two years. That doesn't sound like I want to go back."

Ethan suppressed a grin. Miss Kinsella had a tartness to her, and damn if he didn't like it.

"Why have you waited five years to talk to Charley?" she asked, pointedly changing the subject.

The past hovered, a malevolent force filled with pain and regret, and Ethan wondered if it was possible to overcome it. "We had a falling out some time ago."

"About what?"

He decided to skip the part about Jessica, it being the far less painful incident although the one that ultimately created the rift of silence between them. "When our pa died, things were never the same. We parted ways soon after."

He'd sent letters to Charley over the years when he knew of his whereabouts, usually more often than not—Ethan oversaw the trust his pa had left them. Every time Charley had withdrawn money, Ethan learned his current location. But Charley had never responded to any of his overtures to repair the bitterness that had festered over the years.

"I've come to find Charley and, hopefully, fix the damage," he added. "Any idea where he might be?"

"Not really," she replied. "Word had it he'd been heading north out of town. Once or twice, he'd spoken of the Navajo Reservation. I'm guessing he's headed in that direction."

Ethan nodded. "Then we probably ought to get some sleep. I'd like to head out at first light. Can I ask a favor?"

Her face tensed. Ethan decided she'd be a terrible poker player.

"May I call you Kate?"

After the slightest hesitation, she replied. "Yes, of course."

"Then I bid you sweet dreams, Kate."

She contemplated him as if he'd lost his mind. As they bedded down, on opposite sides of the fire, he wondered if he just might have.

---

KATE BOLTED UPRIGHT AS SOON as she awoke. Her hand flew to her face to shield the bright sun from her eyes but she squinted anyway as her head began to throb. Sweat trickled down her back as she realized sunrise had come and gone. She wanted to kick herself.

She'd overslept her escape.

"Good morning," Ethan said from somewhere. She was still having trouble making heads or tails of her surroundings. "I was getting a little worried. I thought maybe that fall yesterday was worse than it looked. I was having trouble waking you."

She rubbed her eyes and saw him off to her left, tending the horses and her newly acquired donkey. He looked taller than she remembered, and cleaner. He must have shaved. She could only imagine how she appeared—she felt as if she'd been trampled by a herd of horses.

She mumbled something. God, she really wasn't at her best in the morning, but usually she didn't have an audience. She struggled to her knees and Ethan's large hand was suddenly at her elbow. He helped her to stand.

"Coffee's still warm," he said, his voice deep and surprisingly different from Charley's.

She glanced up at him and his blue-gray gaze sent a shiver down her spine, not an altogether unpleasant feeling. The lingering effect of the soap he'd obviously used earlier assaulted her nose and she was appalled that a *clean* man was all it took to intrigue her. She reminded herself she was supposed to be planning her escape. But it would be difficult if her legs continued to feel like Mrs. Finley's less-than-firm strawberry jams.

Embarrassed by her rumpled appearance, she moved away from him and toward the woods for a few moments of privacy. "Thank you," she said over her shoulder. "I'll be right back."

She could escape now. She'd slept in her clothes, including her boots. There was nothing to stop her, except her own fuzzy thoughts. It usually took the better part of an hour each morning before she could function properly. If she ran off now, she was certain she'd probably head in the wrong direction. She glanced at the San Francisco Peaks, quite visible behind her. The jagged top of the volcanic crater still had snow on the peaks. With such a beacon she could hardly get lost. She wanted to go north so she simply needed to move *away* from the sacred mountain of the Hopitu Indians. It was said the *katsinas* lived there, spiritual beings the Indians revered by carving them into wooden figures.

Kate wondered if there was a *katsina* for courage, because she seemed to be lacking that at the moment. Leaving Ethan made sense, and yet it also made sense to travel together.

When she was far enough into the woods, she turned around to make sure Ethan could no longer see her. She quickly took care of business then sat down on a fallen tree trunk and unbraided her hair. A slight breeze rustled the pine and fir trees, and Kate felt calmed by it.

Running after Charley probably wasn't the smartest thing she'd ever done. Well, there were a few others. There was the time she had tried to help a mountain lion cub when she was ten and had gotten a good scratching. The mother had been closer than Kate realized, and she'd been lucky she hadn't gotten hurt worse. Or the time she had followed her brothers into the desert and had drunk a half-filled bottle of whiskey they'd left. She'd heaved the better part of the night and had felt so awful.

But no sense ruminating over those now.

Pursuing Charley certainly didn't lack in foolhardiness. She was alone, a woman, and in the wilderness. She wasn't even quite sure in what direction she should be heading. She had hoped Charley would leave a few clues along the way to aid in the search.

With her hair loose, she ran fingers through the long tresses to smooth out the tangles, then proceeded to plait it again. The action reminded her of weaving, and a sharp longing for her looms moved through her. The repetitive work of weaving often soothed her mind and body and she would get lost in the motions, losing track of time. It suddenly occurred to her that finding Charley might take longer than a few days.

Maybe she *should* stay with Ethan. Why did a part of her warm to the idea?

She pushed that thought aside. For now, she really didn't have a choice. Perhaps by nightfall, she would feel compelled to strike out on her own again. In the meantime, she would have to watch Ethan, in case he…what? Killed her? Oddly, she didn't think he would do that.

But she was smart enough to know that wasn't a good enough reason to drop her guard. She returned to the ashen remains of their campfire, her braid bobbing behind her and her riding skirt swooshing around her legs. The horses and the donkey stood huddled together, packed and ready to go. A tin cup filled with lukewarm coffee and a cold biscuit sat on a nearby rock, which Kate quickly consumed. Ethan was nowhere to be seen.

A few minutes later, he reappeared from the opposite direction Kate had taken. He walked like a man certain of his position in life. It made her think of a blanket woven with a perfect and balanced pattern. "Thank you for the coffee and the food," she said. "Have Whiskey and Brandy adopted the donkey?"

Ethan grinned and her heart skipped a beat. She couldn't remember a man who'd had this effect on her, except maybe Charley, in the very beginning, before she'd gotten to know him, before friendship had replaced any romantic notions. This must be a peculiarity of Barstow men, plain and simple.

"He does appear to be enjoying the female companionship. Can't say as I blame him." He moved past her. "You ready to ride, Sleeping Beauty?"

"Yes," she replied and grabbed her hat. She pushed it on her head and attempted to mount Brandy while standing between the horse and the donkey. Squeezing between the two animals, she tried to get her foot into the stirrup, which proved awkward.

"C'mon you old geezer," Ethan said, and with a sharp whistle and a pull on the donkey's bridle, pulled the animal aside.

Kate hopped up onto Brandy. "Thank you."

She noticed Whiskey gave Ethan room to settle into his saddle, but Brandy immediately took position on her mama's right side.

"We could switch horses," Ethan said. "I might have better luck giving Brandy some independence."

"No, that's fine. I can handle her."

Ethan's mouth turned up slightly into an almost-smile. "Suit yourself." They moved north at a slow pace. "When did you learn to ride?"

"When I was a child. My pa taught me." When Whiskey picked up her pace, Brandy immediately matched her stride and the donkey struggled to keep up. On a sudden thought, she asked, "Do you and Charley have any other siblings?"

Ethan looked surprised. "No. Didn't the two of you discuss things like that?"

"Well, yes, but I was just making sure I hadn't missed something."

"How many do you have?"

"Two brothers. Petey is the oldest, then Owen, then me."

"They live around here?"

She shook her head. "No. They're both back in New Mexico with Mama, helping her and Jim, my stepfather, run the ranch."

"You came to Flagstaff by yourself?"

"Yes. The Finleys took me in. They had known my pa from years before. When Mr. Finley died a year ago I helped Mrs. Finley turn her home, which is quite large, into a boarding house. In exchange for cooking and cleaning, she lets me live there for free."

"What's Charley planning to do once the two of you are married?"

Kate thought she heard a note of disapproval in his voice. Uncertain how to answer the question—she and Charley had certainly never discussed the future—her mind raced for an answer. "He talked of getting some land outside of town and maybe raising sheep," she blurted out.

"I'm glad he was planning to settle down."

In a rare moment, Brandy fell a few steps behind Whiskey, and Kate's conversation with Ethan ended.

She hoped that Charley *would* settle down with Agnes, and that Agnes's family would approve, because Kate had always sensed that Charley wasn't the type to stay in one place for long. It was probably what had drawn her to him at first. Kate didn't want to settle down, either. She wanted to see the world, she wanted to live. She wanted to never be like her ma, dependent on a man.

## Chapter Three

They made good progress the remainder of the day, covering more than twenty miles. Ethan kept an eye out for the three men who had chased Kate the day before, but thankfully saw no sign of anyone, physical or otherwise. He watched the terrain for telltale markings that a person or animal had passed through in the recent past but came across nothing out of the ordinary.

By mid-afternoon, they emerged from the pine trees that had been their constant companion since leaving Flagstaff and entered terrain with less dense vegetation. Joshua trees, shorter and wider than the pines, blanketed the land. They'd have less cover tonight for camp, and with twilight approaching, the air was cooling quickly. A fire would be necessary, although under other circumstances, Ethan would have forgone one. No sense drawing unwanted attention.

But he had clearly shot two of the men. Those wounds would require attention, and that should buy him and Kate enough time to put a fair amount of distance between them and the three bastards. If they were smart, they'd realize Kate's horse was more valuable than the donkey, although in this terrain, that wasn't always true.

A blast of wind hit him in the face, and he planted a hand on his hat to keep it from flying off. It was almost dark, the sky stretching as far as the eye could see, but Ethan spied a rocky outcrop and headed toward it. Hopefully, it would offer enough of a buffer to get them through the night.

"We'll camp here," he said, and turned to see how Kate was holding up. She'd been smart enough to bring proper clothing, wearing a long duster, scarf, and rather large leather gloves.

"I'll collect wood for a fire," she said, dismounting Brandy and running off to search for branches.

Kate seemed to read his mind. Starting a fire was at the top of his list.

He untied and removed the gear on all three animals, including saddles, thinking the donkey's seemed a little heavy. He dug out a small pan and poured water from a pouch into it. The horses each drank in turn, then he offered the pan to the donkey.

"We're gonna have to name you, I think," Ethan murmured.

Kate came up behind him and dropped a handful of branches and twigs. "I already did. I'm calling him Fred."

"Fred?" He grabbed a small sack of oats and filled the pan. Whiskey and Brandy jostled one another for dinner, Brandy finally acquiescing to her mother.

"What's wrong with Fred?" Kate asked. She scratched around the donkey's ears.

"For a woman with a romantic streak, it's a little plain." Kneeling, Ethan added more oats to the pan.

"If you must know, it was my pa's name."

He glanced up at her and saw the pained expression on her face. Then it was gone.

"Fred it is," he replied, and stood.

Another blast of wind and Kate started doing a little dance, clearly cold. He would brush down the animals shortly.

"Let's get that fire going," he said, and moved toward a slab of rock. He began breaking branches on his thigh and stacking them into a pyramid.

"I'll find some kindling," Kate said, and walked back out into the darkness. "I suppose you wanted to name Fred something like Bourbon." Her voice trailed back to him on the wind.

Ethan smiled despite his fatigue from riding all day. Kate returned with an armful of underbrush and smaller twigs. Together they stacked the mass of wood and shielded the burgeoning flame with their bodies, leaning forward to blow on the kindling.

He rocked back on his heels and watched Kate's face, the delicate lines of her nose and cheeks illuminated by firelight. She was beautiful. He lifted his hat and raked a hand through his hair. *She's also Charley's fiancée.* Ethan felt like a heel for even thinking of Kate in any way other than a potential sister-in-law. Hadn't he learned anything from the havoc wreaked by Jessica? And she'd been a potential sister-in-law as well...

It appeared Ethan couldn't find a decent woman on his own. A few years back, there had been Lily, widowed with three boys. Ethan had genuinely liked her—she was warm and funny, and a good mother—but even she had felt the lack of passion between them. She'd remarried a year ago, to a rancher down by Raton Pass, and Ethan was glad for her. Although, he had to admit he missed her boys romping around his place, and he missed her homemade peach cobblers.

"Do you cook?" he asked.

Kate had pulled off her gloves and knelt before the fire warming her hands. "Why? Are you hungry?"

Ethan frowned. That wasn't the answer he'd wanted. "No, I meant do you like to cook back home?"

"I do most of the cooking for Mrs. Finley and her boarders."

"Do you have a specialty?"

"Well, everyone seems to show up for supper on Tuesday

nights. That's when I make chicken and dumplings. So I suppose that could be my specialty."

"That's one of my favorites."

"Do you have any chickens with you?" she asked. "Maybe I could make some right now."

He saw her eyes flash with amusement and a bit of a smile on her lips. Ethan laughed and scratched his jaw, the new growth on his cheeks pricking his fingers. "Can you substitute beef jerky?"

"Sure, but I think I'll only make enough for one. No offense, but I'll stick with a hard biscuit and water."

"No reason for that. I've got beans to go with that hard biscuit." Reluctantly, Ethan stood. Kate was too likable; it was probably best to put some distance between them. "You'd best stay, so we don't lose the fire."

The horses had finished their meal, so Ethan offered oats to the donkey. "Bourbon Fred it is, ol' buddy." Ethan patted him on the neck. While Fred ate, Ethan stacked the gear beside Kate. "This might help to block the wind."

She turned to help him. He hobbled the horses near a cluster of Joshua trees then brushed each in turn. He threw a blanket atop each of his ladies for good measure. He would offer his *own* blanket to the other lady in his life.

"Fred, you're on your own," Ethan muttered.

He returned to the fire, determined to ignore Kate's presence. She'd found his food supply and had opened a can of beans. She was trying to position a small cooking pot on the fire but it leaned precariously.

"I hope you don't mind, but I helped myself," she said as she used two sticks to shift the pot.

It started to topple, and Ethan snatched it with his fingers.

"Sonofabitch." He grabbed his hand back.

"Be careful."

Using her leather gloves she caught the pan before the beans were dumped on the ground. "Are you immune to fire?" she asked, a hint of accusation in her tone.

"It looked like you'd just put the pot in there," he said, squinting in the dark at his hand. "I didn't think it was that hot yet."

She stood and took his hand, her touch startling him more than the burn. "Here, let me have a look." She tugged him closer to the fire. "It doesn't appear bad. I might have some salve that would ease the sting."

Ethan couldn't see her face as she bent over his hand—she still wore her hat and it shielded her from him. All he could feel was the coolness of her fingers.

"I'll be fine." He pulled his hand from hers. "I'm gonna try putting up a tarp to shield the wind."

*And shield myself from you.*

"At least eat something first," she said. "Then, I'll help you."

He nodded. They ate in silence. To the right of the fire, they secured the tarp with rope to nearby trees, creating a small enclosure with the rock face on one side and the canvas slanted on the other.

*Hell.* It was a small space to share with her.

Kate gulped down an entire cupful of water.

"You sure you want to drink that much before bedtime?" he asked.

She poured herself another full cup from the canteen. "I'm a little thirsty." She sat cross-legged in the enclosed intimacy. The tarp shuddered loudly from a gust of wind.

As they settled themselves on a bedroll and a pile of blankets, Ethan put his back to Kate and tried to ignore her movements as she lay down. He thought of the expenses for his ranch for the upcoming month and proceeded to tally them in his head. By the time he fell asleep, he'd tallied expenditures for the next six months.

KATE STRUGGLED TO WAKE UP. She was so damned uncomfortable and was having an awful dream about being chased. Shivering, she'd bundled up behind Ethan's broad backside, automatically gravitating toward him during the few hours she had slept, his warmth drawing her close. She almost didn't want to leave, but her bladder was telling her otherwise.

There was also the fact she planned to escape from Ethan's presence. That was the reason she'd drunk all the water. She knew it would wake her up.

She paused for a moment and rested her forehead against Ethan's warm shoulder blade. She tried to remember why she was leaving him. *He's a ruthless killer.* That's what Charley had told her. It had also been clear that Charley held a lot of resentment for Ethan. But that was of no concern to her at the moment.

She needed to leave, even though Ethan had been nothing but nice to her.

*And he has broad shoulders to protect a girl from the wind.*

Kate's bladder was close to bursting. First, she would take care of business, then she'd pack up her things and head out with Fred. They should be able to get a good distance covered before sunrise.

She rubbed her arms as she left Ethan's warmth, then quickly stood and donned her duster. Her boots were still on her feet. It had been over three days since she'd removed them at all. Wrinkling her nose, she knew it was probably time to rinse out her stockings.

The wind hit her with an icy blast and her teeth chattered as she ran a few feet away from camp to do her business. As soon as she finished—she was forced to remove the coat, cumbersome as it was—she turned back, but a low growl from behind stopped her. Standing perfectly still, Kate slowly turned her head.

Yellow eyes glowed from the shadows, while another growl made Kate tremble.

*Oh God!* Her heartbeat hammered in her ears. Very carefully, she took a step forward, then another, then another, trying very hard to remain as motionless as possible.

"Ethan," she said weakly, but he probably couldn't hear her.

Another step forward. Another growl. Another glance over her shoulder showed the glowing yellow eyes hadn't moved.

Finally, Kate reached the tarp. "Ethan," she said louder. "Wake up." She kicked his foot.

"What's wrong?" His voice was muffled.

"I think there's a bear out there," she whispered urgently.

"A what?"

Suddenly, he stood before her, their bodies touching. A quick glance down showed he held a gun in his hand. As she wondered where he'd been hiding it—the only explanation was he'd been sleeping with it—he placed a hand on her shoulder.

"It's straight behind me," she whispered, face-to-face with his shoulder. "It's been growling at me."

His hand, which had been squeezing her shoulder, relaxed. "I'll check it out." He moved around her.

"Be careful!"

Ethan disappeared into the darkness. Kate strained to see where he'd gone. The wind blew intermittently, and stars filled the clear sky. Her trained eye glimpsed the long white streak of the Milky Way. Cold and worried, she shivered and hugged herself tighter.

Out of the blackness, Ethan reappeared. "It's gone," he said. "You can go back to sleep." He crawled back into their home away from home.

"Was it a bear?" She crouched down and shuffled on her knees to her side of the tarp tent.

"No."

"A mountain lion?"

"No."

"Then what?"

Ethan paused before answering which made Kate suspicious. She hadn't heard gunfire. Had he killed the creature with his bare hands? She searched him for bite marks, torn flesh, or gushing blood, or any combination of the three. No matter how afraid she'd been, she really didn't want an innocent animal killed. And to her shock, she also didn't want Ethan to be hurt.

"I'm not certain," he replied. "But it's gone now. Don't worry, Kate. I'll protect you."

"I had to kick you in the foot to wake you up." The terror she'd felt moments ago was draining from her body with a thud. It didn't make her feel very congenial.

"Well, I shook *you* this morning. I think I could have dropped you off a cliff and you wouldn't have woken up."

"I'm a heavy sleeper," she said, taken aback that he knew something so intimate about her.

"Not tonight, apparently." In the dark, she saw his outline as he pulled the blanket around him again. "You shouldn't drink so much water before bedtime."

The tarp flapped and a gust of wind blew under it. Kate shivered. Lying down, she fumbled with her blanket.

"What about the horses? And Fred? Whatever's out there might attack them."

She and Ethan faced one another in the dark. Looking at him, she wondered if his eyes were open or closed.

"I'm gonna ask you to trust me on this one, Kate. The animals will be fine. Go back to sleep."

He rolled away from her, and soon began to snore softly. Kate realized she'd forgotten to escape, but she didn't much feel like it now. Maybe tomorrow night.

On the other hand, perhaps Ethan was the lesser of two evils. He would probably be able to find Charley more easily than she could. He probably wasn't going to hurt her, or else he would have by now. Maybe his reputation wasn't as bad as Charley had said.

As her thoughts drifted and her eyelids started to close, she moved closer to Ethan's backside.

One thing was certain—being with him was warmer than being on her own.

## Chapter Four

Ethan awoke to a bundle of something wedged against his back. Glancing over his shoulder, he saw that it was Kate. She was curled up next to him sound asleep, as if they'd shared a night of—

He stopped the thought before it could go any further. He needed to get hold of his wayward thoughts. She had simply been cold, and two bodies were always warmer than one. End of story.

Carefully, he stood, trying not to wake her. He soon realized that wasn't going to be a problem. Kate was out cold. He tucked a blanket around her shoulders and indulged a very brief moment of watching her sleep. Much of her chestnut hair had been pushed in disarray from the braid meant to keep it under control, loops sticking up in various directions. She lay on her side with one hand nestled under her face. The tip of her nose was slightly pink, and her lips had an appealing rosy tinge to them. She looked peaceful and serene, and Ethan wondered what kind of dreams filled her head.

He turned from her and their far-too-cozy sleeping arrangement and set his mind on what needed to be done this morning to break camp. The sun had just broken on the horizon and the air was calm and cool, a slight fog settling around him. The whistle of sparrows could be heard in the distance, and the shuffling of squirrels or rabbits shook an occasional scrub brush.

As Ethan got to work rebuilding the fire and tending to the horses and Fred, he couldn't help but think about Kate.

He didn't doubt there were problems between her and Charley. If Ethan was smart, he'd hand-deliver Kate to his brother and then do his damnedest to make certain they worked out their differences. Maybe he and Charley could work out their differences as well. Then he'd ride back to Colorado and look forward to yearly visits from the happy couple. Eventually, he'd become an uncle…

He dropped the bag of oats and half the contents spilled into the dirt. Swearing under his breath, he scooped what he could back into the burlap sack but moved aside when Whiskey and Brandy nudged him with wet noses. They hungrily ate the pile from the ground, grinding their jaws as they chewed.

Ethan made a quick scan of the area for the wolf that was his constant shadow, but Bart had once again disappeared. He'd been close to camp last night and unfortunately Kate had stumbled across him. It seemed prudent not to mention to her that the animal was with him—no sense worrying her unnecessarily. With Bart flanking them, Ethan actually felt safer, but he doubted Miss Kinsella would agree.

With an ease born of habit, he made coffee, fresh biscuits, and bacon. Surely the aroma would awaken Kate, but she didn't budge. Fearing Bart would be drawn in by the aromatic food, Ethan took a plate full of the crisp meat and left it several hundred yards from camp.

With the most pressing chores completed, Ethan proceeded to pack the horses with everything but the tarp, the bedrolls, and the blankets that Kate softly snored upon. Glancing around he realized he had nothing left to accomplish. Not accustomed to wasting precious daylight hours, the restlessness struck immediately. He decided it was time to awaken the slumbering Miss Kinsella.

"Kate," he said softly as he ducked under the tarp and crouched beside her. "Wake up." He nudged her. Nothing. He nudged her more forcefully. She groaned and rolled away from him. "C'mon, Sleeping Beauty," he said loudly. "We'll never find Charley if you sleep late every morning." He squeezed her shoulder and she tried to swat his hand away.

"Just a little longer," she mumbled.

Fred's black and white snout suddenly appeared near Kate's head as the donkey pushed the tarp aside.

"Shoo," Ethan said and waved him off. Then he had an idea. "Wait, Fred. C'mere."

The donkey was surprisingly agreeable, and it didn't take much coaxing since the animal had obviously developed a liking for Sleeping Beauty. Ethan had to admit he wasn't the only one.

Fred licked and nuzzled Kate's cheek and Ethan cringed. She wasn't going to appreciate donkey slobber all over her. Although she tried to push Fred away, she also giggled.

"That tickles," she said. "Stop that." The laugh came from deep in her throat.

Ethan smiled and really did shoo the donkey away this time. No reason the smelly old beast should have all the fun.

Kate opened her eyes. "Blech." She wiped at the drool on her cheek. "Did you make Fred kiss me on purpose?"

"I had to do something to get you up. You obviously never make breakfast at the boarding house."

Kate sat up and tried to pat down her hair, which puffed out on both sides haphazardly. "Well, no, not usually. Mrs. Finley gave up on me after the first week she opened her doors."

"Go eat," Ethan said and with a flick of his head indicated the food he'd left on a nearby rock. "I need to pack up your bedroom."

She crawled out on her hands and knees.

With short, jerky movements he folded the blankets, rolled the bedrolls, and removed the tarp from their rocky camp.

His luck with women was worse than sludge. Ethan couldn't remember the last time he'd found happiness in a woman's arms, beyond the obvious physical satisfaction. Not that he was complaining. In fact, he was becoming quite accustomed to his life as a bachelor rancher. He came and went as he pleased, he stayed up late on Saturday night playing cards with the ranch hands, and his house reflected his own tastes and interests. What more could a man want?

*Children, for one thing.*

"Are you and Charley plannin' to have children?" He stacked the blankets and carried them over to Fred.

Kate looked up, her plate of food balanced on her knees as she sat on the rock, the edges of her dark blue skirt turning brown from resting in the dirt. She hadn't even bothered to fix her hair yet.

"We never really talked about it much," she replied around a mouthful of biscuit and bacon. After a big swallow of coffee she added, "But I've always wanted a big family."

"Yeah, me too."

"I never thought to ask, but do you have any children?"

He shook his head.

"Are you married?" she asked.

"No. Charley must not have told you much about the Barstow clan."

"No, not much."

Ethan was about to ask why when she interrupted him. "Any sign of the bear, or whatever it was, from last night?"

"No." He retrieved the tarp and bedrolls and tied them onto Whiskey. "Whatever it was must have run off." He snatched his hat where it hung on a branch and pushed it onto his head. "You about ready?"

Kate licked her fingers then wiped her mouth with the back of her hand. When she stood, she glanced around.

Ethan took the empty plate and cup. Kate definitely didn't lack an appetite. "Why don't you take a minute for yourself." He looked down at her face and the depths of her dark blue eyes.

She nodded. "Yes, I'd appreciate that."

He couldn't resist. He reached up and touched a loop of hair flopping about near her cheek. "You might want to fix your hair."

She stared at him. Ethan wished she didn't already belong to Charley. Knowing he was precariously close to crossing a line he shouldn't, he stepped back.

---

THEY RODE to the northeast and covered about fifteen miles, by Ethan's estimation, by early afternoon. The sky had looked stormy that morning, but now it seemed definite they'd get rain. Large black thunderclouds shadowed the land, and the wind blew hot and moist. Ethan had some idea of their location—they were headed toward the Little Colorado River—but finding shelter would have to be done the old-fashioned way, with eyes peeled and a lot of luck.

A flash of lightning followed by a crack of thunder startled the horses. Whiskey shook her head and stopped. Kate struggled with Brandy. Fred simply flattened his ears and stood his ground. Rain broke from the clouds and poured down in sheets.

"We need to find shelter," Ethan yelled. They both wore dusters and hats, but they couldn't stay out in this for long. "Keep moving and keep an eye out."

Kate nodded.

With water streaming off the brim of his hat, Ethan thought he spied a rider approaching. Blinking, he looked again, wondering if it was his imagination. Definitely a rider. As they drew nearer, an old man with a long beard reined in his gray horse, the animal's fur matted in clumps. Not the best kept animal Ethan had ever seen.

"Howdy," Ethan said. "We're lookin' for shelter."

"There's some Indian ruins not far behind me. You could hole up there."

"Thanks. Appreciate it. You're welcome to join us."

"Naw. Don't want to frighten your missus, but I stay clear of ruins. Ghosts and bad luck, that's the last thing I need."

Ethan nodded. "Have you seen a man by the name of Charley Barstow out this way?"

"Don't ring a bell," the elderly man replied. "There was a man the other side of the river, a few days ago. A white man with two Navajos."

"What did he look like?" Ethan asked.

"Well, a bit like you, I s'pose."

"Thanks, I appreciate the information."

The old man touched a gnarled hand on the brim of his hat and nodded toward Kate. "Miss."

Ethan kept Whiskey between the stranger and Kate. He seemed innocent enough, but it never hurt to be cautious. The man guided his horse around them and departed.

"Maybe we shouldn't go to the Indian ruins if they're haunted," Kate said as Brandy took up a close position to Whiskey.

"We'll be fine," he said. "We need to get away from this lightning more than we need to worry about a few ghosts. Let's go."

Another half-mile and Ethan caught sight of dwellings built into a rocky escarpment. He and Kate very well could have missed them had the old man not pointed a bony hand this way. They stopped before a series of rooms built beside one another, two and three-stories high, and dismounted.

"Go and see if you can find a dry room," Ethan said. "I'll get the gear."

Kate stopped and stared at him. "You want me to go into haunted Indian ruins by myself?"

Her tone surprised him. She didn't strike him as a superstitious kind of woman. He didn't know what to say.

"Give me your gun," she said.

"To shoot ghosts?" But he handed her the Colt revolver anyway.

"No," she said, grimacing as she took the weapon. "Wild animals. Surely we're not the only ones looking for shelter."

She had a point. He kept his sights on her as she weaved in and out of the ruins while he untied the gear. He threw it in a pile against the outside wall of the nearest dwelling.

Kate poked her head out of a doorway. "All dry and clear in here. We can put the animals next door, it's clear too."

Ethan nodded and led them to the other doorway while Kate grabbed the gear and tossed it into the room. Once he secured the animals, he rejoined her.

"No fire since everything's wet," she said.

"Maybe not." Ethan searched through their gear until he found some branches he'd wrapped into the tarp. He tossed the pile onto the ground.

"Are you always so prepared?" Kate asked.

"Most of the time."

He did a quick scan of the room and found a corner that might be suitable for a fire. He inspected the wall and found an outlet for the smoke. Kate moved about behind him as he stacked the wood and started a small flame.

"The storm doesn't look like it's going to let up anytime soon," she said. "Should we stay the night here?"

Ethan leaned on the ground and blew on the kindling to get the spark to ignite. "Makes sense."

Thunder rumbled, and the rain continued to fall in heavy sheets. Ethan hoped the ruins would hold, but that was an unfounded worry—they'd been here for hundreds of years already. One more night shouldn't make a difference.

With the fire going, Ethan stood and removed his wet coat and hat. Kate had already begun to organize the food and blankets. Ethan shook the tarp out and laid it onto the ground near the fire.

"We'll sleep on this," he said.

Kate put the bedrolls down and then the blankets, both still damp. Exposure to the fire would hopefully dry them out. Kate stacked the food tins and organized the remainder of their gear. She was efficient, and the two of them had settled into an easy routine with one another in no time.

"Are you hungry?" she asked.

"I can wait."

She nodded. "Me too."

Although the storm had darkened the sky considerably, it was still late afternoon. Kate found her book of astronomy and sat near the fire. A small window above her brought in some light and she started to read. Ethan checked the horses and Fred again but resigned himself to spending quiet time with Miss Kinsella. He entered their temporary living quarters and paused.

Kate looked up at him. "Would you like something to read?"

"You brought more than one book?" Ethan only packed necessities. Normally, he would whittle a piece of wood to pass the time but with the sparse supply of dry branches they had with them, that didn't seem a good idea.

"Yes." She scampered to her knees to drag her belongings over to her. She sat back on her coat, which she used as a mat, and pushed wet strands of hair from her face then shuffled through the bag. "Here it is." She handed him a book which he leaned forward to take then stepped back, putting as much distance as possible between them in the tiny enclosure they occupied.

He glanced at the title—*Pride and Prejudice* by Jane Austen.

"It's quite good," Kate said. "I think you'll like the hero, Mister Darcy. You remind me of him."

"How's that?"

"He keeps others at arm's length." She returned to reading the text in her lap while Ethan digested that observation.

He didn't reject people; it was quite the contrary—people kept leaving *him*. Ethan wasn't a complicated man and he'd be the first to admit it.

"I'm not big on reading," he said and handed the book back to her.

"Oh, all right. Wait." She shuffled in her bag again. "I think I have the latest issue of *National Geographic*. Yes, here it is."

Ethan took it and sat against the far wall to flip through the magazine.

"You can look at the pictures," she said, keeping her gaze down on her own reading material.

"Didn't your mother ever curb that smart mouth of yours?" As soon as he said it a part of him wished he could take it back.

Kate looked at him this time, the crackling sounds from the fire filling the space between them. She narrowed her eyes. "My mama told me I'd never get a husband if I sassed him the way I sassed her. But last time I looked, you weren't the Barstow I'm engaged to."

He deserved her temper, he really did.

Charley would have his hands full.

## Chapter Five

"Yá'át'ééh."

Ethan's head snapped to the doorway as Kate gasped. A figure loomed in the opening. As Ethan's eyes adjusted, he saw it was just an old man, stooped and wet. In an instant he decided not to grab his gun and instead stood to greet the visitor. Kate rose to her feet also.

"Can an old Indian warm himself by your fire?" the figure asked, still shrouded in darkness.

Ethan nodded. "Come on in." He stepped aside to let the man enter.

Kate appeared slightly confused but quickly scooped up her two books so the man could sit in her spot by the fire.

"I have traveled far," the old man said as he removed a well-worn cowboy hat and a blanket with rectangular designs on it. Underneath, he more resembled his Indian heritage, with long black and gray hair braided on both sides, a dark blue tunic, and tan trousers held in place with a colorful red sash. Several silver necklaces adorned his chest, one sporting a horseshoe-shaped piece of turquoise inlaid in silver. He wore leather moccasins on his feet, soggy from the torrential storm still going strong just beyond the walls. The man's body looked strong, but his face was etched with layers of wrinkles, telling Ethan he was far from a young man.

"There's certainly no reason to be out in a storm like this. I'm Kate Kinsella." She stepped forward and held out her hand. "It's nice to meet you."

The man gently took it and gazed up at her—he was slightly shorter—and smiled. "This rain is good. It has been dry in our land. You have the touch of the wind."

Kate glanced at Ethan. "Are you Navajo?" she asked. "You speak very good English."

The elderly Indian nodded. "I am called Joe Tohonnie."

"That's your Indian name?" Kate asked.

He shook his head. "No. But you can call me Joe."

"This is Ethan Barstow," Kate said.

Ethan shook Joe's hand and wondered why it felt like feathers fluttering across his palm.

"And you have the touch of the land," Joe said.

Ethan saw that Joe's eyes were dark and colorless, not instilling fear, but definitely a feeling of otherworldliness. Ethan decided the man they'd run into earlier was simply filling his head with spooks.

Ethan stepped back. "Please sit and warm yourself."

Joe sat down, cross-legged, and sighed. "It is good to rest. Do you both travel to *Diné Bikéyah*?"

"Pardon?" Kate asked as she settled beside him.

"You call us the Navajo, but we called ourselves *Diné*. *Diné Bikéyah* is the land we call our home."

Ethan stood to the left of Joe and leaned against a wall that had been around a lot longer than any of them had.

"We're not sure," Kate replied. "We're looking for a man named Charley Barstow. Might you have seen him recently? Ethan is Charley's brother, and they look a lot alike."

Joe angled his head to look up at Ethan. "Your brother rides an unsteady wind. Even the birds stay away."

"So you've seen him?" Ethan asked.

Joe shook his head. "No. I've come looking for you."

A unwanted chill ran down Ethan's spine as Kate sat up straighter.

"Have the two of you met before?" she asked.

"I've never been this far south," Ethan answered. "And I'm afraid I don't recall ever meeting you," he said to Joe.

"Many winters ago, I know your father," Joe said.

"How so?" Ethan asked.

"He was hunting in *Diné Bikéyah*. A bear take the advantage of him and your father lay bleeding. I find him. I heal him."

The chill from Ethan's spine spread to his gut. His pa had spoken once of a bear attack, but he'd never mentioned an Indian named Joe.

"He tell me of his two sons," Joe said. "There was great love in his voice and in his eyes. His wife was gone, and in his sons, she still lived."

Ethan swallowed past the sudden constriction in his throat and inhaled the pungent aroma of burning juniper from the fire.

"What happened to your mother, Ethan?" Kate asked softly.

He looked at her and felt disoriented. Hadn't Charley told her anything? Hadn't she cared enough to ask?

"She died when I was five and Charley was two. She'd been very sick." He and Charley and his pa had been cast adrift without the anchor of Emily Barstow.

"I'm sorry," Kate replied, an unexpected compassion in her gaze. "Charley so rarely spoke of his family. I had no idea."

"The Bear was a man who had lost his touchstone," Joe said. "For some men, the woman of their heart keeps it pumping strong, and when that woman is no longer in this life, the spirit dwindles to nothing."

"The Bear?" Kate asked.

"Calder Barstow, Ethan's father."

Ethan stared down at Joe. That this old Indian had known his pa was farfetched enough, but that he'd found Ethan and Kate camped in these ruins during a rainstorm stretched credibility to the extreme.

"What the hell are you doing here?" Ethan said, not even sure he'd spoken the words aloud.

"Sometimes the spirits will breathe the presence of those we wish to see again."

"I've never met you."

"Then, you do not remember." Joe gazed into the flames. "You were a boy becoming a man, and The Bear had taken you on a journey to spread your wings."

Ethan stared in disbelief at Joe Tohonnie.

"You shot a wolf, but he was not dead. The Bear told you to finish it, but you could not. You tried to remove the bullet so that you could save the animal."

"*K'aayelii*," Ethan uttered, barely comprehending the man's presence.

Joe nodded with approval.

"I don't understand." Kate looked from Ethan to the old Indian. "You were with Ethan when he tried to save the wolf?"

Joe silently agreed, and his midnight eyes moved to Ethan. "We could not save the wolf, but the animal's spirit clings to you yet."

"You called me…something," Ethan said, still trying to find the images in his memory. It had been years since he'd thought of that incident.

"He Who Walks With Shadows."

Ethan acknowledged the name like an old friend. "I'm sorry, K'aayelii, that I didn't remember you." *Nothing like ripping open the past to bring forth emotions thought long forgotten.*

"But you didn't," Joe replied. "Not really."

"This is an amazing coincidence," Kate said to Joe, "you finding us here."

"White man speak of coincidence," K'aayelii said. "There is no mystery. I was looking for you, and now I have found you." He stared directly at Kate.

She shifted where she sat, clearly uncomfortable from the scrutiny. But Ethan had learned in a very short time that Kate never shied from speaking her mind.

"You've been looking for *me*?" she asked, a short laugh conveying her bewilderment. "I *know* we've never met. This is the first time I've ever been this close to the land of the Navajo."

"But you are the wind," Joe said. "You've never stayed in one place for long."

Kate paused. When she glanced at Ethan, he noticed a spark— a flash—of impatience. She didn't like insights into herself any more than he had. He gave her a slight shrug in sympathy.

"I don't mean to be rude, Mister Tohonnie, but I'm here to find Charley Barstow," she said. "He's run off and I need to find him. We were to be married."

It was the *were* that stuck in Ethan's mind. Did that mean she meant to call off the engagement? If that were the case, and Charley suspected Ethan had had anything to do with it, Ethan was certain his relationship with his brother would be beyond repair.

"You are the wind chasing the wind," Joe said. "And you are the key to The Bears' sons. You are the touchstone. I am tired now." Joe took a deep breath. "I would like to rest."

Ethan offered Joe some food but the old man refused. He lay down on the blankets near the fire and soon slept. Kate lay down also, looking weary. Ethan's gaze met hers and she acknowledged him with a half-smile as her eyes closed.

Ethan settled in the corner opposite the fire and closer to the horses. He hadn't thought about the incident with the wolf in a long time. He'd been fourteen years old and his pa had taken him into the wilderness, to spend time together, to have an adventure, to become a man. They'd traveled by horse west of Trinidad, into terrain that was wide and barren. Ethan had taken to it immediately. The desolation offered solace, the endless expanse the closest he'd ever felt to the idea of God and Heaven. He'd had the thought that his ma was here—in the turquoise sky, in the white, fluffy clouds tinged with gray, in the bright sun and the whispering wind. After several days they'd encountered K'aayelii—Joe Tohonnie—who had then ridden with them. Joe and his pa seemed to have a friendly and respectful relationship, surprising Ethan that his pa even knew an Indian. It impressed Ethan.

They'd been away for days when one morning, in the pre-dawn light, a wolf flanked their camp. Ethan saw him, his white-black fur barely visible, yellow eyes watching intently from behind the oak shrubs where the animal hid.

Ethan had grabbed his Winchester for protection. Then it all happened so fast. The wolf lunged forward. Ethan fired the rifle. The animal fell.

As Ethan approached, the wolf still breathed, blood oozing over his magnificent hide.

"I'm sorry." He dropped to his knees beside the animal.

"You need to finish it, Ethan," his pa said from behind him.

In that instant, Ethan knew he couldn't and gave a slight shake of his head. He moved his hands onto the animal, shushing him when the wolf jerked in response, and began to search for the entry wound. He would remove the bullet and try to help the creature. Joe kneeled beside him and together they tried to save the animal's life.

But it wasn't to be. Later that day, the wolf passed.

As Ethan drifted off to sleep, he saw his father and K'aayelii and the wolf, and remembered how sad, how empty, he'd felt when the imposing animal had died in his arms. His pa had never said anything, had simply let Ethan be, respecting what had occurred without judgment.

---

KATE CAME AWAKE WITH A START. She'd been dreaming of her pa and the time they had spent in Colorado when she was a little girl.

Her pa had helped build the rail that ran through Raton Pass and Kate had lived in Trinidad with her ma and her brothers. She was just a little girl, only four or five, but there had been a boy in town that walked with the wolves…

Kate shook off the memory. Old Joe had certainly filled her head with images that had transferred to her dreams. It was pitch black—the fire had long since died—and a deafening quiet filled the air. The storm had stopped, and Kate pulled a blanket around her to shield the cold night air. With her eyes adjusted to the darkness, she finally noticed the empty spot by the fire.

Joe was gone.

Kate scrambled to her feet and looked everywhere, but there was no sign of him. Ethan slept in the far corner, his broad shoulders barely noticeable in the darkness. Kate tiptoed around the small room then peeked into the other one that served as the horse stall—Whiskey and Brandy had both kneeled to the ground, Brandy resting her head on her mama's flank. Kate paused a moment and watched them. They were so peaceful in one another's company, and it squeezed Kate's heart, making her think of her own mama. Fred stood just beyond the inseparable equines, head down.

Kate moved outside. "Joe," she whispered loudly. "Mister Tohonnie? Are you all right?"

The storm clouds were gone and a sky full of stars greeted her. She leaned her head back and beheld the incredible view. It was breathtaking.

Where had Joe disappeared to? She should awaken Ethan but decided against it. At some point yesterday, she had determined not to escape, and now she felt oddly protective of Ethan Barstow, acknowledging a strong need to let him rest and regain his strength. Charley had never told her what had happened to his ma, but watching Ethan's face when *he* told her had nearly broken her heart.

When had she begun to care so much about Ethan's state of

mind? She hardly knew him and would likely not know him for much longer. Once they found Charley, she would handle everything, then move on. After that, she would never see Barstow again.

She watched the stars, little pin pricks against the God-blackened sky. Joe had called her a touchstone but that wasn't true. When things closed in, Kate moved on.

*I'm the wind.*

Joe had gotten that part right.

Kate returned to the room she and Ethan occupied. Joe must have left, impatient to keep going once the storm had abated. Hadn't he said he was looking for them? Obviously, once he found what he was searching for, he moved on as well. She went to Ethan and laid a blanket over him. He hadn't bothered to grab one, leaving the pile for her and Joe.

She knelt beside him, his face turned away from her. She thought of what Charley had told her of his brother. It hadn't been good, or at least, it hadn't *sounded* good. Kate couldn't remember all of it now, except that her opinion of Ethan Barstow had not been high. However, he didn't appear all that menacing now, especially asleep. And God knew that Charley had lived up to far less than her expectations. So, maybe it was possible that Ethan wasn't as bad as Charley had portrayed him to be.

Kate tucked the blanket around Ethan's shoulder and lay back down on her own bed. She said a prayer for Joe Tohonnie, wherever he might be, and a prayer for Ethan's mother. She was, no doubt, the true touchstone.

## Chapter Six

"Where'd he go?" Ethan asked.

Kate shrugged. Ethan had shaken her awake just a few moments earlier. She yawned and wondered if she could make coffee while still half-asleep. Usually, Ethan had coffee and breakfast waiting for her—he was spoiling her and she was beginning to become accustomed to it.

"When I woke up the storm had stopped," she said, crawling on her knees to the pile of gear against the wall. She started rummaging for the coffeepot. "Joe must be a night owl. He must've decided to move on."

Ethan stood in the doorway, bright sunlight framing his outline. Out of the corner of her eye Kate saw him shake his head. "He did it when I was fourteen, too," he said. "When the wolf died, he stayed in camp with me and my pa, but by morning he was gone."

Kate's fingers touched the cold metal of a pot. She grinned and pulled it out. Her smile faded—it was a cook pan. She set it aside and pushed her fingers back into the bag. "Don't you think it was strange he found us at all?" she asked.

The coffeepot peeked out of the bag and Kate sighed with relief. She was halfway to breakfast. Now, she needed to locate the tin of coffee grinds. She crawled to the knapsack that held most of the food supplies and grabbed the metal container of grinds along with the coffeepot, and then shuffled upright on her knees over to the fire.

She would have coffee yet. Ethan's arms suddenly came around her and he gripped the tin with one large hand and lifted it from her. He hovered so close that she felt his heat down the length of her back. Her breath caught and her heart skipped a beat, a response rarely elicited from the nearness of any man. Certainly not with Charley. Maybe not anyone.

"Boiled flour won't taste very good." His voice caused an involuntary shiver down her toasty backside. Then he was gone, and her senses crashed back to earth. He took the coffeepot from her. "I'll make it," he said, and began accomplishing the deed with precise speed.

"The tins all look alike," she said as she sat back on her heels. Stealing glances at Ethan as he started a fire, she was stunned by an immediate revelation—she found him compelling. She found him intriguing. She found him attractive.

*Oh no.*

Kate tried to focus her thoughts. Being drawn to Ethan was the stupidest thing she could possibly do.

Ethan laughed. "I've never met a woman more useless in the morning."

Did he just insult her?

"I'm slow, that's all," she said then realized she wasn't bettering her case. "Slow to wake up," she amended.

"You asked if it was strange that Joe had found us, and yes, I think so, too." Ethan stoked the new flame licking at the wood with more kindling. "But the incident with the wolf was strange as well." He poured water into the coffeepot then sifted grinds from the tin into the pot and pushed the lid on tight. "I really hadn't thought of it in years." He positioned the pot into a niche between the burning pieces of wood.

"Why did you shoot the wolf in the first place?"

Ethan ran a hand through his hair and rubbed the back of his neck. He rested a forearm on one knee as he considered her question, and for the first time, Kate took notice of the differences between Charley and Ethan. While they both had dark hair, Ethan's curled at the nape of his neck with a texture that made her suddenly want to touch it. She gripped her hands together in response. *Oh no.*

Charley was tall and lean, as was Ethan, but Ethan had wider shoulders and a broader chest, a face slightly more chiseled, a narrower nose, and eyes that carried more depth.

"He came at the camp," he said. "I just reacted. But after...I immediately regretted it. My pa wanted me to end the animal's suffering, but I couldn't do it, so I tried to remove the bullet. Joe helped me, but we couldn't save him. He died later that day."

"That must've been hard. Why did Joe say wolf spirit still clings to you?"

"From that time on, I seemed to have an affinity for the animals."

Kate thought of the boy in Trinidad, the one who'd been talked about by the other children, not always kindly. Wolf-boy. The one who talks to wolves. Could it have been Ethan? Had their paths crossed years before? Strange...

"You doin' all right?" Ethan asked. "You look a little pale."

"This journey has been more than I bargained for," she replied truthfully. Kate had honestly believed it would take her an afternoon to find Charley and bring him back to Agnes. If she had known she'd be here, three days later, with a man she hardly knew after having her horse stolen and men chasing her and shooting at her.... She frowned, surprising herself when she realized she just might have come anyway.

"I'd have to agree with you on that one, Kate."

They ate, cleaned up, and packed the horses and Fred. The Little Colorado River beckoned in the distance, and once again

Kate contemplated fleeing Ethan Barstow. For some reason, she knew that once they crossed the path of water carving its way through the rocky landscape, there would be no turning back. But she couldn't seem to muster up the energy to engage an escape plan. Her fate was sealed.

Joe had told her she was the wind, but for now, the wind was content to stay right where it was.

They rode to the east and Kate used her hat to shield the sun from her eyes. Brandy was in fine form, keeping pace with Whiskey, and Kate wondered how Ethan could ignore the fact that their legs bumped against the other at least fifteen times in the course of a mile.

They crossed the flat landscape and made for the shimmering thread winding its way in the distance—the Little Colorado. Scrubs and mesquites dotted their path, and they descended from a plateau to the main water source in the area. As they neared, Kate could hear rushing water. The horses slowed their gait, and a waterfall came into view.

Water poured off the edge of a mesa, crashing down at least two hundred feet. White foam shot droplets into the air and sunlight reflected an array of colors into the mist. Dew settled on Kate's skin.

"Did you know about this?" she asked.

Ethan shook his head. He pulled a map out although it didn't appear very detailed to Kate.

"There is mention of a fall," he said, raising his voice so she could hear him. "But I'd imagine the rain yesterday did this. It'll probably dissipate in a day or two."

Kate watched the cascade of water. The sound of the crashing mass reverberated in her bones and made her feel strangely connected to the land. The pull was almost hypnotic.

"So, we wait here until it dries up?" she asked.

"No. Let's head upstream and look for a crossing." He put the map back into his saddlebag and shifted his gaze to something in the distance. "That doesn't look good."

Kate looked over her shoulder. Three riders approached, some distance away. Kate turned Brandy so she could have a better look. Whiskey moved so close to her daughter that Ethan's shoulder bumped Kate's from behind.

"That couldn't possibly be them, could it?" she asked. Appalled that the three men who had stolen her horse were still after her, and trying her best to act as if she bumped shoulders with men she found compelling every day, she made a decision right then and there. "I'm not giving up Fred."

"Then move it, Kinsella." Ethan pushed Whiskey into a gallop.

They rode the horses, Fred tied behind Whiskey and moving at a good clip, up a rocky incline, climbing above the waterfall to their left. They moved fast, riding parallel to the river. The waterway was wide and although it didn't look deep, Kate had no desire to cross so close to the waterfall. A sickening feeling of falling swept over her at the thought of plunging over the mesa.

Ethan kept pushing forward and Kate thankfully had to do very little to keep Brandy on pace with him. Kate chanced a glance over her right shoulder—the riders were moving at a faster clip. Ethan pulled his gun.

"What are you doing?" she demanded, jolted with panic. She was between Ethan and the men chasing them; was he going to shoot her?

He slowed Whiskey just a bit but didn't take a shot. "Get on the other side of me," he yelled.

Kate pushed Brandy ahead and to the left. Ethan protected her on one side while the river threatened to swallow her and Brandy up on the other.

The three riders gained on them and the sound of gunfire made Kate's heart slam into her chest.

"Ride low, Kate," Ethan commanded. He shot several times in

succession and the three riders were forced to scatter. "We need to cross. Look for a low spot."

Kate started searching the shoreline. They'd moved about a quarter-mile upriver from the waterfall so the current should have lessened but Kate really didn't want to test that theory.

"I don't know," she said. "It all looks pretty much the same."

"Then let's go. Remember to hold tight to Brandy, especially if it gets too deep."

Kate's mouth went dry as she turned her horse to the left and splashed into the muddy waters. It wasn't deep and Brandy moved swiftly. The horse jostled Kate up and down as the water rose to Brandy's belly, and Kate's boots got wet. Brandy started to slow, fighting the current, and Kate saw Ethan, Whiskey, and Fred still on the shoreline. She swung her head around to look over her other shoulder. One of their assailants closed in, and Kate panicked. She should do something. She tried to turn Brandy around, but the horse resisted.

"Of all the times to become independent," Kate growled. "Go back to mama, Brandy." The horse stayed the course.

Kate searched the shoreline again. Ethan had dismounted and shooed Whiskey and Fred into the river. The two animals moved toward her, kicking up a flurry of water. Brandy wouldn't turn around so all Kate could do was wait for them to catch up. She watched with mounting concern as Ethan took cover behind a scrub brush with a gun in one hand and a rifle in the other. Enemy number one took aim at Kate. Ethan opened fire as Kate fell off Brandy's back and into the water.

The current pulled her feet from under her and she frantically tried to hold onto something but lost her grip on Brandy's saddle. She moved down river with surprising speed. It wasn't deep, but her feet slipped repeatedly every time she tried to dig her heels into the soft bottom. Her hat bobbed behind her, pulling the drawstring against her neck. She choked as much from that as from the water splashing onto her face, into her mouth, and up her nose.

*I have to stop*. She'd fly off the waterfall any second. Her arms flailed to find anything. She tried to swim against the current, stroking with one arm then another but gasped for breath.

Her foot caught on a spindly branch protruding from the swirling fluid, and she jerked to a stop. Grabbing the smooth wood with both hands, she prayed it would hold. She was able to partially stand, with the water just below her breasts, but the strong current made it impossible to move. She must be close to the waterfall.

*Help! Help me!*

In the distance she heard a voice. "Kate. Kate!"

"Ethan!" She hoped he could hear her. "Ethan! Over here!"

She searched for him on the western bank.

"Kate!"

He was behind her atop Whiskey. Brandy and Fred were with him, as unhappy as Kate if their agitation was any indication.

"Hang on," he yelled. "I'm gonna get you."

He detached a circle of rope from Whiskey's saddle, unwound it then positioned himself partially in the water.

"I'm gonna throw you the rope! Grab onto it!"

She nodded, although she doubted he could see her response. Her hands felt slippery on the thin wood she grasped, and her breathing came in short, rapid bursts.

Ethan spun the rope above his head and cast it upriver from her. The current brought it to her, and she reached out to grab it as it floated by, but she missed it by inches. She spun around her wooden anchor and almost lost her grip entirely. In a panic she struggled to grab back on, screaming and crying.

"Katie! Honey, look at me," Ethan said.

Her back was to him now, and she was terrified to move. "I can't, I can't," she chanted to herself. If she yelled, the force of her voice might dislodge her from the only thing keeping her from rushing over the waterfall.

*Get hold of yourself, Kate*. But she couldn't. Her arms were paralyzed, and she could hardly breathe. She needed to grab the rope again when Ethan tossed it to her, needed to extend one hand from the safety of her barely-there tree. *Move your arm.* She closed her eyes and prayed for courage as a sob escaped. She couldn't bring herself to let go. As long as she held on, she survived. If she let go, the water could push her from her only anchor. She squeezed her eyes shut again.

Her mama flashed through her mind. She hadn't spoken to her in two years, had barely corresponded via letters, and now she would die and there would be no more opportunities. "I'm sorry, I'm sorry," she chanted. But her mama couldn't hear her. Neither could Owen or Petey. Or Mrs. Finley. She'd die, and she was only twenty years old.

"Katie! Look at me." Ethan's voice was louder, closer.

She lifted her gaze, trembling so much the hair hanging in her face shook. Ethan was in the water, coming toward her.

"What are you doing?" she cried. "I can't grab you."

With broad strokes, he moved toward her from upriver, and within seconds was upon her. The current brought him to her quickly and as he wrapped his arms around her, the protruding branch snapped. Kate screamed and then was yanked back. Ethan held her, something held Ethan, and they weren't going anywhere.

Kate struggled to keep her head above water. Ethan pulled her to him, and she clung to his neck, holding on for dear life.

"Grab hold of the rope," he said, his face near hers. "In case the knot doesn't hold."

He shifted her on his hip, and she reached out to grab the lifeline. Her fingers felt so weak she had trouble holding on. Ethan let out a sharp whistle and Kate winced. Whiskey was on shore, a rope knotted on the horn and wound around her flank several times. The horse leaned hard, digging her hooves into the dirt, and started moving upriver, and Kate and Ethan slowly began shifting in the same direction.

"Oh, my God," she said. "We'll pull her in, Ethan."

"Let's make sure we don't," he replied, heaving.

He was trying to dig his feet into the sandy bottom to help Whiskey in any way he could, so Kate shifted and tried to do the same. But her strength was gone, and her feet were pushed into Ethan's legs.

"Just hold on, will you?" he said through clenched teeth.

So Kate gripped the rope with one hand and wrapped her other arm around Ethan's neck, burying her face against him as Whiskey slowly pulled them from the river. When the pressure lessened, and they were finally free from the current, Ethan lifted her from the water and carried her to shore. He dropped her to the ground then sat himself, breathing heavily. Kate pushed a clump of hair from her face.

"I can't believe," she said, pausing for several short breaths, "that Whiskey did that."

Ethan glanced at his horse. "Neither the hell can I."

## Chapter Seven

E than took a hot biscuit from the pan and shuffled it from hand to hand before tossing it into Kate's lap. It was well past sunset, and they had ridden farther than was probably wise, considering Kate's condition, but Ethan wanted to make sure they lost the three riders who had pushed them across the river too soon in the first place.

Kate gingerly broke off a piece of biscuit and ate. She sat cross-legged before the fire, a blanket wrapped around her. He knew she wore little underneath—he'd had to help disrobe her once they'd finally stopped—but it was more than her state of undress that had him distracted. She could have died today, and the thought didn't sit well with him.

He probably shouldn't have started a fire, but he decided to risk it. Kate was pale and trembling, and she needed food and warmth. Ethan poured coffee into a cup then moved to sit beside her.

"Drink this," he said and put the cup in her hands. They shook enough that he had to help her take a sip.

"Thank you," she said, and when she looked at him, her eyes filled with tears.

He set the coffee to the side then took her hands into his. "Take some deep breaths, Katie. Everything's fine now." Ethan would have to deal with his own reaction at some point, but for now Kate needed him, so he pushed his own fears to the background.

She smiled through her tears. "No one calls me Katie," she said. "Just my pa."

"It's a shame I'll never meet him," Ethan responded truthfully.

She stifled a sob. "I miss him so much sometimes." The tears poured from her eyes now. "I don't think I've ever gotten over losing him. And in my anger, I pushed my mama and my brothers away. I've really messed things up with them. And I could've been swept over the waterfall and killed, and it's been forever since I told my mama I loved her." She tried to catch her breath and hiccupped.

Ethan put an arm around her although he felt awkward. He shouldn't touch her, but anyone sitting beside her would be hard-pressed not to offer comfort. And that was all he was doing, he reminded himself.

"You've got a chance to make amends," he said over the top of her head. "Sometimes we all have to ask forgiveness from the people we love." He thought of his relationship with Charley. "We have to make the effort, even if it's the hardest thing we've ever had to do."

She nodded and her hair brushed against his chin. She sniffed and wiped her nose with the back of her hand. She fit very nicely into the crook of his arm. Ethan needed to escape so pulled back and tried not to memorize the feel of her against him—warm and soft and comfortable. He moved to the opposite side of the fire.

"What happened to the men chasing us?" she asked. She wiped her eyes and adjusted the blanket around her more tightly.

"The one who got the closest must have been the one I didn't shoot before." He squatted and threw another branch onto their small campfire. Sparks flew into the air and Ethan was grateful they had clear skies tonight.

"What did you do?"

"I shot him." Her eyes fixated on him. It was the same reaction she'd had a few days ago when he'd introduced himself to her, when he'd had the feeling she was about to run from him.

"You shot him in cold blood?" she asked.

Ethan frowned. "No. He shot at you and then you fell from Brandy and were swept into the river. I thought you might've taken a hit. So I blew his shoulder out, threw his gun into the water, and raced across the river to help you."

The firelight danced across her features, illuminating her smooth skin and blue eyes. For a moment, Ethan's chest squeezed, and he couldn't breathe. Kate Kinsella called to something deep inside him and he couldn't explain it, couldn't understand it; he could only be bowled over by it.

"Oh," she said. "It was very noble of you to stay behind and protect me. Thank you."

But he had the distinct impression that Kate wasn't being entirely sincere. It didn't really bother him—he hadn't defended her because he expected recognition or thanks—but he was confused.

"I promise I'll do my best to look after you," he said. "I'd hope Charley would do the same with the woman I planned to marry."

"Is there someone…." Her voice faltered.

"To marry?" he asked. He shook his head. "Never found the right one."

"I could never understand how my ma could marry another man after my pa died."

"Was her new husband unkind?"

"No. Jim is a good, hard-working man. I just think his expectations for life have always been a little high, and I disliked living with him being disappointed all the time. It made me… anxious."

"Why was that?"

"I guess I felt responsible. That it was somehow all our faults, this new family he had suddenly adopted. I just wanted my pa back and no one could ease that pain. Least of all my mama."

"It must have been hard on her, widowed with three children," Ethan said. "You can hardly blame her for remarrying." He thought of Lily and her three boys. Maybe Ethan should have married her. But if he had he wouldn't be sitting here with Kate, and, despite everything, he didn't want to be anywhere else at the moment.

"I suppose you're right," she agreed. "Did your pa ever remarry?"

"No. Losing my ma pretty much broke him. He never found anyone else. He died about seven years ago. I stayed on to run the ranch and oversee the trust. That's how I tracked down Charley's whereabouts, through the trust."

"Charley has a trust?" Kate asked in surprise.

Ethan scratched his cheek. Charley's track-record with women was deplorable. Obviously, he didn't believe in an open and honest relationship, and Ethan teetered on the edge of telling Kate to forget his brother and get clear while she still could. But he had no business doing that kind of meddling, especially since under normal circumstances Ethan would have likely courted Kate himself with everything he had to offer. She was a woman worthy of some effort. And *effort* had always been a foreign word to Charley.

"Yeah, Kate." Ethan sighed. "I hope you haven't already given Charley your life savings."

Her silence was evidence enough and Ethan knew he'd give Charley an earful when he found him. "I'll pay back every cent. How much?"

"Why would you do that?" she asked. "It wasn't your doing."

"Maybe not, but I run Barstow Enterprises now and Charley's a part of that, poor reflection that he might be at times. We don't take advantage of innocent women. How much, Kate?"

"Charley said he'd get it back."

Ethan rested a forearm on his knee. There were times in the past few years when he'd honestly missed his little brother. But this wasn't one of them. "I'll let it drop for now. When we find Charley, we'll square everything up. Alright?"

Kate nodded in silence.

Ethan almost asked why.

Why would Kate agree to marry Charley? She was intelligent and funny and pretty all the way down to her toes. There had to have been a whole line of men waiting to catch her eye, and while Ethan knew Charley shone with a light all his own, he also thought Kate would have been smart enough to see through it.

But he didn't ask. It was none of his business, just as the feelings of warmth and protectiveness he was beginning to feel for her were none of his business. And desire…he needed to steer clear of such foolishness.

"You should get some rest," he said. "I'll keep watch for a while."

Her eyes grew wide. "You think those men are still behind us?"

"I doubt it, so don't worry. The sorry ass—," he cleared his throat. "The one I shot will have some cleaning up to do on that shoulder. If we're lucky, infection will set in on all three of them and if their limbs don't start falling off, they might just keel over dead."

Kate's expression was unreadable, but she appeared a bit stunned. Ethan realized his description of their assailant's fate was a little gruesome, but he wouldn't take it back. That was the second time they'd tried to kill her, and that didn't sit well with Ethan. Not at all.

Kate lay down and pulled another blanket over herself. "Goodnight, then."

"'Night, Katie." He could at least indulge himself a nickname with her. She tucked a hand under her cheek and closed her eyes. Ethan watched her and felt glad she lived.

KATE SURFACED FROM SLEEP SLOWLY. Her dreams had been full of rushing water and sadness over the estrangement from her mother. But in the midst of it had been Ethan's strong arms, holding tight, an anchor that hadn't disappointed her. Yet. She opened her eyes and saw that he'd already been up, made breakfast, and packed as much of the camp that she wasn't lying upon. If nothing else, he was efficient.

He had offered to repay the money Charley had borrowed from her, an unexpected surprise. She wasn't a total fool, or at least, she wanted to think she wasn't. She'd known there was a chance Charley might never get that money back to her. But his enthusiasm to make a life for him and Agnes had swayed her, so she'd offered to help. He'd needed money for an investment, something to do with a mine in Navajo Territory, although she was embarrassed to admit she didn't know much more than that. It had seemed like a good decision at the time, although now she could see how it might appear to Ethan, that Charley had somehow taken advantage of her. Maybe he was right. She wasn't romantically tied to Charley, but perhaps she wasn't any different than Agnes, sitting back in Flagstaff, pregnant and waiting for him. What if Charley had never planned to return to either of them?

She covered her eyes from the bright sun and rolled onto her back. The one thing she'd felt certain of was his love for Agnes. But he wasn't engaged to Agnes, he was engaged to *her*. Charley had begged her to keep up the façade of their engagement because Agnes's family didn't like him, and it was the only way to throw them off track, but if Charley truly loved Agnes why didn't he stand up to her pa?

A smattering of white clouds hovered above her. *What am I doing out here?* That was easy, she was looking for Charley. *But why?* To remind him that Agnes was pregnant, and the babe needed looking after. But maybe she was chasing Charley because she really did want her money returned. If that was true, then she should accept Ethan's offer and head home. But that didn't truly cover all the reasons for her behavior, either.

She'd struck out on her own at the age of seventeen to be independent. A part of her had been terrified, but she'd also relished the freedom. Embarking on a search for Charley had simply been another part of her restless, independent-seeking self looking for a challenge.

She sat up and spied a plate with two biscuits and several strips of bacon and a cup of coffee beside it. Ethan, who had clearly enjoyed shooting those men chasing them—something that didn't sit well with Kate—seemed to be the exact opposite of her self-indulgent fiancé. If only she'd met Ethan first. And if only he wasn't a killer who obviously enjoyed killing. But dwelling on what-ifs got a person nowhere. Hadn't Kate learned that when her pa had been killed almost twelve years ago?

She sat up and realized she only wore her undergarments. A flush of embarrassment washed over her. Ethan had helped her undress last night. The last man to see that much of her was her brother Petey, by accident, when she'd just started blossoming into womanhood. He'd needled her so much about it that she'd laced the sugar bowl with salt and he'd spit his morning coffee all over the kitchen floor. That memory brought a slight smile to her lips.

Kate found a pair of wool trousers and a crumpled maroon shirt inside her satchel. She'd filched them off Petey before she'd left home. Although he was two years older, they were of the same height, so the clothing should fit fairly well. As she stood and quickly dressed, pulling the shirt over her head and buttoning the trousers, she realized she needed suspenders for the sagging pants. As she searched in her bag for them, a wave of homesickness for her brothers washed over her.

She and Petey had taken after their pa, in looks and temperament. Frederick Kinsella was a man of small stature but big on dreams. He'd often tell them stories of far-off places like

Russia, Egypt, and his home country of Ireland. Although he'd come to America as a youngster and had no firsthand recollections of his homeland, he repeated the tales his own pappy had shared. Kate wondered if one day she might visit Ireland.

Owen, on the other hand, took after their ma. He was taller than all of them and far more practical and reliable. If a chore needed to be done, he was the one who'd finish it. A year older than Kate, he often acted as the man of the house, especially after the death of their pa.

If Owen were here, he'd challenge Ethan to a fight for daring to look; and if it were Petey, well, he'd probably ask Ethan for a job. Petey had always wanted to return to Trinidad; for that matter, so had Kate. Her pa had been alive there, they'd been happy, and they'd been a family.

Kate shoved the ends of the shirt into the trousers, slipped a suspender onto each shoulder, and rolled the sleeves to her elbows.

"Mornin'."

She jumped and spun around.

Ethan stood a few feet from her, his hat casting a shadow across his stony features.

"Morning," she replied and tried to catch her breath. His sudden appearance jolted her completely awake, more so than any cup of coffee could have ever done. "Where were you?"

"Checking behind us, making sure there was no sign of trouble." His expression was so flat and lacking in warmth that Kate immediately wondered what she'd done to make him so thoroughly dislike her. But that was ridiculous. It wasn't as if she cared about such things.

"We ought to get going. It's tough getting a late start every morning." He moved past her and leaned down to throw more dirt on the campfire ashes.

Kate felt like a child who'd been chastised for getting her hand caught in the cookie jar. "Right," she said. "Sorry. I'll try to stop sleeping in." She needed to go back to drinking water before bed.

She snatched the plate and stuffed several pieces of bacon into her mouth then gulped down half the coffee, dumping the rest. Ethan gathered up her blankets and they bumped into one another as they both moved toward the horses.

"Sorry," she mumbled around a mouthful of food.

Ethan looked at her as if she'd suddenly become a lizard. She tried to bring her lips together, but a piece of biscuit fell out of her mouth. She chewed faster and swallowed hard.

"Now that you've enjoyed breakfast, are you ready to ride?" he asked as he mounted Whiskey.

She nodded and stuffed the used cookware into her saddlebags, then climbed aboard Brandy and cinched her hat.

They headed slightly northwest into flat and featureless terrain with mesas rising to the east. Kate likened them to tabletops for the gods. They saw no one and the day grew warm. Ethan pushed them hard and they stopped barely ten minutes for a lunch break. He conversed with her as much as a piece of wood might.

---

FRUSTRATED from enduring Kate's close proximity for hours, Ethan decided it was high time he broke Brandy of her overwhelming fondness for her mama. How was he supposed to keep his distance if Kate rode so close to him all day? It was his own damn fault, of course, for not being stricter with his favorite mare. Ethan had a soft spot for Whiskey and honestly saw no problem allowing her to dote on her offspring. But it was a problem now. Kate Kinsella was a problem.

Movement off to the right caught his eye.

An object flew toward him and he jerked forward in reflex as Kate screamed. The rock smacked her in the face and pushed her from Brandy.

He struggled with Whiskey's reins as the horse snorted and stepped backward, wanting to bolt, but Ethan held her steady with one hand while pulling his gun with the other. He shot in the direction of the hidden attacker. Or attackers? It couldn't be the three bastards who wanted their donkey back. If it was, they were damned persistent. Ethan decided he would pay for the damn animal and be done with it.

He slid off Whiskey's back and crouched low. He shot three more times as he rounded Brandy's backside, hoping she wouldn't kick him in the head. As he reached Kate's side Whiskey and Brandy bolted, leaving a cloud of dust in their wake and Ethan and Kate without cover. Fred was nowhere to be seen.

There was no return gunfire, so Ethan scooped Kate into his arms and ran quickly behind a rocky outcrop, keeping his gun pointed and ready. As he released her to the ground, he saw blood oozing between her fingers where her hand covered her left eye.

"Jesus, Kate, are you all right?"

"What was that?" She looked dazed.

"I think it was a rock," Ethan replied. "Move your hand and let me have a look."

She complied and Ethan saw an open gash but luckily it had missed her eye. Still, it was nasty and needed immediate attention.

"You're gonna be fine," he said soothingly. She was going to have a humdinger of a scar, especially if he didn't get it stitched up, but he didn't really want to break that news to her yet.

"I'm bleeding a lot," she said, staring at her bloodied hand.

"I know." Ethan reloaded his gun. "Face wounds do that. I'm gonna take care of these sonsofbitches," he said, anger filling his thoughts. "Stay here. I'll get you cleaned up in no time."

"Ethan—"

He ignored Kate's plea, stood, and advanced on their attackers.

"You worthless jackasses!" he yelled. "Come on out and show yourselves." With his arm stretched long, he fixed his gun on the last known location of the rock thrower. No more shots in the legs or shoulders. If they didn't surrender this time, he would kill them. Kate's safety demanded it.

He heard the scuffle of rocks and dirt as someone, or several men, started to retreat. Ethan made a wide arc and moved quickly to the assailant's hideout.

"I'll shoot," he warned, his finger resting on the trigger and close to doing just that.

He stopped short at the faces that stared back at him, wide-eyed and innocent.

The attackers were three young Indian children.

## Chapter Eight

Kate pulled the end of her shirt free from her trousers and applied one of the ends to her bleeding face. She wore a camisole beneath, so she was at least still presentable for traveling with her fiancé's brother. Yes, presentable was important. Her hand trembled as she took a steadying breath and closed her eyes. Her face stung and her head throbbed. And she'd fallen from an animal yet again. She was young and strong, but a body could only take so much.

Where was Ethan? She feared he'd gone off to shoot someone. She struggled to stand on wobbly legs, still holding the end of the shirt to her face. The material was wet with blood but luckily it matched the maroon color. She peered around her rocky hideout.

Ethan stood with his gun pointed at three children.

Kate gasped. "My God, what are you doing?" She stumbled over to him.

"They threw the rock at you," he said. "They were planning to rob us."

Kate didn't know what to say. She tugged at her shirt so a dry portion of cloth covered the wound. She would need Ethan's help in cleaning it.

Two boys and a girl stood motionless watching them. They were dirty, their dark-skinned faces smeared with sweat and dust, and they looked scared and desperate.

"Do any of you speak English?" she asked.

The oldest one nodded slightly. His straight black hair was cut short and by his height—nearly as tall as Kate—she guessed his age to be about thirteen or fourteen.

"Are the three of you all alone out here?" Kate said.

The same boy nodded again.

"They look terrible, Ethan," she said. "We should feed them. They attacked us because they're scared." She turned back to the boy. "Isn't that right?"

Another slight nod of his chin.

"If you three promise to behave yourselves, I won't tie you up," Ethan said, lowering his gun.

Kate was appalled. "Of course we won't tie you up." Then she whispered angrily to Ethan, "What a horrid thing to say."

"You're too trusting, Kate. And your face looks like hell."

"You're too kind," she said sarcastically.

"I'll get the horses." Ethan handed her the gun. "Keep an eye on the rock posse." Then he disappeared to the east.

Kate let the gun hang at her side, but she didn't put it on the ground. Not that she had any intention of using it on the children, let alone scaring them with it by waving it in their face the way Ethan had been doing, but she worried one of them might grab it and hurt themselves.

"What's your name?" she asked the oldest boy.

"Agayotsay," the boy answered.

Kate frowned. "Ah-guy-oat-say," she muttered to herself. "A-guy-oat-stay." She cleared her throat and smiled, trying to convey friendliness with only one eye working. "I'll just call you Guy."

She looked at the girl, with a round face and fearful expression. Kate guessed her age to be nine or ten. "And what's your name?"

"Mashilaywi," the girl answered softly.

"Mah-shee," Kate said, nodding. "It's nice to meet you. And your name?" she asked the youngest, who appeared five or six.

"Popay," he said, his voice still that of a young child, high-pitched and sweet.

"Oh good, an easy one," Kate said with a laugh. "Popay. I'm Katie Kinsella. Where are you children from?"

They all stared at her in silence.

She tried again. "Are you Navajo?"

Guy shook his head.

"Hopi?"

Guy nodded. A man of few words. He and Ethan ought to get along famously.

"Mister Barstow and I have come from Flagstaff. Do you know where that is?"

"*Neuvatikyao*," whispered Mashi.

"Pardon me?" Kate asked.

"The sacred mountain where the katsinam live," Guy replied.

"Oh, yes, you mean the San Francisco Peaks. There *is* something sacred about them, isn't there? Especially during the winter months when they're covered with lots of snow." The children stared at Kate, and she knew she rambled.

Ethan reappeared with the horses and Fred. He pointed to a bit of shade. "The three of you sit there," he said to the children.

They slowly complied. Ethan handed each of them dried meat and a canteen of water to share.

"We'll make something else once we set up camp," Kate said. "Some hot biscuits and beans. I might even have a treat somewhere in my things."

Ethan stood and glared at her. "A treat? They knocked you off your horse with a rock, Kate. They're only getting the necessities until we can figure out what to do with them." He held a hand up. "Don't argue with me. Come over here and let me have a look at your face."

Ethan grabbed a small bag from Whiskey and ushered Kate

several feet from where the children sat, slowly chewing their meat and watching the two of them. As an afterthought Ethan went back to the horses and guided them to the other side of their position, placing themselves between the animals and the children.

"You think they'll steal Whiskey and Brandy?" Kate asked.

Ethan raised an eyebrow. "How long have you been on your own? Why don't you just paint a bullseye on your forehead?"

"Don't you believe in extenuating circumstances?" Kate asked.

Ethan kneeled beside her—the children still in his sights—and gently pulled away the blood-soaked end of Kate's shirt from her wound. The cloth stuck and had to be tugged; Kate tried to push Ethan's hands away as she winced.

"Are any extenuating circumstances worth this?" he murmured quietly.

Ethan wet a cloth with water and wiped the gash for several minutes. Kate tried to keep still and not whine, but several times "ouch" escaped her lips. Ethan unscrewed a small bottle then paused a moment.

"What's that?" she asked.

"Whiskey. Hold still, this might sting a little."

She nodded. She wasn't going to be a baby about this. Ethan poured the liquid on the wound and it immediately ran down the side of her face and into her ear. A sharp stinging sizzled from the gash and Kate clenched her teeth and took several steadying breaths. Ethan grasped her hand and she squeezed hard.

"I'm gonna do it again, Kate. I don't want you getting an infection. And I'm gonna need to stitch it up."

"Yes, of course. I'm fine, really." She spit the words out in a rush.

More whiskey, more stinging. Then Ethan retrieved a bar of soap from their supplies and washed his hands with water from his canteen. From somewhere, he produced a needle and thread and sterilized them with the alcohol.

"You're awfully prepared," she said, leaning back against a rock. She hoped she wouldn't cry, but she was close to not caring.

"Yeah," Ethan said grimly. "Drink some of this." He handed her the flask he'd used on her face. "It'll help take the edge off. I'll work as fast as I can."

She drank the liquid and coughed as it burned down her throat.

Ethan stopped to look at her. "Try to hold still." he leaned over and pierced her skin with the needle. Kate closed her eyes, but tears escaped anyway.

"Easy, sweetheart," he said soothingly. "You're doing fine."

The needle pricking her flesh hurt beyond reason, and the sounds of the thread moving through her skin made her nauseous.

Kate gripped her hands into the ends of her shirt and twisted tightly. She kept her eyes closed and desperately tried to hold back the sobs that were pushing at the fragile barrier of her self-control.

"Almost done."

Kate swallowed hard and took several rapid breaths.

"Finished," Ethan said. "I'll cover it for now so it stays clean." He placed a folded cloth over the stitches then wound a bandanna around her head and tied it into place. He took hold of her hands, untangling them from her shirt, and she opened her eyes. "Are you all right?" he asked.

She nodded, but the tears burst forth anyway. Ethan brought a hand to her face, opposite the wound, and he brushed the wetness away with the pad of his thumb. She was surprised by the pained look on his face. "Is it bad?" she asked.

"As long as it doesn't become infected, no."

"I suppose the scar will make my eye bulge," she blubbered and sniffed loudly.

Ethan smiled and smoothed some of her hair from her face. "I've always thought women with bulging eyes were quite attractive."

Alarmed, she stared at him.

"Don't worry," he reassured her. "It'll swell and be sore and look nasty for a while, but in time the worst of it will fade."

She strove to maintain her composure. She had never been a woman to dwell on her appearance, but then she'd never had to worry before that her appearance would draw unnecessary scrutiny. "I can always pull my hair forward and wear a bigger hat," she said, finally getting the sobbing under control. She felt a little better, with minimal shakiness and light-headedness.

"A little scar won't make you less beautiful." He stood. "Stay here and rest. I'll set up camp. It's time our three little helpers pulled their weight." He brought the horses back to the children and went to work.

Kate rested and watched. She *was* tired. Ethan was stern with the children but not overly cruel and they responded to him, moving gear and collecting firewood. Her eyes began to close as she leaned against the rock and watched them. Kate didn't know what to think about Ethan anymore. And the fact that she needed to figure it out—needed to figure *him* out—confused her. She was simply too weary to sort it all out in her mind.

*A little scar won't make you less beautiful.*

To her mounting confusion, Ethan's opinion mattered to her. When had that happened? She stopped fighting her tiredness and dozed.

———

"KATE. KATE." The distant sound of her name brought her from the meadow where she played with her pa, the yellow wildflowers bathed in sunlight and the air filled with the trills and whistles of hawks and sparrows and songbirds. She reluctantly let go of the memory, the vividness of the dream giving her the only opportunity to be with her pa again, to experience with *all* her senses what it was to have him in this life again.

"I'm sorry to wake you." It was Ethan, and his face was close to hers. She missed her pa. And Ethan had a way to him that reminded her of her father. Hovering in the land between sleep and wakefulness, Kate reached for Ethan and his warmth, his comfort, and his security. She placed her arms around his shoulders and buried her face into his neck.

"I've made a pallet for you by the fire," he murmured. "You should lie down." His arms moved under her back and beneath her knees. Without effort, he lifted her.

Kate snuggled closer and Ethan's arms tightened around her. It felt nice and she sighed, her lips making contact with his bare skin just above his shirt collar. He was warm against her mouth.

"No," she protested sleepily as he gently released her to the ground.

"Get some rest, Kate." He covered her with a blanket and smoothed back her hair.

Briefly opening her eyes, she saw a starry night sky and a strong fire burning, three bundles lying around it.

"Are the children all right?" she asked.

"They're sleeping." Her eyes met Ethan's and she saw caring and confusion in their dark depths.

Unsure what it meant and too sleepy to think clearly, she curled up on her side and closed her eyes again. "Hmmm, that's good."

"Sweet dreams," Ethan said quietly.

She sighed and slipped beyond wakefulness. This time, Ethan awaited her in the meadow.

---

ETHAN MOVED BACK to his place near the fire—the children had his bedroll and all the extra blankets—and tried not to look at Kate, or think of Kate, or wonder...

*Did she just kiss me on the neck?*

His body thrummed with the inevitable response to an overture from a woman who attracted him on far too many levels. He doubted she meant to arouse him, but it didn't quiet his male reaction any less. Had she been any other woman, he would have explored the possibilities with her, but the truth was, he'd never before met a woman like Kate.

He ran a hand through his hair. He had no right thinking of her this way. He had no right thinking of her, period.

He kept vigil over the slumbering forms of Kate and the three children who watched him as if he were a bear about to bite their heads off. But if they tried to hurt Kate again, Ethan suspected he might do just that.

It was a long while until he slept.

# Chapter Nine

K ate awoke uncharacteristically early. She sat up as sunrise broke across the land. Ethan slept to her right and the Indian children slept to her left. Her face felt puffy; she put her hand on the cloth covering her wound, making it difficult to see out of her left eye, and knew it had swollen quite a bit during the night. It was sore and throbbed with pain.

Ethan's face was turned away from her as he slept on his back, one hand resting on his ribs and the other arm bent behind his head. He snored softly and Kate tried to remember her dreams. If she wasn't mistaken, they'd been filled with Ethan.

She shifted her attention to the Hopi children and realized only Guy and Popay were present. Mashi was gone. Kate slowly stood, noticing the blood-stained shirt she still wore. She needed to clean herself, but first she would look for Mashi. The girl couldn't have gone far.

As Kate walked, a slight breeze pushed against her and the early-morning chill sharpened her senses. She stopped to hear the sounds of the desert. The wind whispered in her ear and a feeling of isolation overtook her. A clear blue sky encompassed a landscape that extended beyond what the eye could see, brown and tan and a hint of green where flora struggled to grow, fighting to survive.

Kate scanned the horizon. From the corner of her good eye, a black head bobbed up and down. Mashi disappeared, then darted from her hiding spot with surprising swiftness. Concerned the girl was running away, Kate followed quickly, but to her relief she realized the child wasn't trying to escape but instead chased after something. Kate saw a jackrabbit bounce from side to side. Slowing to a walk, she decided to sit and wait for the girl to complete her morning exercise.

When Mashi had finished chasing the rabbit, the girl ran directly to Kate as if she knew she'd been there the entire time.

"You look like an Indian, Kay-tee," Mashi said, her trim body heaving and dark eyes sparkling. Her short black hair, shorn into a bob, clung to her sweaty face. She pushed it back in frustration.

Kate smiled and touched a hand to the bandage around her head and her own brown hair flowing loose, down to her lower back. "I suppose I do," she said. "Why are you running around?"

"I always run with the jackrabbits," the girl replied. "You sleep a long time. Agayotsay is sorry about the rock. We are all sorry about your face."

"Well, maybe you'll think twice before throwing something next time."

"It was all Agayotsay's idea."

Kate smiled. "Is he your brother?"

Mashi nodded. "Popay too."

"I also have two brothers. And the oldest often had harebrained ideas that got the rest of us into trouble."

Mashi sat beside her. "What kind of trouble?"

"I was about your age when Petey told me he would show me where a bunch of rattlesnakes lived. He led me into an old mine shaft then he left me there. I got lost and couldn't find my way out."

Mashi inhaled slowly. "What happened?" she asked, eyes wide.

"Some of the men from my stepfather's ranch found me. I'll admit I was scared, but I never let Petey know. Mama tanned his hide good and he had to shovel the barn twice a day for a week as punishment."

"Did you see the snakes?"

Kate shook her head. "No, thank goodness." She laughed, wincing when the stitches strained on her swollen face. "I really didn't want to see them, but I didn't want Petey to think I was afraid, either."

"The Hopi aren't supposed to do our Snake Dance anymore," Mashi said solemnly.

"Why?"

"The *Bahanas*, the white people, tell us it is wrong and that we should believe in their god. We are to become questions."

Kate frowned, confused. "Oh, you mean Christians."

Mashi nodded. "They have given us new question names."

"What's yours?"

"Mary."

"That's a nice name," Kate replied. "But it can be difficult if you don't really like it. I have two names, but I don't really like the other one." She glanced at Mashi. "It's Martha."

Mashi smiled.

"At least if you have to use Mary, you can still keep Mashi in your heart," Kate continued.

Mashi appeared to consider the suggestion.

"Have you and your brothers run away from a Christian school?" Kate asked tentatively.

Mashi sighed. "We just want to go home. I miss my mother and father."

"How long have the three of you been out here?"

"Many days. People chase us. But we hid and got away from them."

"That's impressive," Kate murmured, wondering what on earth

she and Ethan should do with them. "Don't you think your folks are scared, wondering where you are?"

"Yes. We try to get home. But every time we see a *Bahana* we think they are here to take us back to the school. So Agayotsay attacks them to scare them off and to steal some food. We have been hungry."

"Did Ethan—Mister Barstow—give you more food last night?" Kate asked suddenly, hoping that Ethan had treated the children well.

"Yes, but he was very angry at us."

Kate didn't know what to say.

"He was mad about what happened to you," Mashi added.

Kate hoped he hadn't scared them too much. "I see," she said. "Well, I'll talk to him and we'll try to get the three of you home. Let's go back now and have some breakfast."

As they stood something fell from Mashi's shirt. Kate leaned over and picked it up. It was a small cradle doll, carved from wood.

"This is lovely," Kate said as she handed it to her. "Did you make it?"

Mashi shook her head. "No, I got it when I was a baby. It's a *tihu*, a katsina doll. This one is called *putsqatihu*. It's my favorite, but I was supposed to give it up at school."

Kate leaned down so she was eye-level with the girl. "There is nothing wrong with standing strong in your beliefs. And some *Bahanas* are wrong—we are not all the same."

Kate straightened and they began walking back to camp. "What is your god called?" she asked the girl.

"*Masau'u*. He is the God of Death, and of Fire, and rules this World. But we also have *Gogyeng Sowuhti*—Spider Grandmother. She helps us a lot."

"Spiders and death and fire." Kate rested a hand lightly around Mashi's shoulders. "I'll try hard not to make you mad."

Kate was rewarded by a smile on the young girl's face.

ETHAN GLANCED up from the cook fire and saw Kate approaching with Mashi. She laughed as the ends of her shirt, not bound by the suspenders, blew gently upward. He rummaged through the sparse clothing he had brought with him, not realizing he'd been swearing under his breath until he noticed Guy staring at him. He glared at the boy as he stood then tossed the dark blue shirt at Kate, who had reached the campfire.

She barely caught it as it headed toward the fire. "Good morning," she offered. "Is there some reason you're throwing clothes at me?"

"You should change out of that bloodied shirt." They needed to find Charley, and fast. Then Ethan could disentangle himself from this woman he would soon call *sister*.

She tossed the shirt back at him. "I have clothes. I'll just be a few minutes, then I'll help make breakfast."

She walked past him and Ethan forced himself not to move. "How's your face?" he asked quietly. Her eye and upper cheek were quite swollen.

"It stings a little." She looked away as she brushed past him.

The brief, whisper-like touch of her shoulder against his made her blush, and with a sudden, sharp clarity, Ethan realized she knew.

*Kate was aware of the attraction between them.*

And what was worse, she felt it too. At least, he thought—he hoped?—she did. It brought a sickening clarity to the situation. It was Jessica all over again. Five years ago, he'd become entangled with a woman attached to Charley. It hadn't mattered that he hadn't wanted her, that nothing had ever happened, that it had all been a huge misunderstanding. It had still cost him his relationship with his brother. And in the wake of the death of their pa, and Ethan's recent homecoming after chasing the ghosts of guilt and remorse, the situation had gone from shaky to terrible in no time flat.

Ethan had thought it couldn't get worse, but in the form of Kate Kinsella, it had. He did want her. He was in a dangerous place that didn't even come close to what had happened with Jessica.

But he was older and wiser now, wasn't he? He could keep his feelings to himself. He need never let Kate know how he felt about her.

Kate moved off for some privacy, so Ethan concentrated on breakfast. When she returned, she was well-covered with another white shirt buttoned to her collarbone. But her hair was still down.

As if reading his mind, she said, "Can you help me remove the bandage? I'd like to braid my hair."

Ethan nodded and untied the bandanna. Peripherally, he was aware of the children watching them as if they were a vaudeville show. He supposed if he were young, he'd find his own behavior amusing. He gently tugged the bandage from the stitches and inwardly flinched. The gash was swollen to twice its size, black and purple, with blood crusted around the stitches. Just looking at it hurt, so he could only imagine how it must feel. Kate was going to have one hell of a scar. *And if Charley ever says one word about it, I'll deck him.*

Distance, he reminded himself.

Kate's scar and Charley's reaction were of no concern to him.

"How does it look?" she asked.

He stared into her blue eyes and couldn't lie. "You're gonna have a nice little memento from our time here."

She looked beyond him to their company sitting by the fire watching every damned second of what went on between the two of them. "It's all right," she said quietly. "It could have been so much worse."

The wound had to hurt like hell, and all Kate worried about

was reassuring the children. Ethan turned away before he did something stupid, like touch her again.

*Shit.*

It was all too clear that Kate Kinsella had slipped past his defenses—the anger and protectiveness over her safety had overwhelmed the obvious logic of the situation. He'd certainly given Guy, Mashi, and Popay a piece of his mind last night about what they'd done to her, and he'd never been so cold with children before in his life.

"Ethan, Mashi told me they've run away from boarding school. We really ought to see them safely back to their family."

"I know." He poured coffee into a cup and handed it to her.

"Thank you." She took it, sat on the ground then set the cup before her.

"Guy told me he might have seen Charley through here three days past," Ethan said. "A detour to First Mesa will cost us too much time." Ethan felt a mounting pressure to find his brother.

"First Mesa?" Kate asked.

"It's where their village, Walpi, is located. I estimate it to be more than forty miles from here." He removed the biscuit pan from the fire and tossed hot rolls at each of the children. They caught them and ate quickly. He dropped one into Kate's lap since she was busy braiding her hair.

"You're not suggesting we leave them here," she said.

"Guy, can you find your way home?" Ethan questioned.

Guy nodded.

"This is absurd," Kate said vehemently, releasing her half-braided hair and staring up at him. "I'm not going to let the three of them go off on their own."

"We'll give them supplies and Fred," Ethan said calmly. "They should be home within a day or two."

Kate let out a frustrated huff, then resumed braiding her hair— but the result was a loose mess. She quickly tied off the end, pushed her handiwork over her shoulder and stood. "You honestly believe this is a good idea?" she said quietly to him, but her eyes flashed with anger, the swollen one struggling.

"Ask Guy how long they've already been on their own," Ethan countered.

"Ten sunrises," Guy answered.

Kate stared at the boy. "That's appalling. You're lucky none of you has been seriously hurt."

"All right, Kate," Ethan conceded. "The other option is we take them with us to Tuba City."

"And then what? Dump them there? That's almost as bad as leaving them here in the middle of nowhere."

"There's a settlement at Moenkopi, near Tuba City." Ethan took a swallow of coffee. "We can drop them there. Surely someone can get them back to where they belong."

"Is this true?" she asked Guy.

Guy shrugged his shoulders. "We do not want to go to Moenkopi. The *Bahanas* will find us and drag us back to school. We will take your donkey and go home ourselves. I know the way."

"How do we know you're telling the truth?" Kate asked, her voice turning lethal.

Ethan sighed. It was a helluva time for her wariness to suddenly kick in. "They're not our responsibility," he said to her.

"Is that how you live your life?" she accused. "Shirking your responsibilities because it's not convenient?"

"Of course not," he replied defensively, irritated by how the day had begun. "What's your point in picking this fight?"

"I'm not fighting with you. I just don't understand your attitude."

"I want to go home," Popay said, his sweet voice interrupting them.

Ethan and Kate turned to look at him, and she immediately started nodding. Ethan suppressed the urge to roll his eyes. It wasn't that he felt unkind toward the children, but Guy was old enough to see the brood home. Although Ethan had to admit he wasn't certain Guy would do that now. *Hell*.

"All right," Ethan said, caving in. "Everyone pack up. We're headed to Walpi and we're riding fast." As soon as the words were out of his mouth, he realized Kate was probably not up to a hard day's ride. While he was certain her swollen face looked much worse than it really was, he wasn't prepared to bet money on it. And he knew if he asked Kate, she'd deny it—all for the sake of the willful children who'd caused it in the first place.

And then there was Popay. He was quiet and sweet and scared, and Ethan would only be more of an ass if he rode the poor child hard. Right then and there he knew he had to stop taking his frustrations out on these youngsters. Kate was right—they had an obligation for their safety, whether it fit into his schedule or not. Kate didn't fit into his well-ordered life, and God only knew how Ethan was going to untangle himself from her presence.

Kate and the children hustled to roll blankets and pack up the gear, although Guy was less than enthusiastic.

"You didn't think to live out here on your own, did you?" Ethan said to him.

Guy looked up and his closed expression was surprisingly fearful. "If we return, the *Bahanas* will still come and take us back to school." He shook his head. "It is easier to live out here, alone."

"Maybe for you," Ethan said. "But what about Mashi and especially Popay. They're too young to survive out here for any length of time. I can't give you answers for the rest except that it's undoubtedly an issue between your elders and the U.S. Government."

"Have you ever lived under the yoke of another's will?"

Ethan thought of his own headstrong ways in his younger days, actions that had led to other people's pain and suffering.

"You'd do well to follow guidance when it's given." Ethan grasped his shoulder. "It might just save you from yourself one day. It's not the yoke that matters, it's the way we deal with it that does."

Guy acknowledged Ethan's words with a bowed head. He raised his eyes and the fear was gone. Resolution had replaced it. "Then I will go home."

"And I'll make sure you get there."

"Your woman seems to think you won't," Guy said.

"I've changed my mind. And Kate isn't my woman. She's to marry my brother."

"Then she is to marry the wrong brother." Guy raised an eyebrow and appeared far older than he was. "You want her, so choose her."

"They say too much schooling is a bad thing." Ethan gave Guy a friendly shove toward the horses where Kate and the two younger children were busy at work. "I'll give you a lesson on extenuating circumstances tomorrow."

Guy ruefully shook his head, but Ethan caught a brief glimpse of a smile on his face.

## Chapter Ten

They rode east all day toward flat-topped mesas in the distance. Mashi rode with Kate, Popay with Ethan, and Guy rode Fred. Ethan had reapportioned the gear, so Fred didn't have such a heavy load, but the donkey appeared slower than usual to Kate. She wondered if he was feeling well.

By nightfall, the mesas loomed closer and Guy said they were within a morning's ride to Walpi. They set up camp under a clear sky. Kate and Ethan prepared a meal with little conversation, an easy routine settling between them. She had left the bandage off of her wound and the swelling had subsided a bit, making it easier to see the task at hand.

As they sat around the campfire, Popay and Guy took turns making animal sounds—hooting like an owl, or howling like a coyote. They all laughed when the boys tried to growl like a mountain cat. Kate had never seen Ethan really laugh and it transformed his face and his manner into something quite magnetic. Ethan was a mystery to her, but he was also just a man.

It was better if he *remained* a mystery.

"I have one that none of you will guess," Mashi said. She

began making high-pitched screeching noises. Kate was amazed the girl could raise her voice to such an octave.

"A hawk," Popay answered.

Mashi shook her head.

"A mouse," Ethan said.

Mashi grinned and shook her head again, obviously proud she could stump them all.

"A turkey that's been stung by a bee," Kate offered.

That made the children giggle and Ethan grin, his warm gaze lighting a fire in her belly. *The man certainly has Charley's charm.*

"Do you give up?" Mashi asked.

Everyone nodded.

"It's a bat."

"How do you know what a bat sounds like?" Guy asked.

"I am more quiet than you," Mashi argued. "They speak, and I listen."

"Then listen to this." Everyone jumped at the raspy male voice from the darkness.

Kate stood and whirled around at the sound of a gun being readied. She pushed Mashi behind her and searched the darkness for whoever was out there. A chill went down her spine and fear made her heart pound. This threat was real.

"Don't try it," another voice said from behind Ethan.

Kate glanced at Ethan over her shoulder and realized he'd tried to retrieve his gun. More than one man surrounded them.

The man in front of her materialized from the darkness. His paunch-bellied front side and mustache that curled past his upper lip brought instant recognition to Kate. He was one of the three men who had stolen her horse, chased her when she'd taken Fred from them, and then tried to shoot her at the waterfall. He held a pistol in one hand and swaggered toward her.

"Well, well, well. We finally caught up to you, little lady. It's about time." He suddenly pointed the gun at Ethan. "Stay put there, mister. Unlike you, I'm of no mind to shoot anyone. Harry and Rufus," he yelled. "Come on. We found the donkey."

Two more men, both tall and lanky, appeared behind Ethan—one limping, a bandage tied around his thigh, and the other sporting a shoulder wound.

"All right," the one in front of her said, waving his gun at them. "All of you go over there."

Kate backed up slowly, making sure Mashi stayed behind her. Guy held Popay in his arms and Ethan moved in front of the boys as well as Kate. They all stood together in the boundary of firelight encircling the small camp.

"Where's the donkey, Clive?"

"Over there," the one holding the gun on them replied. "You get the saddle, Rufus, whiles me and Harry watch the little mixed-breed family."

"Got it," Rufus replied, sporting the shoulder wound, his baggy pants and unshaven cheeks smeared with dirt. He loped off to the left, then ran back, heaving and looking confused, and then ran to the right. "I found him," he yelled. With great exertion he returned with the saddle in his arms and dumped it to the ground. "My shoulder sure hurts," he moaned.

"Is it there?" Clive asked, ignoring the man's complaint.

Rufus turned the saddle over with his good arm and began tugging at flaps of leather that protruded. Kate thought the saddle must have really dug into Fred's back and felt bad that she hadn't thought to check during the time the donkey had been with her.

"Dammit, Rufus," Clive said. "You're as useless as a three-legged dog. Do you have your knife Harry?"

Harry put his gun down, his dark shoulder-length hair looking greasy where it stuck out from under his bowler hat. He looked so much like Clive, the one pointing the gun at them, that Kate guessed they were related. "Yep, I got it." He pulled a dull blade from his backside and began stabbing the saddle forcefully. His face bulged as he attempted to pull the sewn flaps of leather apart, finally rewarded with a ripping sound as it gave way.

"Is it there?" Clive asked excitedly.

Harry pulled a large black bag out the size of his hand. He opened the pouch and poured the contents—a pile of gold nuggets —into his grimy palm. They sparkled in the firelight. Kate peered around Ethan's shoulder, shocked.

"No wonder Fred was so sluggish," she murmured. "Those must be awfully heavy."

Ethan's hand went behind him and he grasped hers. His touch was firm and warm, and Kate was grateful for it.

"We got it, so let's go," Harry said.

Clive glanced back at Ethan. "We better tie 'em up. Wouldn't want you comin' after us, shootin' us again."

"I wouldn't have taken the donkey if you hadn't stolen my horse," Kate said. Ethan gave her hand a squeeze, a warning she knew, but she ignored it.

"I didn't steal no horse," Rufus said, removing his hat to reveal a balding scalp. "I *saw* a horse eatin' grass, all by her lonesome. I simply acquired a loose pony."

"She had a saddle on her, you imbecile," Kate retorted, leaning around Ethan when he tried to step in front of her again.

"There wasn't no rider anywhere," Rufus defended himself. "I didn't have all day to sit around and wait and see if she belonged to someone. Listen, lady, you shouldn't have taken the donkey. You had no right."

Kate tried to step forward, but Ethan exerted a considerable amount of strength on her hand. She wasn't sure if she gasped from Rufus's ridiculous rules of ownership or Ethan's painful squeeze.

"Kate," Ethan said under his breath. "Relax darlin'."

"Wait a minute." Harry stood and limped closer to her, his bandaged leg stiff. "I know you. Did you just call her Kate?" he asked Ethan.

Ethan remained silent, still firmly holding Kate's hand.

"What're you blathering on about?" Clive asked.

"She's Charley's woman."

Clive squinted his eyes at her. "You sure?"

"What's your name?" Harry asked her. When she didn't answer he pointed a gun at her.

Ethan shoved her behind him.

"Not you," Harry said. "Get outta the way. I wanna talk to *her*."

"If you're right, Harry, maybe we oughta take her with us," Clive said.

"Now, why would you want to do that?" Ethan asked.

"'Cause this is only half our gold," Clive said. "Charley Barstow has the other half. And if we threaten to kill her, maybe he'll give it back to us to save her life."

Harry reached around Ethan and grabbed Kate's arm, yanking her apart from the group. Ethan started to stop him but suddenly Rufus pointed his gun at Guy and Popay.

"No," Kate said, fearing these crazy men would shoot one of the children.

Harry dug his fingers into her upper arm hard, causing her to wince, and stared at her like he needed glasses.

"I dunno, Clive," he said. "She looks pretty bad. You seen her face? I dunno if Barstow'll want her."

"It's not her face he'll be interested in," Clive said, talking as if he were speaking to a child. "Is there anything wrong with the rest of her?"

Harry looked her up and down. Kate yanked her arm from him. "You're disgusting," she said.

"Take me," Ethan said. "I'm Charley's brother."

Clive deposited all the gold back into its holder then approached them. "That right?" he asked. He looked from Ethan to Kate. Then he looked at Kate again. "What the hell happened to your face? You do look pretty beat up. Is this guy doin' that?" He jerked his chin at Ethan.

"Of course not," Kate replied. "I just had an accident, that's all."

"Well, I don't recall Charley sayin' he had a brother," Clive said to Ethan. "So, thanks for the offer, but I think we'll take her instead."

"But Charley doesn't want her anymore," Guy said, putting Popay down and stepping forward. "Ethan does."

"Ethan? Who's Ethan?" Clive asked, looking confused.

"I am," Ethan answered.

"It won't work if you take her as a way of getting your gold back," Guy continued. "Charley doesn't want her anymore."

Kate stared at Guy. She knew he was only trying to help but she wondered if he had the gift of prophecy. *And did Ethan really want her?*

"So you stole your brother's woman?" Clive asked Ethan.

Ethan didn't answer.

"Well, hell." Clive spit on the ground. "We sure can't use you then. Charley won't give us the gold for a two-timin' relative makin' moves on his woman." He turned to Guy and said, "Thanks for the advice, Indian." He stepped back. "Tie 'em up and let's take all their horses and gear."

"You've been more trouble than you're worth," Clive said to Ethan. "And you got nothin' better to do than steal a skirt from your own brother. It's mighty shameful, that. Harry, here, is my brother and I'd never do that to him, no matter how mad I got at him. And I've been pretty darn mad at him at times. And Rufus is my cousin, once or second removed, can't remember exactly. But I wouldn't do that to him neither."

Harry started to drag Kate away from Ethan and their campsite. "I will not go with you," she said, digging her heels into the ground.

"C'mon, Miss…Miss…what's your name?" Clive asked.

"It's none of your damned business!" she yelled.

"All right," Clive sighed. "You want me to shoot one of those youngins'? I will, if you don't cooperate."

Kate stopped struggling and her eyes caught Ethan's. He shook his head ever so slightly. She looked at Guy and Popay, and lastly at Mashi, and knew she would do anything to protect them. At some point in the last day they had all worked their way into her heart. Including Ethan?

Harry dragged her into the darkness, tied her hands tightly before her and then struggled to get her atop Whiskey. With his injured shoulder he was so inept at it they fell to the ground twice. Kate almost kicked him in the face, but the thought that Clive or Rufus might shoot Ethan or the children stopped her.

Rufus and Clive tied them up and with a backward glance Kate saw the camp quickly disappear from sight as the darkness encompassed her and three gold-crazy ruffians hot on Charley's trail.

---

ETHAN SPENT the next several hours trying to free his hands and feet from the ropes, frustration and anger welling up in him. He found it almost incomprehensible, considering the behavior of Clive, Harry and Rufus, that any of them could possibly tie a decent knot. But apparently they could, because despite his struggles, he couldn't free himself.

Popay had cried for a time and Ethan had done his best to comfort the boy, but thankfully he slept now. Guy and Mashi were also dozing. As Ethan sat in the darkness and the fire burned down to a barely glowing pile of ash, he vowed that if anything happened to Katie Kinsella, he would hunt down the donkey gang and make each one of them pay…very dearly.

---

ETHAN SLOWLY OPENED HIS EYES. The sun blazed in the sky and he felt stiff as he lay on the ground with his hands tied behind him. A shadow crossed his vision.

"The *Bahana* is awake." An Indian man leaned over him.

Ethan lifted his head and looked for Guy, Mashi, and Popay.

"The children are fine," the man said, his face round and smooth, his dark hair cropped short and tied with a bandanna across his forehead. "We have untied them, and they are eating. I am called Yuteu. Let me free you."

The Indian cut through Ethan's ropes with a knife.

"How did you find us?" Ethan asked.

"He showed us," Yuteu said, looking off into the distance.

A wolf stared at them a few hundred yards away, his ears standing upright in concern and alertness. "Bartholomew."

Ethan was glad he hadn't lost his companion, the familiarity of the animal's black and white hide a boon to the dispiritedness he felt.

"He is loyal to you," Yuteu said. "He sat with you as we approached, but then he ran off. He is wary of strangers."

"Yes, he is," Ethan agreed, rolling his shoulders to relieve the soreness. The wolf had even steered clear of Kate, and Ethan knew she wasn't threatening. As he thought of her, though, he realized that wasn't true. Kate was stubborn enough to speak her mind, and God knew she was a threat to Ethan's self-control.

"There's a woman that was traveling with me," Ethan said. "The men who tied us up took her. Can you take the children back to Walpi so I can go after her?"

Yuteu nodded. "Agayotsay has already told us. We will give you a horse and supplies."

"That's generous of you. Thank you."

An older man approached, still fit and trim, but the lines around his eyes conveyed his wisdom. He wore a collared shirt, leggings and leather moccasins, and strings of colored beads hung from his neck. His dark hair was also cropped. "It is the least I can do for the man who tried to help my children. I am called Masito." He held out his hand, and Ethan stood and clasped it.

"It's a pleasure to meet you," Ethan said honestly. He glanced toward Guy, Mashi, and Popay where they sat eating and said, "Try not to be hard on them. They do you proud."

Masito nodded. "Agayotsay is too much like me. It is a source of pride and frustration for my wife. They all speak kindly of the woman traveling with you. I would offer to ride to get her back, but I must take my children home. There is much to be dealt with there."

"I understand," Ethan said. "I'll try to repay the horse and supplies. I hope you won't think me rude, but I'd like to leave right now."

"A woman like Kay-tee should not be lost. The children will want to say goodbye."

Ethan walked over to where they sat and kneeled down before them. "I'm glad your father found us."

"Will you save her?" Mashi asked, her eyes round with worry.

Ethan nodded. "With every ounce of strength I have. I promise."

"I should have done more last night," Guy said. "We should have fought those men before they could take her."

"No, Guy, you did the right thing." Ethan placed a hand on his shoulder. "Kate didn't want any of you to get hurt, and neither did I. I don't think those men will harm her. I'll get her back."

"And then you must take her as *your* wife," Guy said. "Do not listen to what that *Bahana* said last night—your brother will forgive you if it's meant to be."

Ethan honestly didn't know what to say, his own feelings and thoughts on the matter far from clear. Guy was young and hopeful, while Ethan wasn't. He knew the price for careless, selfish actions. Taking Kate from Charley wasn't something Ethan would do lightly. And this presumed, of course, that Kate felt the same toward him, a conclusion Ethan wouldn't even dare to consider.

"I'll see you all again," Ethan said, his throat tightening. He hadn't thought saying goodbye would be this difficult. Popay launched himself into Ethan's arms and Ethan held tight. Mashi wrapped her arms tight around his neck and kissed him on the cheek. Guy didn't move but held his hand out in a handshake. Ethan respected his restraint. "I promise to come visit," he said, and knew he meant it.

"Bring Kay-tee," Mashi said. "Tell her I will teach her how to chase jackrabbits. And how to screech like a bat."

Ethan set Popay down and stood. "I will." He swallowed against the lump in his throat.

"And give her this," Mashi said, holding out a wooden cradle doll. "She will know what it is."

"That looks important to you," Ethan said. "Maybe you should keep it."

"No. I know Kay-tee will keep it safe."

Ethan put it in his shirt pocket. He ruffled the top of Popay's head and turned from the children who had snatched a part of his heart like a bolt of lightning.

Yuteu brought a horse to Ethan that was as black as the night. "She is called Alo. She is a good, strong horse."

From the looks of her, Ethan had to agree. "I'm grateful. I'll find some way to repay you."

"No," Masito said. "Keep her. We are even. Alo is my best horse. But those three," he looked back at Guy, Mashi, and Popay, "are my best children." He smiled, the love in his eyes unmistakable.

Ethan nodded. "Until we meet again."

"When we see your wolf, we will know you are not far," Masito said, picking up Popay.

Ethan mounted Alo. "If I can't find my way, then I'm sure he will."

With a final glance, he bid farewell to the Hopi and their land.

## Chapter Eleven

K ate decided Clive, Harry, and Rufus were the most inept
criminals she had ever met. But then again, she hadn't
really ever met any before, so perhaps she shouldn't pass judgment.

They had been traveling for two days when Harry began
groaning and whimpering. In the late afternoon shadows, Kate
tried to ignore him by pulling her hat lower onto her head with her
bound hands, tied at the wrist. She still rode Whiskey, and Brandy
was right beside her, so she was grateful for their familiar company.
And Fred trailed behind somewhere. She tried not to think of
Ethan and the children. Clive had collected most of their supplies
and loaded them on the horses, so Ethan, Guy, Mashi, and Popay
would have no food or water. She decided immediately after
leaving that Ethan would find some way to free all of them and she
felt certain he would make sure the children made it home to
Walpi. The fact that her captors hadn't harmed any of them made
Kate feel somewhat certain they wouldn't hurt *her* either. Ethan
would doubtless never find her, but she knew he probably wouldn't
be looking. His goal had been to find Charley, not her. She did have
his horses, but if she found Charley she would simply give them to
him and ask that he return them to Ethan. It was better this way,

she knew, not to ever see Ethan again. Truly it was, but she had a hard time convincing herself.

"I'm not doin' so good," Harry said, hunched over his horse. Actually, it was Kate's horse Pick, the one they'd stolen from her and for whom she had taken Fred in exchange. When this was all done, she'd definitely take Pick back. Fred too, for that matter.

Kate looked at Harry. His face was pale and he sweated profusely. "You look feverish," she said, not feeling very charitable.

Clive moved his horse closer to Harry's. "We're almost to Tuba City. We'll find you a doc there. I'm sure it's that bullet still in your leg."

"There's a bullet still in his leg?" Kate asked, aghast at the way these men lived their lives.

"That fella you was with shot him and we couldn't get it out," Clive remarked. "Hang on Harry. We're almost there."

"That man, Ethan," Rufus said, "shot me twice in my shoulder, but lucky for me we got it all out."

"Lucky for you," Kate murmured. Ethan had certainly doled out punishment on these men. They deserved it, didn't they? Or did Ethan hurt men who were of no-account without bothering to hear their side of the story? She knew these men had tried to hurt her, but they honestly didn't seem that dangerous to her now. She felt certain that in due time she could plan an escape.

It was nightfall when they entered the town of Tuba City, a collection of wooden buildings and shacks scattered in the darkness. They stopped at the first beat-up hotel they found.

Since her legs weren't tied, Kate dismounted. Rufus came up beside her. "Don't try nothin' funny," he said, towering over her. Kate had to turn away before she passed out from his bad breath.

"And what am I supposed to say when someone asks why I'm tied up?" she asked sarcastically.

Rufus took her hat off and stuck it in one of her hands. "Keep this in front of 'em. No one will notice."

Kate considered screaming for help but there didn't seem to be anybody around. Clive went into the hotel.

He returned and pointed down the street. "Harry, the doc's down there, in a building painted blue s'pposedly. I ain't certain if he's white or Indian, so be sure and ask. There's a room waitin' when you're done. Good luck."

Kate frowned. "You're just sending him off on his own? What kind of brother are you?"

"You just watch that mouth of yours, missy," Clive said, twisting the end of his mustache with dirt-encrusted fingernails. "You've been full of lip the past few days and I don't mind sayin' I'm tired of it. God knows how Charley's gonna put up with you. Which reminds me. Rufus, you keep her with you."

"What?" Rufus exclaimed. "You mean I gotta share a room with her?"

"Well, we can't get her a room by herself. She's our hostage."

"But I was plannin' on gettin' me a sportin' woman," Rufus whined, greasy strands of hair clinging to the shoulders of his filthy black jacket. "We got all that gold. I want a bath and a big steak dinner."

Clive slapped his cheek. "We ain't usin' the gold for that. Now, keep your voice down."

Kate leaned forward to hear the conversation better.

"It's investment capital," Clive whispered. "Remember? That's what Charley said."

"What are you investing in?" Kate asked.

Clive caught himself. "Well, that's none of your business," he huffed.

Harry moaned again and leaned against a wooden post.

"I don't think he can make it to the doctor on his own," Kate said.

Clive glanced at his brother. "Yeah, you're probably right. Harry, git on your horse and ride down the street." Clive moved to his side. "Yep, now that's it." He helped Harry climb atop Pick. "We'll see you when you're done. Good luck."

Harry rode off in misery.

"By the way," she said, "that horse he's riding is mine. And I want her back."

"Why?" Clive asked. "You ain't goin' nowhere."

"I meant when this is all done. You'll return Pick to me."

Clive watched her then shook his head. "Don't you ever shut up?"

"You gotta take her," Rufus said.

Clive sighed. "I'll be honest with you Rufus, I don't wanna. I'm plum weary and need some peace and quiet. Maybe she'll be your *sportin' woman.*"

Rufus looked thoroughly disgusted and Kate wondered if she should be offended.

"No thanks," he mumbled.

"I'm not a *sporting* woman." Whatever that meant. Kate had some idea, but she chose not to envision Rufus's version of such an evening. It was enough to turn her stomach.

"You sure?" Clive asked. "You got yourself in a nice triangle with Charley and his brother—the sonofabitch who kept shooting at us, by the way."

Kate had to repress the desire to slap her hat across Clive's face, bound hands and all. "I am not involved with Charley's brother. And for your information, I'm looking for Charley to break off our engagement, so I doubt he'll give up all your gold just to get me back."

"You're gonna break up with him?" Clive asked, surprised. "Why didn't you say that before?" He scratched his cheek, mumbling to himself. "All right, all right, lemme think. Well, here's the deal, miss, miss...what's your name?"

"Miss Kinsella," Kate answered through clenched teeth. It was at least the tenth time Clive had asked her name in the last two days.

"Right, Miss Kinsella. You need to wait to break up with Charley until *after* we have the gold back. Got it?"

Kate rolled her eyes. "Yeah, I got it." She thought about running off into the darkness, wondering if she could lose them. Maybe. Maybe not.

"Rufus," Clive said. "Let's tie her up in Harry's room. He won't be back for a bit anyhow. When he returns, we'll figure out what to do with her then."

Rufus appeared visibly relieved.

"Maybe we'll just have to take her in shifts," Clive said. "It seems to be the only fair way."

They dragged her into the hotel, and Kate marveled they had any sense of fairness at all.

---

KATE SLUMPED in frustration and let out an uneven scream. Clive had tied her to the end of a wrought iron bedframe, her hands stretched above her as she paused to catch her breath. The scar on her face snagged on her shirtsleeve and she turned her cheek to relieve the discomfort. It felt crusty and sore and the thread Ethan had used to stitch it up needed to be removed. She could only imagine how it looked and wondered if it might be possible to find the doctor in town and have him do it. Harry still hadn't returned; hopefully that meant he was with the doctor right now.

Hopefully?

God, it sounded as if she cared what happened to these three imbeciles. They'd caused her nothing but trouble. And Clive had tied her ankles together so tightly that she couldn't feel her feet anymore. Her efforts to free herself, which she'd struggled with for more than two hours she guessed, had produced no results.

She leaned her head against the metal frame, the cold surface pressing onto her uninjured cheek. The wind howled outside, and she wondered at the suddenness of it; the night had been calm when they arrived in town earlier. The grit of the dirt on the floor collected in clumps on her rear end and the bed linens smelled musty and well-used from body odor. Moonlight shone through the only window in the room and Kate tried to think how she could escape. She closed her eyes and tried to calm the discouragement swirling in her mind.

"*Yá'át'ééh.*"

Kate jerked her head up. She'd been sleeping. It was still dark in the room and the structure creaked as a blast of air whistled loudly around the wooden supports. Had she been dreaming?

"*Yá'át'ééh.*" It was an old man's voice. She hadn't dreamt it.

She spun her head around and saw a shadow standing in the corner. It moved toward her and to her disbelief it was Joe Tohonnie.

"Mister Tohonnie?" she whispered. Even though she didn't fear him, goose bumps rippled down her back.

"Greetings to you, Kate Kinsella," he said, his voice low and rhythmic, as if he were chanting his words.

"What are you doing here?" she asked. "How did you get here?"

"You called me," he replied matter-of-factly.

"I did?"

"I am particularly good at hearing the many voices of the wind. And yours is strong tonight."

"The wind outside *is* strong," she said. "It's good that you came inside. I can't believe you found me."

"Our paths converge," he stated. "What is so strange about that?"

Kate didn't know what to say. She shrugged her shoulders, although it was difficult in her awkward sitting position on the floor. "Might I ask a favor, as long as you're here? Could you untie me?"

"Of course." He moved toward her. "You are near to the land of my ancestors. I believe it calls to you. We await your arrival. And the wolf will guide you."

Kate opened her eyes. She lay on the floor of Harry's rented hotel room, alone in the darkness, the wind still blowing relentlessly outside. As she sat up, she realized her ankles and wrists were untied, the ropes lying to the side. She picked one up and examined it, looking closely in the dark then quickly scanning the empty room.

"Mister Tohonnie?" she asked. But she knew he wasn't there. She wasn't sure if he'd ever been there. Someone had untied her though. Or some *thing*.

She tossed the rope aside and shook off the creepy feeling that washed over her. She didn't believe in spirits or destiny or even sometimes—though she'd never admit it to anyone—in God. The day her father died she had lost the magic of life. And it seemed she'd been striving every day since to find it again.

Perhaps she had managed to loosen the knots herself after all. She must be more exhausted than she'd thought. But regardless of how it happened, she was free. She stood but her legs gave out under her and she slammed to the floor; her feet were still numb from the ropes that had cut tightly into her ankles. Carefully, she stood again and limped to the door. Cracking it open, she peeked into the hallway. All clear. She slipped from the room.

"No," a man grumbled loudly from the bottom of the stairs. "I won't pay that much just to have a bullet pulled from Harry's leg."

*Clive.*

Kate's heart raced as she moved to the opposite end of the hallway. Heavy footsteps pounded up the stairs.

"You gotta pay it," Rufus said. "It's only right. He's a doctor."

"And that means he can charge an arm and a leg?" Clive asked. "It ain't right. And there's somethin' wrong with it, besides."

Kate hid in the shadows at the far end of the hallway hoping neither of the men would see her. They opened the door to Harry's room and went inside. She would have little if no time to escape before they realized she was gone. Rufus didn't completely close the door behind him. Kate tiptoed as fast as she could past the room she had occupied for the last several hours and moved quickly down the stairs, her legs still aching from misuse.

"Where'd she go?" Clive roared as Kate ran out into the street. She looked right then left. The road was dark, windy, and deserted. The sound of loud thumps on the stairs told her Clive and Rufus were right behind her.

She darted around the building and then ran behind another, and then hustled toward the end of the street.

"Spread out! We'll git her!" Clive yelled.

Kate moved around a trading post but sensing a presence from behind, she jerked her head around and stared. A four-legged creature ran past, disappearing.

With a hand on her chest, she struggled to calm her breathing. *It was just a dog.*

She peeked around the building and saw Clive walking down the street carrying his gun. Rufus wasn't in sight. She needed to find a place to hide but most establishments looked closed. Movement to the left caught her eye. *Joe Tohonnie?* Maybe she hadn't dreamt him after all.

The shadow moved across the street and disappeared behind a blacksmith building. Kate ran to the other side of the street, hunching over to hide herself. Once she made it to the blacksmith, she glanced around.

"Joe?" she whispered. "Mister Tohonnie? Is that you?"

No answer but the wind. Kate began backing up toward the rear of the building, dread gripping her stomach. She swallowed hard, feeling uncertain. Staying close to the structure, her heart wouldn't stop pounding and her hands were clammy from fear. She swallowed hard again then turned to run but was caught short, letting out an involuntary gasp when the four-legged creature cut her off with a growl.

The animal's yellow eyes glowed by the light of the moon and he watched her with rapt attention, his body poised for attack.

A wolf.

Another low growl emanated from deep in the animal's throat and Kate fought the urge to flee. The wolf's head easily came to her chest; he would have no trouble chasing her down and ripping her to pieces. The gash on her face would pale in comparison to what he would do to her.

A commotion from behind startled her. Someone grabbed her, and in a frenzy Kate fought back, kicking and straining against the iron grip the man exerted around her waist. His hold loosened and Kate fell to the ground. She grabbed a loose board, and screamed as she swung it around, hitting the man's leg. But he didn't go down. She scooted backward and scrambled to her feet. The man grabbed her this time, facing her. Thinking it was Clive or Rufus, she continued to struggle.

"Katie! Katie! It's me. It's Ethan." He held her tight against the building. A sob escaped from deep inside her throat, a maelstrom that matched the wind roaring in her ears, and then Ethan's mouth was on hers.

Hot, insistent, devouring. She molded into him, her lips and tongue hungry for the sudden and consuming contact. She pushed her body against his, clinging to his broad shoulders, desperate to be closer still.

*He didn't abandon me.*

His mouth crushed hers and she felt on fire, head to toe.

"Rufus, you find her?" Clive yelled in the distance.

Ethan broke the kiss, and Kate reeled back against the building. "Let's go," he said and grabbed her hand, pulling her behind the blacksmith building.

"Wait." She tugged his hand to stop him. "There's a wolf." Her voice shook—either from the men chasing her, the wolf challenging her, or the man who had just devastated her defenses with one kiss. She could take her pick. She'd had a busy day.

"He's with me," Ethan said quietly. "He won't hurt you." The wolf suddenly appeared. "Bart!" Ethan cocked his head. "Come."

"Get back here," Clive yelled.

Kate looked over her shoulder and saw him in pursuit. He began shooting. Ethan ducked down and pulled her with him.

"Dammit, Clive!" Ethan yelled. "Give it a rest!"

"Bring her back," Clive said. "We need her!"

"I need her more. Run, Kate."

She did as he said, remaining hunched over. Ethan stayed behind her. The wolf—Bart?—ran to the left of them, disappearing over a slight rise in the terrain. Kate rounded a corner and saw three horses waiting.

"Get on," Ethan said, lifting her atop Whiskey.

He jumped on the other horse, the hide dark as night, and Brandy trailed behind. In a flash, they rode at a fast clip through town and into the desolate expanse of desert—into the home of the Navajo.

# Chapter Twelve

E than opened his eyes, the sky a light blue as the sun hinted its presence to the animals slumbering through the night. And to the people. He leaned against a rock, his back stiff and his body tired from too little sleep, but the bundle snuggled in his arms felt nice and much too right. Ethan indulged holding Kate because he knew that shortly it would be over.

He kissed her last night because he damn well wanted to. He'd missed her, he'd worried over her, and when he'd found her in the dark streets of Tuba City, any amount of reason and restraint he possessed had deserted him… and he hadn't tried to stop it. She'd been as hungry as he'd been…if Clive hadn't been chasing them, Ethan knew, with a grim finality, that he could have easily seduced her right then and there.

Ethan closed his eyes and clenched his jaw, fighting his own unruly feelings for Kate Kinsella. She was engaged to his brother—Ethan had already crossed a line and accompanying it was a good amount of guilt—and come hell or high water she was off-limits. He should be *thanking* Clive for saving him from a huge mistake. Ethan wasn't about to assume because Kate's response was so…

unrestrained…that she was ready to begin an affair with him. He wouldn't do that to her. She deserved better and Charley deserved better, as well.

Kate stirred against him; they'd ridden for a long while last night before stopping to rest. She had crawled into his arms and he'd let her, he'd wanted her to. But now it was time to end this, it had already gone too far.

*She's marrying Charley, for chrissakes!* One day she would have his brother's children, Ethan's nieces and nephews.

Ethan rubbed his eyes and swore at himself under his breath. His relationship with his brother just barely existed—this would surely crush it to pieces.

He carefully removed himself from Kate and stood. She leaned against the rock, sighed, then scratched the top of her mussed hair, most of it hanging in a limp braid over her shoulder. She wrinkled her nose then sneezed, which startled her awake.

She groaned. "I don't suppose you've made any coffee," she said, her eyes focusing on him. Then she smiled.

Ethan's gut clenched. Kate was lovely and bright and funny, and Charley was damn lucky to have found her because if Ethan had found her first…life would be different. But there was no point in going down that road.

"I can't believe you rescued me," she said. "I didn't think you would."

"Why would you think that?"

She shrugged. "How are Guy, Mashi, and Popay?"

"Their father found us, Masito. He's the one who gave me the horse and supplies to find you. He's taking them back to Walpi. Maybe once we find Charley, you and he can stop in and see them on your way back to Flagstaff."

Kate's expression became closed.

Ethan shifted his stance and glanced at Whiskey, Brandy, and Alo several feet beyond, resting and waiting for the journey to continue. He needed to set things right.

"Kate, about last night, about the kiss…"

He looked at her as she watched him, her expression stark and pale.

"You regret it," she said quietly.

"I'm sorry. I never should've done it. I had no right."

For a long moment she said nothing, her eyes focused on the ground before her.

"I don't know what came over me," he continued, "but I promise you're safe with me. It won't happen again."

She nodded, appearing a bit lost then chewed on her lower lip a moment. "Can I ask you something?"

Ethan waited.

"Have you really murdered men in cold blood?"

"What?" Ethan stared at her.

Kate stood. "Charley did speak of you a few times. He described you as…."

When she hesitated Ethan prompted her, suddenly curious what Charley had said about him. "As what?"

"He described you as somewhat ruthless, and crazy. He said you were responsible for a terrible incident with a stagecoach. That afterward, you roamed around with a posse, that you robbed people and hunted down criminals, but innocents as well. He said after your pa died that you stole all the money left to the both of you, that you never gave Charley his rightful share. He said you stole a woman from him."

Ethan heard the words and the bitterness laced around them, but he also knew the thread of truth that coursed beneath, at least in parts of it, and it left him hollowed out. He couldn't change the past, no matter how hard he'd tried these past years to do right. Maybe he'd been delusional to think he could even try.

"Is any of this true?" Kate asked.

"Some, yeah."

"Would you care to explain it to me?"

What he'd done in the past had been the actions of a

headstrong young man. He'd acted first, never pondering the consequences, and people had died because of it. He'd vowed never to repeat that life path again. But how could he explain this to her? She'd turn away from him for certain. And he realized he couldn't completely push her away. Not now. Maybe not ever.

"Kate, you're safe with me. I'd never hurt you." He knew that deep in his bones.

The look in her eyes told him she wasn't so sure.

---

AFTER A MEAL of corn and squash, supplied by Masito, they rode northeast. Kate was atop Whiskey, Brandy close beside her, carrying all the gear. Ethan seemed to prefer the jet-black horse—the two of them rode some distance ahead. It was best this way, she knew, keeping space between them. It shouldn't have surprised her that he regretted kissing her last night. She'd been all over him. What must he think of her? She was still engaged to Charley.

What a mess.

Kate didn't know what to think about her conflicting feelings for Ethan Barstow. And he hadn't denied the stories Charley had told about him, had even agreed that some of it was true. Which parts? And did it matter so much? After spending time with him, Kate had seen a shining goodness in Ethan that spread a wide circle. Didn't that count for something? Everyone made mistakes. Maybe he'd atoned for his.

And then there was the kiss.

Just the thought of it spread warmth deep into her belly, igniting a desire to touch him again, to have him touch her, his hands on her, his mouth....

Kate shook off the memory and pulled her hat lower on her head and scanned the vast, endless desert before them, blue sky and white fluffy clouds completing the picture. The isolation of the area made Kate feel small and insignificant. All her worries and cares—in the end it would come to nothing. She missed her ma again. When this was over, Kate decided, she'd return to New Mexico and visit her family.

Ethan spoke to her very little all day. They moved at a steady pace, in what direction Kate had no idea. That she had planned to find Charley alone now seemed foolish. She'd probably be dead by now. Perhaps it was Divine Providence that she'd crossed paths with Ethan. Perhaps it was fate that they had met.

Should she tell him the truth of her and Charley's engagement, that he really loved another girl, that he'd gotten her pregnant and run off to make his fortune? Kate suddenly realized how trite she might sound saying this to Charley's brother. And for what gain? That Ethan might scoop her into his arms and kiss her senseless like he had last night?

What if he didn't believe her? What if he thought her a wanton woman, saying anything to regain his attention, willing to sacrifice Charley's character and motives in the eyes of his brother for her own selfish wants?

Uncertain about her own motives, she did nothing.

They made camp in a ravine that offered some protection from the wind. Ethan made a fire while Kate rummaged for food. The horses whinnied off to the left.

Ethan stood and approached her. "Mashi wanted you to have this." He handed her the wooden carving the girl had possessed.

"She did?" Kate took the doll, touched by the gift.

"She was worried about you."

"I think she called it a *tihu*."

Without warning, Ethan cupped one side of her face, shocking her to stillness.

"Where's your wound?" he asked.

"What do you mean?" Kate tried hard not to react to Ethan's touch, but as his warm fingers rested on her cheek, a nervous excitement shot through her body.

He ran his thumb gently above her cheekbone, near her eye,

where Guy had hit her with the rock. With a racing heart, she brought her hand to her face to feel for the stitches and the crusty scab. God, what a sight she must be. Her fingers brushed his and she couldn't meet his eyes.

"The stitches are gone," he murmured. "There's only a faint scar." His hand moved to her jaw line and gently turned her face toward him.

For a moment Kate thought he might kiss her, then realized he was checking the other side of her face. Abruptly, he removed his hands, and she immediately missed the strength of his touch. She wanted it back. She chanced a glance at him and saw, only briefly, the confusion swirling in his eyes, the frown marring his handsome face.

"How did it heal so quickly?" he asked.

Kate looked away and ran fingertips over the bump of scar tissue—all that was left from her wound. "I don't know. I saw Joe."

"Where?"

"In Tuba City." It seemed odd now. "Maybe he did something."

"Such as what?"

Feeling silly to continue down this line of reasoning, she shook her head. "I don't know. Hasn't anything unexplained ever happened to you?" She looked directly into his eyes.

He matched her gaze. "Yeah. Twice." He turned and walked away.

Kate felt the wall between them as if Ethan had built it himself with bricks and mud. It was better this way. There was no sense even worrying over it, thinking about it, contemplating the other side….

But she felt an overwhelming sadness, and deeper loneliness than she'd experienced in a long time.

They slept on opposite sides of the fire, and in weariness, Kate dozed on and off all night. Her dreams were filled with the dark desert, the howling wind, and the search for a safe haven. She sought a faceless enigma just beyond the shadows of her own mind. *Ethan.*

Kate awoke with a start. It was still dark, but light was spreading in the sky to the east. Dawn would soon be upon them. It was so unlike her to awaken early. She felt tired but didn't want to sleep anymore. As she sat upright, a glance across the burned out campfire told her Ethan was gone—his blankets and bedroll already collected and tied together in a heap near their food supplies. Apparently, she wasn't the only one who couldn't sleep. *Serves him right.* Anger still brewed just below the surface of her emotions.

If Ethan didn't want her then why did he kiss her? Why couldn't he have kept his hands to himself? It was unfair to ignite a desire in her body and then leave her hanging. Shocked and annoyed by her thoughts, she stood and began folding and rolling the most uncomfortable bed she'd ever slept upon.

It didn't help that some of what Charley had said about Ethan was true—he'd possibly killed men, stolen from others and from Charley, and taken a woman from him. Was she deluding herself to think there was any good in Ethan? Was she simply the next person to be taken advantage of by him? Was the woman he'd stolen waiting for him at his ranch?

Kate brushed her teeth but didn't eat. Her stomach was in knots anyway—food didn't seem very appetizing. She paused in the pre-dawn haze and listened; nothing but the stillness of the desert. It called to her and melted into her bones.

She walked several yards from camp, took care of business, then noticed something move off to her right. It slithered along the ground.

A snake.

Since it was moving away from Kate, she felt safe enough to allow her curiosity to take over and follow. She wondered if it was a rattlesnake. Since they were dangerous, she wouldn't get too close, just follow it a little way.

The snake slipped quickly around rocks and underbrush, moving straight but contorting its body in an S-shape. Kate trailed behind and tried to move quietly. She got close enough to see the thick body of the reptile, the diamond-shaped head, and the rattles at the tail—most definitely a rattlesnake. It disappeared under a rocky overhang. Kate paused and waited for it to reappear; the steady sound of her breath filled her ears, but the creature didn't show itself. Finally, she turned away and headed back the way she had come.

Moving slowly, she relished the time alone. Ethan had made it difficult to think straight. As the stars disappeared and the sky turned a pale blue, she scrambled uphill to have a better look at the sunrise. She scanned the flat horizon, the Arizona desert spreading out in all directions around her. Kate could feel the peace and power here. She wondered at her own place in the world, her own power to make her way, much the way the snake had cut effortlessly through the sand.

If only life and the choices made were that easy.

Movement to the north caught her attention, and she watched for a moment until a man appeared. It was Ethan. Even at a distance she knew the outline of his shoulders, the taper of his waist, and his long legs. She strained to look more closely because she thought she saw a dog with him.

No, the animal beside him was large and much bigger than a dog or a coyote.

A wolf.

Ethan played with it as if it were a beloved pet.

Kate stared, mesmerized. Maybe it was simply the chance to watch Ethan with his guard down, but she drank him in like a woman thirsting for water after days of going without. His tall, lean body was relaxed, and he smiled and ducked and ran when the wolf pounced on him. Then he sat and scratched the animal's ears as his face was given a good licking.

A yellow light sliced across the landscape as the sun broke the horizon. Ethan turned toward it, and she was so aware of him that she noticed the change in his demeanor immediately. She glanced to the sunrise and saw two men on foot, their long hair flying behind them, coming toward him.

When she looked back at Ethan, the wolf was gone.

# Chapter Thirteen

E than met the two Indians on an open expanse of desert. Sunlight poured over them, bringing the landscape alive with vibrant hues of orange and red. Ethan could understand why the Navajo and Hopi tribes called this area their homeland.

There was a magic to it.

Not unlike a certain woman he knew.

He pushed Kate from his mind, but she never stayed out for long.

The two men facing him were on foot, wearing knee-high moccasins, leather leggings, long brown tunics, and colorful blankets draped around their shoulders. A red band of cloth was tied around the head of the shorter one; both men had long, black hair flowing loose. Ethan noted they were armed, knives at their hips, but he didn't feel imminent danger—and they were far enough away from Kate and the campsite. She was safe, for now.

"Mornin'," he said, nodding.

"*Yá'át'ééh*." The shorter Indian held out his hand to Ethan. His youthful features made Ethan guess he was eighteen or nineteen years old.

Ethan accepted the gesture and shook the young man's hand.

He looked to the other Indian—taller, with large gold hoops in each ear, shrewd eyes gazing down a long nose and sculpted cheekbones not unlike the red rock that had begun to surround them, his defined chin jutting forward—and guessed he was older.

"We watched you with the wolf," the younger one said, his round face encompassing dark eyes. "Where do you go?"

"North," Ethan replied.

"I am called He Who Casts Light. I am also called Lee." He gestured to his companion. "This is *Dziditháshii*." He paused and frowned. "How you say…scorrpeeeon."

Ethan nodded. "Scorpion. Got it." That one wasn't to be messed with. "Ethan Barstow."

"You travel from the south but that is not your point of origin," Lee said.

"No. I'm looking for my brother. His name is Charley. Maybe you've seen him?"

Lee was silent as a breeze lifted the ends of his hair from his shoulders. He murmured something unintelligible to Scorpion, who agreed with a slight movement of his chin. "There is a white man, he travels with Luci."

"Who's Luci?" The flair of hope that Charley might be carrying on with some woman, leaving Kate newly detached, startled him. He clamped down more tightly on his own desires.

"Luci is…Luci. One of our wisest elders." So much for the demise of Charley's engagement. "It is said she lead the white man because her husband told her."

"Who is her husband?" Ethan asked.

"Joe Tohonnie."

Ethan paused. "Do you know where Luci has gone? Could you tell me how to get there?"

"We take you," Scorpion said, his voice deep and gravelly, leaving in its wake an uneasiness in Ethan.

"Luci hard to find when on quest," Lee added.

Ethan considered the offer. In the vast expanse of the Navajo stronghold, tracking Charley would be challenging to the extreme. He'd known this but hadn't said anything to Kate about it. Talking to her was a lure anyway. The less interaction he had with her, the better. If he did go with Lee and Scorpion, he'd best leave Kate behind—except that Clive, Rufus, and Harry were probably still back there, somewhere. He didn't want to send Kate away, anyway. He wanted her company despite the torture being with her brought him. And if she were with him, he could protect her. He could think of nothing worse than losing Kate's light in this world, even if that light would never be his to hold.

Knowing he took a risk traveling with two strangers, Ethan nodded slowly. "I appreciate the offer. I've a woman with me." They would know soon enough.

Lee nodded. "You fetch her. We wait. Maybe we speak to the wolf."

"Bart doesn't make friends easily," Ethan said.

"Maybe the wolf says you are a man to trust," Scorpion responded, but his tone sounded skeptical.

Ethan wished that were true. But time—and his own lustful inclinations toward a woman who would one day be his sister—had shown that good intentions were an illusion for him.

Good intentions had lost him his pa. Good intentions had forced a wedge between him and his only brother. And good intentions had placed him in the company of a woman who shook the very foundation of his life.

He turned to fetch Kate.

———

LEE AND SCORPION didn't have any horses, something Ethan thought peculiar, but he did the only thing he could—he dispersed the gear among his three horses and offered Whiskey and Brandy to the two Indians. With reluctance, he put Kate behind him on Alo, her hands holding as little as possible to his hips, her breasts pressed time and again between his shoulder blades, her thighs touching his, a constant and painful reminder of how much he wanted her.

But he would ignore it. The alternative was to let her ride with one of the Navajo men, which was out of the question. There was no way in hell he'd let either of them touch her, however innocent it might be.

Kate was silent for a long while, accepting their new traveling companions without much of an argument. Ethan was loath to admit it, but he'd been hoping for more of a fight from her—antagonized friction between them was better than quiet consent. It gave him far too much time to simply think about her.

"Where's your wolf?" she said.

"How do you know about my wolf?" he asked over his shoulder, never really looking at her.

"Well, in Tuba City you told me, and then this morning I saw you with him. He's been following us for some time, hasn't he?"

"Yep."

"It was him that I saw before we crossed at the Little Colorado, wasn't it?"

"Yep."

"How did he get across the river?"

Ethan shrugged. "Probably went upstream and waited. The flow likely died down in a day or so."

"Did he follow you all the way from Trinidad?" She leaned a bit further around his shoulder.

Ethan was so aware of her he wished he had eyes in the back of his head so he could see the dirt on her face, the disarray of her hair, and the circles under her eyes from the same bad night's sleep he'd had. He wanted to see her without any barriers. He stared straight ahead.

"Bartholomew has become attached to me. He beds down under the porch on my ranch."

"Why has he stayed away from you since you came from Flagstaff?"

Ethan laughed softly. "Well, sweetheart, that would be because of you."

"Why? What's wrong with me?"

*Not too damned much.*

"He's skittish is all. And wolves don't really like donkeys, so I'm sure he wanted to give a wide berth to Fred. He doesn't know your scent, so he's understandably wary." *I should have walked away the moment you fell off that donkey.* But Ethan never could have done that. He'd caught Kate's scent and he'd never had a chance. He could walk away now, but it was too late—he suspected he'd never be able to fully erase Kate from his mind.

"Well, now you're making me feel bad." She shifted back directly behind him and took her hands from his waist. They weren't moving quickly, so she really didn't need to hang on to him. He contemplated kicking Alo into a gallop.

"I never meant to scare off your pet," she added.

"I wouldn't quite call Bart my pet. But don't worry about him, he can take care of himself. I don't think he was ever part of a pack. He's accustomed to being alone."

"Like you?"

The personal question took Ethan aback. Sharing with Kate was dangerous territory, despite his burning need to know more about her.

Besides, he wasn't really alone. There were plenty of people around him at the ranch—his housekeeper, the ranch hands, the occasional woman. He adjusted his hat.

"Nothin' wrong with being alone," he murmured.

The horses kicked up puffs of red dirt as they followed a trail across a stretch of flat land with crimson cliffs rising to the right. Clumps of Indian rice grass and snakeweed, along with the blackened and distorted specters of juniper trees, dotted the expanse. The uniformity made it difficult to determine distance, so Ethan kept an eye on the cliffs.

"How'd you find Bart?" Kate asked, apparently not content to let silence prevail between them.

"I've had trouble from mountain lions time and again getting at the cattle. About four years ago, I was patrolling one of the boundaries during the night when something spooked my horse. Whiskey threw me and bolted, and I became disoriented. I'm still not sure where the cat came from, but all of sudden there I was—face to face with one very unhappy female. I figured out later she had kits somewhere, and she wasn't about to let me get past her that easily. When I fell, I'd lost my gun, and my rifle was on my horse."

"And Bart saved you?"

Ethan laughed. "He made an amazing amount of ruckus which helped me get out of there, then he trailed me all the way home. After that, I started to leave food out for him, as a favor, and over time he became used to me, to my touch."

"You were very patient."

"With a creature like him, that's the only way to be." Ethan hoped that if he was patient enough with his feelings for Kate they would eventually fade to mere fondness.

He grimaced and willed the increasingly awkward desire for this woman to die a fast death. He could see no reasonable restitution of his thoughts from making love to her all night long to mere fondness and general apathy, friendly to her during the Christmas holidays while playing with her children. Charley's children. He clenched his jaw and tried not to enjoy her touch against his backside. But, damn it all to hell, he did.

It was late afternoon when Lee and Scorpion stopped at the base of a small mesa.

"We walk now," Lee said.

"To where?" Ethan asked and swung his leg over the horn of the saddle. He jumped down, then helped Kate dismount. Her unsmiling mouth and heavy sigh signaled her exhaustion. Ethan rested his hands on her shoulders longer than he should have, unable to stop from comforting her. A half-smile reached her lips and eyes, and Ethan felt unduly pleased by her response.

"To'onoh," Lee replied. "He lives just beyond." He nodded toward the mesa. "We will see if he is home and if he met with Luci."

"Who's Luci?" Kate asked quietly.

"I should have mentioned it," Ethan answered, forced to lean close so their conversation was private. "Lee seems to think Charley is traveling with her."

"Oh."

Kate's disappointment cut at Ethan. Did she miss Charley more than she was letting on?

He couldn't leave her hanging. "It would seem Luci is Joe Tohonnie's wife," he added.

Kate looked at him questioningly, the scar near her left eye reddened from their day in the sun. He drank in the blue of her eyes and filed the memory for nights when he was very alone, and very lonely.

"I'm sure she's quite old," he added.

"Oh." Kate looked confused.

*Welcome to my world.*

"Do you want to stay here?" he asked her. "You look tired."

"No, I'll go."

He moved aside and let her follow Lee and Scorpion, who had already moved a good distance up the hill on a switchback trail. Ethan tied off all three horses and glanced at the sun.

"How long will this take?" he yelled to the two Indians.

"Not long," Lee replied.

Ethan pulled his rifle from its scabbard on Alo and followed behind Kate's steady gait.

"You will not need that," Lee returned.

"It goes anyway."

As the sun sank toward the west, they crested the mesa and came to a hogan several hundred yards away with a makeshift corral nearby. Ethan noted fresh sheep droppings and possibly dog excrement, but no animals present. The place was eerily quiet, as if the resident had fled in haste.

Two crows landed on the hogan's mud roof in a flurry of black wings and cawed loudly at them. Superstitions aside, Ethan knew animals were keenly aware of changes in the environment long before men.

Lee knocked on the door, then entered when there was no answer. It was apparent no one was home. Scorpion started for the doorway, but then abruptly turned and began walking a perimeter around the homestead. Lee unhooked a strand of beads that hung above the entranceway.

"What's that?" Ethan asked.

Lee frowned. "Juniper berries."

"Does it mean something?"

"Maybe. Can be ghost beads." Lee carefully hung the strand back in its original location.

"So, To'onoh was afraid of ghosts?"

Lee glanced around the interior of the small dwelling. A pallet lay on one side, and a table and chair occupied the other. Another table held what looked like satchels of herbs or spices. There were jars filled with different powders with markings Ethan didn't understand. The place looked recently occupied, orderly and well-kept.

"He seem to be afraid," Lee said quietly.

Ethan walked back outside and noticed that Scorpion had stopped and was now digging in earnest with a sharp, pointed rock while Kate watched the two crows. Keeping her in sight, Ethan approached Scorpion, Lee behind him. "What's going on?" he asked.

Scorpion unearthed an object wrapped in a red cloth. Carefully, he laid it on the ground and uncovered the item, revealing a large, round clay pot with a small opening on the top. Lee knelt down and conversed with Scorpion in Navajo.

Kate moved to stand beside Ethan. "Is something wrong?"

"To'onoh is a medicine man," Lee said. "The crows alert us that all is not right. To'onoh has used his powers for bad."

"What does the pot mean?" she asked.

"To'onoh has placed a curse on those on the pot." Lee held up the clay piece and turned it slowly with his long, brown fingers. He pointed to several stick figures. "These are men. The lightning above show they will be struck down by such a force."

With the sun setting, the haze of dusk descended quickly. A chill ran down Ethan's spine as the wind picked up force. He glanced at the sky. It was cloudless, but a strong gale could appear at any time.

"Why would To'onoh place a curse and bury it right next to his home?" Kate asked. "Wouldn't that curse him too?"

"Maybe," Scorpion replied, his deep voice jarring in the ensuing twilight. "Maybe no."

Kate rested her hands on her hips. "Do you know who's been cursed?"

Lee glanced at the night sky. "It would seem that it is us who have been."

"You mean you and Mister Scorpion?" She gestured toward them with her hand.

"No." Lee held up the pot again. "It is all here, in the markings. The yellow indicates me, He Who Casts Light. The scorpion can only mean Dziditháshii. And here," he pointed to a small gray and white figure, "here is The Wolf. And the bent over trees indicate a strong wind. The wind buffets all of us. You are The Wind."

Ethan felt Kate shiver beside him, and he couldn't stop himself —he placed an arm around her shoulders and pulled her close.

Ethan feared that fate had just spoken to Kate, guiding her to this place, to him. He feared it was his punishment—to want a woman he couldn't have—for leaving his pa that fateful day years ago.

## Chapter Fourteen

"A curse? Is this a joke?" Kate whispered to Ethan as they sat near the campfire at the base of the mesa. The sky was pitch black, sprinkled with hundreds of stars, and Kate scanned for the most prominent constellations out of habit—Orion's Belt, Cassiopeia's W, the Big Dipper.

"Depends what you believe, I suppose." Ethan pushed at the firewood with a stick, orange embers sparking and flying upward.

Lee and Mister Scorpion were still gone, having left a while ago to do…something. Kate wasn't quite sure. A part of her hoped they would return so she wouldn't have to be alone with Ethan. On the other hand, *all* she wanted to do was be alone with Ethan.

"They had to be fabricating all that nonsense about you and I being painted on that pot." She continued to whisper since the last thing she wanted to do was offend their two traveling companions. She feared something even creepier could unfold.

"What about Joe Tohonnie referring to you as the wind?" Ethan asked quietly. "Or the fact that the wound on your face healed so quickly and with hardly a scar?"

Kate touched the soft indentation of skin near her left eye. "It certainly doesn't feel like much of a scar. Ethan, this is all starting to seem rather unsettling to me."

"Would you like to leave Lee and Scorpion behind?"

Ethan had hardly glanced at her since their conversation had begun and it was starting to annoy Kate.

"No, that wouldn't be too smart, would it? They're the best lead we've had on Charley yet."

"I can find my brother, with or without their help. But if we part ways with them then you have to stay behind too." Ethan turned his gaze on her then and the intensity she saw there shook her clear down to her toes.

"Do you want me to stay behind?" she asked, her voice breathing the question into the stillness of the Arizona desert.

"No."

He held her eyes a moment longer then returned to watching the fire. Kate felt Ethan's desire for her as if he had touched her, making her tremble as heat spread deep and low in her belly.

She looked to the stars, the patterns always a source of peace, but the safe haven eluded her, all due to the overwhelming presence of the man beside her.

She wanted to cry, and she wanted to scream. She wanted her longings for Ethan to go away, to loosen their grip on her mind and —God help her—her body. She ached for Ethan in a way that surely wasn't ladylike or proper.

*What was wrong with her?*

Lee and Scorpion returned and sat across from them.

"What now?" Ethan asked.

"This curse is a problem," Lee said. "We need to find medicine man to remove."

With exasperation, Kate said, "Is that really necessary?"

"We do not want to be struck down by lightning."

"Well, I certainly don't want to either, but don't you think we can find shelter if a storm hits? There are precautions we can take…the curse is just the power of suggestion."

"Perhaps, but bad spirits will plague us."

"I choose not to believe that."

Lee shrugged but looked to Ethan. Unflinching, Ethan stared across the fire then nodded slightly. And that was that. She never would have suspected that the reserved, closed Ethan Barstow was superstitious, but it seemed he was. Of course, after watching him with the wolf this morning, she should've realized there was far more to this man than he let the world witness.

"I'm going to sleep." She shuffled on her knees to grab her bedroll and blanket from the pile of gear she and Ethan had deposited earlier. "I hope you all won't be struck by lightning come morning," she mumbled.

It wasn't like her to be so sarcastic, except maybe to her brothers, and her ma from time to time, but she was tired and tense and feeling more than a little frustrated.

"Goodnight, Kate."

Her eyes locked with Ethan's and he gave her a half-smile that looked more pained than happy.

She lay down, closed her eyes, and tried to ignore the warm tingling in her body that took the better part of the night to calm down.

---

KATE AWOKE groggy the next morning, and in a fog ate the biscuit Ethan gave her. In no time, she was seated behind him once again as they headed north. She longed for Fred, despite all his jostling. Sitting this close to Ethan all day was nothing short of agony.

Lee had wrapped and carefully stowed the hex pot; Kate wondered what would happen if it got broken. Would the curse go on forever?

By mid-afternoon they came upon the Red Lake Trading Post, a partial two-story structure located on a barren rise in the terrain. Animals were in residence in the back—sheep, chickens, dogs, burros, and horses—and Kate wondered if Ethan would purchase another mount for her to ride. She didn't have enough funds to do so herself. Later, after he'd replenished their supplies of water, flour, sugar, baking powder, coffee, bacon, beans, and oats, he presented her with a gift. Not a horse, but a bar of soap. She didn't know if she should be grateful or insulted. Was her smell so unpleasant? She held her tongue nonetheless, taking the soap and murmuring a thank you. They shared a meal of mutton, boiled potatoes, and goat's milk served by an elderly Indian woman, which Kate devoured alongside Ethan, Scorpion, and Lee. The meal was the most delicious food she'd eaten in what felt like forever. With a full stomach, her energy returned and her mood improved. When another horse never materialized, she climbed aboard behind Ethan, determined to ignore his close proximity as best she could.

As they made camp that night, Lee told her of a small spring nearby where she could bathe if she so desired. She could only surmise that all of the men had tired of her grimy appearance and odor, so she took his suggestion and gathered a change of clothes and a hairbrush then followed the man.

Ethan was suddenly right behind her.

"What are you doing?" she asked, the words almost an accusation. She was desperate to have a moment's peace from him.

He checked his gun before putting it back in the holster at his hips. "Goin' with you," he replied. "And here," he handed her the soap, "you forgot this."

She frowned. It would be nice, she had to admit, to feel clean again. It had been many days since she'd had a chance to freshen herself. But her time alone had suddenly become very crowded.

"*He's* going with me." She thrust a thumb in Lee's direction, several feet in front of her. "It's not necessary for you to go."

"You're not his responsibility, you're mine. And in the middle of the desert, water attracts all sorts of animals. I'll feel better if I'm with you."

"I'm not your responsibility," she shot back. With her improved spirits gone, she was now tired and frazzled and fed up with her desire for this man. Why wouldn't he just leave her alone? "I've been on my own for a while." She turned and began walking toward the watering hole.

"The day Charley proposed to you was the day you became a part of the Barstow clan," Ethan replied, keeping pace with her. "It's my duty to look out for you."

"Charley and I aren't married yet." Temptation to share the whole truth pressed on her.

"Don't let me be the reason you don't."

"You've made that very clear." Her temper did a slow boil.

"What else can I do Kate?" His low voice strained in frustration.

She looked at him as he walked beside her. He wouldn't meet her eyes, instead, watching the terrain. She didn't know what to say. *You could kiss me again. I could tell you the truth. We could be together.* But all those sentiments remained lodged in her throat, coated by a wave of uncertainty about the outcome of such an admission.

"Promise me you won't let my actions turn you from Charley," he said, still not meeting her eyes.

Kate couldn't speak, wanting to say so many things but unable to begin.

"Charley's very lucky to have you," he continued.

Ashamed of lying, she remained silent.

When they reached the spring, Lee smiled and nodded, his youthful face eager to please. He pointed to the water then turned to walk back to camp. Kate looked around. There was little privacy. So much for shedding her clothes and getting a good cleaning. Dejected, she set her belongings down and sat at the edge of the water and ran her hand idly through the fluid. Out of the corner of her eye, Ethan paced back and forth then circled the water hole. He'd pulled his gun and was obviously scouting for trouble.

She rinsed her face and hands then rolled her sleeves up and washed off her arms. She removed her boots and stockings and dipped her feet. It felt nice after spending all day in the sweat-soaked footwear. She thought it would also be nice to rinse her clothes, at least the shirt she wore, since the white fabric was now a dusty brown. She wondered how she could do that without being half-naked. Ethan would probably look at her as if she were a tease. Agnes had been a tease, and Kate had never liked that aspect of her friend.

Kate resigned herself to rinsing out her stockings.

"What about the poor animals that have to drink that water?" Ethan asked, rounding his way toward her again.

Her hands stopped above the pool, wet stockings dripping into the water. "I didn't think of that. They're not that dirty," she said quickly.

"I can smell 'em from here."

She brought the dripping garments over dry land and wrung the last of the water from them. If he was chiding her, she was in no mood for it. She released a frustrated breath. "What makes you happy, Ethan? Because you sure aren't happy right now. And I have no privacy thanks to you so all I can do is rinse my stockings, but you don't like me doing even that."

He stopped. "I'll go sit over there, with my back to you. Do what you need to do. Call me when you're done." He looked back at her. "Or if there's trouble." He didn't wait for her reply but moved to a rock and sat with his back to her. He began to fiddle with his gun.

Kate scanned the area, accosted by a sudden play of nerves but quickly pushed the suspenders from her shoulders and began to unbutton the oversized shirt she wore, pulling it over her head. She removed her trousers but left on her camisole and knickers. She couldn't bring herself to stand fully naked with Ethan in her sights, despite his turned back. She leaned over the edge of the water and began rinsing her upper arms and legs.

A slight movement behind her made her freeze and stand

perfectly still. Slowly she looked over her shoulder. A wolf stood not far from her, his yellow eyes staring at her. She wondered if it was Bart. She hoped it was Bart. But, pet or not, would she be safe with him?

She should yell for Ethan but sensed if she did it would likely startle the animal. Carefully, she turned around. The wolf—with a black snout and face, and ears with white fur—took a few steps closer. He stood almost to her chest and his paws were huge. Rooted in place, Kate remained with her feet in the pool of water, stunned by how breathtaking he was.

He must be thirsty, so she painstakingly stepped out of the liquid and moved away from the spring, Ethan now behind her. The wolf's ears flicked a few times then he moved toward her again. Never taking his eyes from her, he put his nose to the water and began to drink.

Kate didn't move.

He was…magnificent. He raised his head, and she sensed his wary acceptance of her. Kneeling, she wondered if he might approach her; tentatively, she held out her hand.

A breeze blew the thick mane of hair around his neck. A chill spread over Kate's barely clad body but she didn't dare move, knowing that any sudden movement would scare the animal.

He raised his nose to the wind and flicked his eyes to a point just behind her then returned his attention to her. He lifted a thick paw and stepped slowly forward, but then he stopped, and Kate waited. Dusk was now upon them, and in the muted gray haze, she felt time fall away.

As the wolf moved closer, she stretched her hand out, and the animal gently sniffed her fingertips. In the back of her mind, she hoped Ethan wouldn't start yelling or making any noise about why she was taking so long.

ETHAN'S IMPATIENCE and concern were equally matched. Before he realized what he was doing, he glanced over his shoulder and froze.

Kate knelt with her back to him, shoulders and buttocks barely covered by some thin undergarment. To his disbelief, she was befriending Bartholomew, his wolf who approached no one. His mouth went dry at the sight of them of her. He held himself in check, not wanting to startle Bart. The animal was still as wild as they came.

He drank in the sight of her since he surely would never get another chance to learn the soft, shapely curves that were hers alone. Her brown hair trailed down her back in a loose braid, her skin pale in the twilight. As she bonded with the wild wolf, Ethan sensed Kate's own spirit, so wild in itself. It was as if two forces of nature had finally stopped their headstrong journey and paused long enough to find peace in the other's presence. He knew he intruded but was profoundly grateful he had some small entry to the world that Kate and Bart inhabited.

# Chapter Fifteen

K ate decided the next morning that Lee was superstitious after he chastised her for eating with her left hand. Mister Scorpion shook his head and hushed him on the subject, but Lee told her that ghost spirits use their left hand in that way. If she continued to behave in this manner, they might have to conclude she was a spirit. Not certain what to do with this information, she decided henceforth to try to remember to eat with her right hand.

"Have you always been a lefty?" Ethan asked over his shoulder as they rode.

As she sat behind him, she tried to ignore his masculine and totally distracting self. "Yes. But I think I can accommodate Lee and use my right hand. My brothers teased me endlessly about it, so I became adept at using both hands. It helps when I weave."

"What do you weave?"

"Blankets and rugs. I learned the technique from Mrs. Finley, who learned it from the Navajo."

"It must take a fair amount of time to finish one."

"Yes, sometimes weeks."

There were no clouds, just a few wisps on the horizon, so she felt certain lightning wouldn't strike anytime soon. Glancing behind, she noticed that Bart followed, which made her smile. The smile soon vanished, however, when her breasts reacted to contact with Ethan's shoulder blades every time she turned to look at the wolf.

The sensation left her wanting, and she knew Ethan was the only solution. Her mind dwelt again and again on the kiss in Tuba City. It had been deep and intense, overwhelming, dark and compelling. No one had ever kissed her that way, as if the contact were more important than breathing. She was beginning to think it was true.

"Bart seems to like you now," Ethan said.

"I've never been accepted by a wild animal. He's beautiful."

"Just be careful. *Wild* is the key word."

"But he's never hurt you?"

Ethan shook his head.

"Doesn't anything hurt you?"

"Not speaking to Charley in five years has."

Kate stared at the back of Ethan's neck, at the dark hair that lay in an enticing pile at the nape.

"What if he doesn't want to see you?" she asked.

"That's why I've come in person."

Kate wondered at the rift between the two men. She had thought it was due to Ethan's notoriety as a man wont to meting out his own form of justice, but the more she came to know him, the more she began to doubt this reputation. Was she being foolish for thinking this? *I don't really know this man.*

But her heart whispered that she did.

Was that childish? Wasn't it time for her to grow up?

Her ma had told her time and again—*you don't always get what you want or deserve.*

They crested a mesa and beyond saw a settlement.

"Navajo," Lee confirmed.

As they neared the dwellings—domed hogans made of wood and packed mud—small children in tunics and trousers ran to greet them. Several adults approached, the women in shin-length dresses tied at the waist and moccasin-clad feet. Kate couldn't take her eyes from the colorful blankets across their shoulders, certain the women had likely woven them. Lee and Scorpion dismounted so Kate took the opportunity to slide off Alo and separate herself from Ethan's constant touch.

Lee spoke in Navajo then gestured toward Kate. Ethan dismounted and came to her side.

"Doba is a medicine man," Lee said.

An old Indian, stooped and wrinkle-faced, bobbed his head several times. His thinning, gray hair reached his shoulders, and a blue bandanna was tied around his forehead. When he smiled, many of his teeth were missing.

"He will help us," Lee continued, "but not until dusk. They have offered you food and shelter, so we will stay."

"Do they know anything about Charley and Luci?" Ethan asked.

Lee conversed with the old Indian and several other younger men then turned back to them. "Luci passed through here three days ago with a white man of same height and face as you." He gestured to Ethan. "They go to the Sacred Lands."

"Can you take us there?" Ethan asked.

Lee nodded.

"Are you sure we can't leave sooner?"

"No. There is much need for this ceremony." Lee left them.

Kate sensed Ethan's impatience, but he returned to Alo and began to unpack their gear. Several women came forward and guided Kate to a small hogan.

"For you," one woman said. "And your man."

Surprised, Kate was about to protest but instead looked back at Ethan as he tended to the horses and smiled at some of the children. She glanced around the settlement and realized these people had little. Fussing about the accommodations would be small of her. And trying to explain that Ethan wasn't *her man* was probably not worth the effort. It would only be for one night.

"Thank you." She smiled warmly at the women and was guided inside the dwelling.

---

ETHAN WONDERED where the hell Kate had disappeared to. It was dark after he'd tended to Alo, and then had discussed everything from raising sheep to the seeming drought upon the land with the Navajo men around an outdoor campfire. Lee translated, but many of them spoke snippets of English. They'd eaten a meal of corn mush, Lee saying they were not to ingest anything else lest they contaminate themselves for the ceremony.

Finally, Kate emerged from a hogan wearing a colorful blanket around her shoulders, her hair swept away from her face and pinned in the back. He acknowledged her with a tilt of his head and she returned a slight smile. The women must have helped her clean up because she looked different. Beautiful…almost radiant.

"We go now," Lee said.

Ethan stood and went to her.

"She is to come also," Lee added.

"She's allowed?" Ethan asked, knowing that women weren't always accepted into Indian religious ceremonies.

Lee nodded.

When Ethan was close enough, he put a hand at the small of her back and guided her as they followed Lee.

"Where have you been?" he asked.

"The women said I needed to be cleansed before I could attend the ceremony."

"Didn't you tell them about the spring last night?"

"It involved a little more than just a bath." She hesitated. "They had to make certain I wasn't in the midst of my…woman's cycle. It could disrupt the energies."

Ethan hid his surprise at Kate's frankness and remained silent.

Lee stopped before a hogan and gestured for Kate to enter. She pushed aside the blanket and passed through the doorway, followed by Ethan, then Lee. Doba sat on the far side of a central hearth with a small flame burning, awaiting them. He nodded as they took a seat, his eyes dancing with what appeared to be amusement, his wrinkled face creasing deeply as he smiled. Ethan sat on the dirt ground beside Kate, close enough that their legs touched. It was fine by him. He'd missed seeing her the past few hours. Sometimes, simply being with her was all he needed…for the moment.

Lee sat beside the elderly medicine man.

Scorpion appeared at the doorway and Doba immediately spoke in Navajo, waving the man away. Lee argued with the medicine man while Scorpion entered the dwelling and took a seat beside Kate.

As Doba shook his head, Scorpion spoke, giving what Ethan thought was an ultimatum. But it was impossible to say without understanding the exchange.

"What's going on?" he asked Lee quietly.

"It is of no concern," the young Indian replied. "Scorpion will stay."

Ethan had the impression that Doba didn't like the man.

A young Navajo woman appeared, her slim figure clad in a colorful blanket similar to Kate's, her black hair bound at the nape of her neck and flowing down her back. "I am Nascha. I am daughter of Doba. I will assist." She gave a wary glance at Scorpion's profile and moved to a position beside the old man, sitting cross-legged like the others. She glanced to Ethan and then to Kate, acknowledging them with a slight nod. "We are always pleased to have visitors."

"I'm Ethan, and this is Kate."

Ethan felt even more prickly tension in the room, and from the corner of his eye saw that Scorpion's gaze bore into this woman.

She shifted uncomfortably and cast her eyes downward, but the taut line of her lips showed her rebellion of his scrutiny.

Doba began to chant. After several minutes, he stopped and removed the cloth wrapped around the pot from where it sat before him. He began removing items from inside—a pouch filled with what looked like dried herbs; a piece of bone which Doba promptly dropped to the ground. Nascha used a piece of cloth to retrieve the item as Doba spoke. "A human skull bone," she translated. "We must not touch direct."

More items emerged—rocks of various colors, a collection of dried berries, more bones—but Doba directly handled these remains, so Ethan guessed they were animal. There was also a torn piece of a weaving.

When Kate caught sight of the image on it, she gasped.

"What's wrong?" Ethan asked.

"That's from one of my blankets. I always weave an insignia of a bear in the right-hand corner." She pointed at it. "That's the bear."

Her shocked tone did little for Ethan's taut nerves.

Ethan frowned. "Why would that be inside the pot?"

Doba spoke, and then Nascha said, "It is not clear what this means."

"Did Charley have one of your blankets?" Ethan asked Kate.

"Yes. I gave him one. That could be from it." She took a deep breath. "So it was Charley who did this? Why would he want to hex me?"

Doba's nasal monotone filled the space as he spoke, waving a crooked finger over the items.

"He say the weaving may mean a bear," Nascha said.

"An actual bear?" Ethan asked. "Wait. Joe Tohonnie called my pa 'the Bear'."

Nascha's quick intake of breath caught Ethan's attention.

"Do not speak the name of the dead," she whispered. "It will invite a bad omen."

"You mean my pa?"

Nascha shook her head. "No. The other."

*Joe was dead?* Ethan exchanged a stunned glance with Kate, but it made a strange sort of sense. "I didn't know," he said. "I'm sorry. Scorpion and Lee didn't tell us."

Nascha glanced at both men, censure evident in her gaze. "Then they violate the traditions of the Navajo."

Ethan began to wonder if Lee and Scorpion had hidden motives, considering the discord evident between them and Doba and his daughter.

After an awkward silence, Kate spoke. "There's a curse upon Ethan's father?"

Nascha spoke in Navajo to Doba who then responded.

"Doba believe the bear is for you." Nascha's gaze rested on Ethan.

The old man spent long moments examining the outside of the pot, etched with stick figures and lightning bolts. At last he spoke, which Nascha translated.

"The figures are of men, perhaps Lee and Scorpion, perhaps other men you have traveled with. They can be any figures." She addressed Kate directly. "But the woman marked on the pot is not you, yet it is."

Ethan suspected he knew. What the hell was Charley up to? And did he still harbor so much resentment for him that he would take the time to curse his own brother and the woman that had torn them apart five years ago?

"A betrayal in the past?" Nascha asked.

Doba closed his eyes, chanted, and entered a trance-like state.

Kate rubbed her forehead.

Doba's eyes flew open, and he spoke briefly.

Nascha seemed to hesitate. "He say the curse cannot be broken."

"Why?" Ethan asked.

Nascha looked to her father. He spoke again.

"He say there is a wall, a fog, he cannot see past. There is something that is not finished. You should be cautious and not follow unknowns." She lowered her voice to a whisper, her eyes flicking toward Scorpion. "You should not follow spirits."

Unease snaked down Ethan's spine.

Scorpion appeared fed up, and Lee openly argued with Doba and Nascha in their native tongue, then the two Navajo men abruptly left the hogan.

Kate hung her head.

"Are you alright?" Ethan asked, suddenly concerned.

"My head aches."

Nascha stopped her side conversation with Doba and turned her attention to Kate.

"One last thing," she said, picking up the cloth that held the piece of human skull. She carefully tossed the item into the fire.

Kate wavered beside Ethan and he put an arm around her shoulder. In a short time, she lifted her head and looked groggily at him. "The pain has stopped."

Doba nodded, crossing his arms and rocking slightly forward and back.

"We are done," Nascha said.

Ethan pulled Kate to stand. "I would say thank you but I'm not sure for what," he said to the old medicine man.

"You will be safe here this night," Nascha replied.

He guided Kate from the dwelling. "You need to get some rest. Show me where you're staying."

She leaned against him. "I'm afraid we're staying together. They think you're mine. Or I'm yours. Or something like that. It seemed more diplomatic to let them think that. I hope you're not angry."

"It's hard to stay angry at you, Kate."

The wind blew hard against them, so he held her arm as they walked through the village to the far side and entered a smaller hogan. The burning hearth filled the area with a soft glow. Their bedrolls laid out, the blankets atop them. It appeared warm and cozy, and Ethan wasn't sure if he should be glad he would have Kate nearby tonight—her presence was definitely a tonic to his dispirited soul—or if being with her would be more of the frustrated torture he'd endured the past few days.

But he was tired, too tired to let the awkwardness creep up between them. Kate moved to her bed, removed her boots and the colorful weaving, and lay down. Ethan did the same, reclining beside her.

"Does Charley really hate you so much?" Kate asked.

Ethan stared at the dancing shadows flickering across the ceiling from the firelight as the wind howled outside.

"I didn't think so," he replied. "But I'm beginning to think I never understood him as much as I once thought."

"How did your pa die, Ethan?"

"Every year he would come to Navajo country. He seemed to love it here. I'd been away for a while, chasing my own demons I suppose, but then I returned so I came with him on his yearly journey. While we were here...we got separated." He paused, hardly believing this was the story of the end of his pa. "And he disappeared," he added quietly.

"What do you mean?"

"I searched and searched but I could never find him."

"So you had nothing to bury? Were you even certain he was dead?"

"No. Charley and I waited a year for him to return. But it was during that time that Charley began to accuse me."

"Of what?"

"Of killing him."

Kate went quiet.

"It's not true, Kate." The old wound began to ache, of not knowing his pa's fate, of finally leaving Navajo country to return home and resume as normal a life as possible, all the while holding out hope that Calder Barstow would show up one day with one hell of a story.

"I believe you." Her hand found his, the touch warm and accepting, supportive, almost loving. Since the day he'd lost his pa, Ethan had had little of that.

"Charley painted a dark picture of you," she said, "and to be honest, when you first found me, you scared me. During those first few days, I tried to get away because I was afraid you might hurt me. But Bart always kept me close to you."

The acceptance from her meant more to him than he thought possible, and the urge to pull her to him welled up inside with such ferocity that for a moment he couldn't breathe. Even his wolf had conspired to keep this woman nearby.

It was so damned unfair.

*I'm in love with my brother's fiancée.*

He'd wanted to believe he could find some measure of happiness again, someday, putting the misdeeds of his past to rest, putting the loss of his pa to rest. But why did it have to come in the form of the woman his brother planned to marry?

It was clear there would be no peace for him in this lifetime. *Time to accept it and move on.*

He closed his eyes and removed his hand. "You really should stay away from me."

And with that, he rolled away from her.

## Chapter Sixteen

K ate awoke abruptly from men's voices beyond the Hogan. She quickly pulled on boots and threw on a hat since her hair surely was a mess. Once outside, she stopped at the sight of Ethan arguing with Clive, Rufus, and Harry, her one-time captors.

"Like hell I will," Ethan said, his voice firm but tinged with impatience.

"Look, I know we shouldn't have took Caroline."

"No, no, Clive, her name is Kathy," Rufus interrupted.

"Well, whatever the little lady calls herself," Clive continued, waving off his cousin. "But you gotta understand—we really, really need to find Charley. And we're not too prideful to admit we need your help."

"I ought to hog tie the three of you right now and get the law on your asses for taking Kate," Ethan said, tying gear onto his horse. "Why would we willingly ride with you?"

Beyond the arguing men stood Fred the donkey. Kate winced from the bright sunshine as she stepped from the shadows of the hogan. "I'd at least like the donkey back," she said. "And while you're at it, my horse Pick, too."

Clive looked at her. "What the hell are you talkin' about? We can't give you those animals."

"They belong to *us*," she said in exasperation, her temper rising. Actually, Fred didn't belong to them, but she wasn't about to remind Clive. She'd become fond of the donkey and wasn't about to abandon him.

Clive started nodding, slowly at first, then more emphatically as his mind processed the information. "All right, it's a deal."

The three of them moved off to tend their own horses while Ethan turned his gaze on her. It was direct and shot straight to her toes. He seemed angry.

"Ethan, they're quite harmless," she said, attempting to ignore the shaken feeling she frequently felt in his presence.

"I'm not convinced of that." He returned to secure his gear atop Alo.

"Maybe they can help us?"

"I can't imagine how." He yanked the cinch of the saddle. "And I'll have to sleep with one eye open to make sure they don't nab you again."

"Look at this way. If lightning is to strike us all down, isn't it better to surround ourselves with other bodies to take the hit?"

Ethan stared at her. Then he laughed, transforming him from darkly compelling to utterly handsome. It squeezed her heart and made her take an involuntary step toward him. He could cast a line and reel her in, so willingly would she go.

"You better eat something," Ethan said. "As soon as I'm packed, we're leaving."

She nodded and went to retrieve her belongings, then gratefully took the food one of the women offered, a type of Mexican tortilla and a hollowed-out gourd filled with cooked squash. She quickly ate. When she approached Ethan—Lee and Scorpion nearby—she realized she could ride Pick now, instead of riding double with Ethan. It relieved her, but at the same time she felt a sharp twinge of disappointment.

She greeted her horse, who responded with a whinny, and rubbed the mare's neck. "It's good to have you back girl." At least Clive, Harry, and Rufus hadn't mistreated the animal.

"But I don't have a horse to ride," Harry said. "Now that they have 'em all."

"What happened to your horse in Tuba City?" Kate asked.

Harry huffed. "He got stolen."

"You'll ride Fred," Ethan said.

"Who's that?" Harry asked.

"The donkey."

"He can't ride Fred," Kate said, alarmed. "He's too big for the animal."

"Harry's a little smaller than the other two," Ethan said.

"Am not!" Harry proclaimed. "Besides, I wanna ride a horse."

Kate noticed that Scorpion and Lee had acquired different horses, obviously from the Navajos they'd encountered, so they would no longer need Whiskey and Brandy.

"He could ride Brandy," Kate said quietly to Ethan, referring to Harry.

"And who're you riding?" he asked. "Whiskey?"

"Did somebody say they've got some whiskey?" Harry's voice rang with hope.

Ethan looked at Kate and raised an eyebrow. She laughed and said, "You have to admit, this is all a little confusing."

"Do you really want to be close to *that* all day?" Ethan threw a glance toward Harry.

He referred to Brandy's propensity for sticking close to Whiskey, and he was right. Whoever rode those two would be quite chummy for the trip. A part of her hoped that Ethan would give up the black stallion and return to his own horses. But who would ride Alo?

"I'd thought to ride Pick," she answered.

Nascha materialized from the growing crowd. "I'm going too."

Ethan considered the woman, and then shrugged. "Why the hell not? The more the merrier."

Kate frowned. "Why are you coming?" she asked, unable to hide her annoyance. "Since you and your father weren't able to lift the curse, we're all supposed to be hit by lightning. Surely you don't want to put yourself at risk."

"I am not at risk. I was not painted on the pot."

"You have a point."

"I come to help, just in case."

"Do you have a horse?" Ethan asked.

"I do not," she answered, raising her chin. "I should ride with you?"

Kate didn't like that idea as an unexpected surge of jealousy flowed through her. Nascha was quite lovely with her flawless brown complexion, dark eyes, and trim figure. What if Ethan took a liking to the woman?

But Ethan shook his head. "No," he said. "Time to play musical animals again."

Scorpion stepped forward. "She will ride with me."

Kate didn't miss Nascha's stiff spine at the offer and her steadfast refusal to look at the Navajo warrior. She wondered what was going on between the two while at the same time feeling a bit relieved. Nascha was likely coming on this trip for the tall, brooding Navajo man rather than for the tall, brooding white man.

"No," Ethan said. "She can ride Brandy." His gaze swung to Kate. "You ride Whiskey. Harry can ride Pick."

It all made sense. Kate and Nascha would be chummy friends, no doubt for the best. Kate stroked Pick's nose, sorry to let her go to Harry, but she could at least keep an eye on them. Pick nudged her hand and bared her teeth.

Kate smiled. "Sorry dear. But I'll be nearby."

They all climbed aboard their respective animals, and amidst the flurry of farewells and good wishes, Kate cast a longing glance at the giant weaving loom near the hogan of one of the elderly Navajo women. Regrettably, she'd had only the briefest chance to inspect it the previous night. She'd need days, maybe weeks, to appreciate the artistry these women put into their weavings, the language barrier making it difficult to exchange information beyond admiration and smiles.

Kate returned her focus to the task at hand as eight riders went in search of Charley Barstow and Luci Tohonnie.

---

ETHAN'S PATIENCE was pushed to the limit. He concluded that Kate was the only sane one in the bunch.

Lee rode ahead of them, leading the way, but Ethan was beginning to suspect more and more that the Navajo man followed a hawk flying overhead than any known direction to the Sacred Lands. Scorpion seemed to be no help at all as he rode stone-faced at the end trailing behind Nascha, the Navajo woman also clearly uncomfortable. Ethan was ready to tell them to find a bush and get it over with.

That bit of advice could be applied to him and Kate.

To push that ever-persistent thought from his mind, he focused on Clive, Harry, and Rufus. Kate insisted on riding nearby, so Ethan cut his horse between her and them.

"You're riding too close to Miss Kinsella," Ethan said.

"It's all right." Kate leaned forward on Whiskey to keep Clive in her sights. "They were about to tell me how they know Charley."

"Charley told us he was gonna strike it rich," Harry said.

"How was that?" Ethan asked.

Rufus answered, "He said he was privy to special information about a copper mine."

"Hey," Clive yelled. "Shut yer trap."

"I don't understand," Kate said. "You all gave Charley gold to find copper? Why didn't you just hang onto your gold?"

Clive glared and cut off his brother and cousin when they tried to speak.

"Obviously they thought the investment was worth it," Ethan said. "Tell me what you know about this copper mine." He looked directly at Clive.

"Why? So you can steal it away from us?" the man accused.

Ethan shifted his hat and grimaced. "If you want my opinion, you're gonna end up with nothin' no matter how you look at it. But if you know the location, we might be able to find Charley faster. Then you can at least get your gold back."

They rode in silence a moment and Ethan was glad Kate stayed where she was—out of reach of these three idiots. The fact she was also close to him was beside the point. Nascha, atop Brandy, was ever on Kate's left but appeared disinterested in the conversation.

"He spoke of a Navajo chief called Hoskinnini," Rufus said. "He was goin' to look for him."

"Anything else?" Ethan asked.

"Look, we don't think Charley's the bad sort," Harry said. "Even though he *did* put a bun in that girl Agnes's oven."

Ethan stared at Harry, stunned. "What did you say?"

Clive hit Harry on the back of the head.

"Ow! Why'd you do that?"

"'Cuz Kathy there," he pointed at Kate, "is gonna marry him." Clive shook his head and sighed. "You're so thick, we oughtta use you for syrup on flapjacks."

"I thought she was breakin' up with him," Harry muttered.

Surprised by the turn of the conversation, Ethan turned his attention to Kate, but she faced away from him. The first thought through his mind was maybe there was hope where she was concerned, after all. His second thought—what a total and complete ass his brother was.

"Kate," he said softly, "what's goin' on?"

She smiled half-heartedly then shrugged.

"Did you know about this other woman?" he asked.

She kept her gaze on Whiskey's mane. "Yes."

"Was this before or after you became engaged?"

She hesitated. "Before," she stammered. "No after. I'm not sure."

"Why didn't you tell me?"

She bit her lip. "I'm not sure. I didn't know you very well and it's rather personal, don't you think?"

"Since when have things not been personal between us?" he asked, his irritation rising swiftly.

"Look," she said, her voice rising, "I've come searching for Charley to take him back to Agnes. I'm trying to do the right thing here."

"Are you going to break off the engagement with him?"

"Yes, that was the plan," she answered, again refusing to meet his gaze.

"If you want my opinion," Harry said to Kate, "that Agnes is no match fer you. You're much prettier and you've got a bosom that tempts a man a mile away—"

Ethan pulled his gun and pointed it at Harry's chest. "Shut up."

Harry swallowed nervously. He nodded, his chin jerking up and down.

Ethan slowly holstered his firearm and tried to gather his thoughts.

Charley had apparently cheated on Kate then run off to find a copper mine. She was chasing him to break things off, and had been planning to all along.

It felt like a punch in the gut.

Ethan kicked his horse into a gallop to catch up to Lee, who rode at least a quarter mile ahead. Kate was freer than she'd let on. If she'd had any interest in discovering what was between the two of them, she could have. She didn't need to stay so true to her engagement to his brother.

Ethan could only conclude one thing—he wanted her far more than she wanted him.

The entire day had just gone to hell.

## Chapter Seventeen

Kate sat by the campfire in a foul mood. She must be tired—God knew riding across the Arizona desert was monotonous and never-ending—because she wasn't normally so surly. She glanced around at the faces of her companions. Strangers and yet she had become accustomed to their presence. But the one she really wanted to see was nowhere to be found. Ethan had managed to avoid her for the remainder of the day after learning of Charley's supposed infidelity.

Was she suddenly afflicted with a contagious disease? Could Ethan not even bring himself to look at her? She didn't understand it. Was he angry about her not telling him what Charley had done? Or was he simply disappointed in his brother?

Ambivalence pushed against her. Should she tell him the truth? That she wasn't really engaged to Charley, that it had all been a charade? That she'd lied all along? She'd done it to protect Agnes and the baby she carried, but somehow Harry had known anyway. It wasn't such a big secret after all.

Ethan's dismissal of her left a gaping ache in her chest. Exhausted and disheartened, she couldn't eat any of the food Lee and Nascha prepared.

When Ethan reappeared out of the darkness her heart leapt, but he wouldn't look at her, making her humiliation acute.

"We have food for you," Lee said and handed Ethan a plate with beans and a meat Kate suspected was prairie dog.

"Thanks." Ethan took the meal and moved to retrieve his gear. "I'm up on the ridge tonight. I'll keep watch."

Kate stared—completely stunned—as he turned and left. Just like that. He hadn't glanced at her or spoken to her. He treated her as if she didn't exist.

It felt like a slap in the face.

She was shocked…and hurt. Didn't he feel *anything* for her? Because, God knew, she felt something for *him*.

In a daze she sat with the others, nodding and mumbling when they spoke to her, and then helping to clean up the food and set up blankets near the fire. She lay down and tried to sleep, tried not to think about Ethan off in the distance…somewhere.

Damn the man! He wasn't worth all this aggravation. She closed her eyes, but tears burned behind the lids. Pursing her lips, she took a ragged breath through her nose, then rolled onto her back and looked at the mass of twinkling lights in the sky.

Her eyes outlined the constellation of Leo, with its distinctive backward question mark, and Lyra, the harp, but she quickly tired of one of her favorite activities.

She soon heard snoring from Clive and Harry and sleeping sounds from everyone else. The fire had burnt down, and darkness now engulfed the camp. Before she could think better of it, she shot off the ground and grabbed her coat, and then stalked off into the night to find Ethan's solitary camp.

---

ETHAN STARTED AWAKE, his vision filled with the starry sky. He'd dozed, which surprised him. A muffled thump caused him to sit upright.

"Ethan." The voice stirred his senses. *Kate*.

"What's wrong?" he asked, resisting the urge to go to her. "Did something happen?"

"No. Everything's fine." She trudged toward him. "I came looking for you since you seem to be avoiding me."

He could hear the annoyance in her voice.

"Can I sit?" she asked.

In the dark all he could see was the faceless outline of the woman who haunted his dreams and every second of the day besides. Just being near her made him feel like he couldn't breathe.

"Yeah," he replied.

She sank to her knees a few feet from him.

Ethan rubbed his eyes and braced himself to not react to her proximity. He could do this, he reminded himself. *Just don't look at her*.

"Can we talk?"

"Can't it wait till tomorrow?" He stared into the inky darkness, the land varying shades of shadow.

"I don't think I can wait until tomorrow." She paused. "Something isn't right between us and I don't like it. Why are you avoiding me?"

"I just needed to be alone. Our traveling party has grown in number, of late."

"Aren't you worried about leaving me with Clive and Harry and Rufus?" Anger tinged her voice.

"You assured me they aren't a threat. Are you telling me I shouldn't take you at your word?"

Silence filled the space between them. When at last Kate spoke, her voice floated on the night air, barely discernible. "Yes."

Ethan waited.

"I haven't been completely honest with you," she said. "Charley and I aren't really engaged, well we are, but it's not because we love each other."

Ethan's heart skipped a beat and his gaze sought hers in the blackness. "What are you saying?"

"Charley is with Agnes, and yes, she's pregnant, but her family doesn't approve of him, and in a panic, he told everyone he and I were engaged. I wasn't going to go along with it anymore and that's why I came looking for him—to bring him back to Agnes. He doesn't know about the baby."

"Why would you lie about it?"

"I was just trying to help them. Aggie's pa is prominent in town and can be difficult to deal with. He really didn't like Charley, and Charley didn't help things by getting into fights at the saloon. I guess Aggie's pa pulled a gun on him, demanding to know what was going on between him and her, and he decided to cover his tracks by saying he was engaged to me. He begged me to go along with it, at least for a while."

"Why didn't you just tell me?"

"I was afraid of you in the beginning. Charley didn't have nice things to say about you, and I had no reason not to believe him. I tried to get away from you, but you suggested we search for Charley together, and I couldn't think of a good reason not to. Except of course now...now that there's..." She gestured her hand between the space that separated them. "...this between us. I didn't expect to like you at all. You weren't anything like I thought you'd be. And now you're mad at me, and you have every right to be because I'm a liar, but I'm not usually. I thought maybe you wouldn't appreciate me speaking about a deception that your brother was a part of. Family is family."

"Kate—"

"I'm sorry, Ethan. I should've told you. But as time went on, I became afraid to tell the truth. I worried what kind of woman you'd think I was." She stopped to catch her breath.

"Kate, I've only ever thought you were amazing. I've tried my best to stay away from you, all the while wondering how the hell I was gonna live with you as my sister."

"Then why are you out here? Why are you trying to get away from me?"

"It just seemed that if you felt anything close to what I feel for you then you would've come to me sooner."

She went silent.

"Kate, I told you that two unexplained things have happened to me. One was losing my pa, but the other was meeting you. I've given you a lot of thought, more than was warranted, considering I thought you were promised to Charley. The truth is, I want you as more than a passing fancy. But I was prepared to walk away, and I still am, because I don't want you if it's not in your heart."

Her face was stark within the shadows of the night, and the sight of her twisted his heart. Could he honestly let her go? Now that he knew she wasn't truly betrothed to his brother, he felt certain that if he pressed, she would yield to him. Was he desperate enough for her that he would take her under any terms?

"You ask so much," she whispered. "Sometimes it scares me."

"I'll take care of you. I promise."

Still kneeling, she moved closer. He reached his hand up and touched her face. Leaning forward, he kissed her, the contact feather light. When she didn't pull back, he brought his mouth to hers again, lingering, and her lips softened, welcoming the contact, and his mouth melted into hers as both hands cradled her head. She grasped his forearms, returning his kiss, first tentatively and then with a slow-building urgency. He rose to his knees and drew her to him, fitting her into his arms, and even through her coat her soft curves molded to his hard angles, softening the brittle edges of his existence. To have here was more than he ever hoped. He trailed his mouth along her cheek and across her neck as he buried a hand into her hair. A faint smell of sage underlay her scent, beckoning him with hunger and a desire that slammed into him.

God, he wanted her.

He willed himself to slow the pace.

He kissed her again, and she turned her head to the side, giving him a wide opening. He went deep, holding nothing back. Kate matched his hunger, her arms wrapped tight around his shoulders. He released her long enough to push the duster from her shoulders, then brought her body into contact with his, needing to feel her against him.

"Kate." He leaned his head downward, trailing his mouth to her collarbone. He brought a hand to one breast, feeling the shape of her despite the barrier of her shirt. She gasped and wrapped a hand around his neck as he came back to her mouth and took her in another breathless kiss.

---

KATE FELT the power of Ethan's desire and it fueled her own; a desperate, overwhelming craving to be close to him. She'd never been kissed like this, never felt the force of sex so tantalizing, so near. It excited and frightened her at the same time. But hadn't she come to this? Hadn't she all but asked him for this?

"Kate," Ethan said, his voice strained and hoarse as his breath mingled with hers. "I'm sorry. I can't seem to hold back."

"I'm not very experienced with this," she whispered.

"I know." He kissed her, lingering for a moment, then sat back on his heels. He took her hand. "Maybe we should talk."

He lay down and drew her beside him. "I'll try to behave," he added.

She nestled in the crook of his arm, resting her head against his shoulder, and his arm drew her close, warming her in his embrace.

"I've never been with anyone before," she said, glad he couldn't see her face, feeling embarrassed by the admission. Her lack of experience bothered her.

"That's nothing to be sorry for." He kissed the top of her head.

She moved closer to him, the length of her body flush against his. It felt so nice to be near him, to touch him, to release the frustration from being so god-awful drawn to him. She could feel his heartbeat beneath her hand, strong and fast, and wanted to be a part of him, to have her heart beat near his, with the same rhythm, the same need. An urge to shed her clothes overcame her, to touch her skin to his with no barriers. What would it feel like? Should she tell him the impassioned thoughts she had of him, of them together?

She moved her hand to the buttons at the top of his shirt. Carefully she loosened one, then another, then slid her hand underneath the cloth and made contact with his bare chest, her fingers encountering chest hair and warm skin. She leaned toward him and kissed his neck. The arm that encircled her tightened, and his hand slid to her buttocks, urging her closer. She shivered and arched her back slightly. He rolled to face her and as his mouth took hers she was forced to pull her hand from inside his shirt, so she came from underneath, her palm sliding up his bare back.

"Kate, can I touch you?"

She nodded, murmuring an affirmative noise. His long fingers slid beneath her shirt, beneath her camisole, and didn't stop until reaching her breasts. Her breath caught as he gently squeezed, the sensation causing a cascade of desire to pour through her body. She rolled to her back and he kissed her—hot, deep, unrelenting. Reason fled, and only the needs of her body made sense.

The assault continued, and Kate joined as a full participant, tugging at Ethan's clothes as he helped to remove hers. Every chance she had she touched him, hungry for the skin to skin contact, wanting to please him with her body, hoping that he found it to his liking. At the same time, she was so ravenous for his that she no longer cared about her inhibitions.

When he had her naked and beneath him, he hovered above her, trailing his mouth from her neck to her breasts. The sensation caused her to gasp and arch her body to his, desperately seeking contact. His hand trailed along her ribs to her hip then between her legs. The touch jolted her, and she let out a startled cry; Ethan stopped and kissed her, then began slow ministrations in the most private place she could imagine on her body. Slowly the tension dissipated, only to be replaced with a new pressure, mounting in need deep inside. He gently nudged her legs apart, and she felt the strain of him entering her. She hesitated as she wondered if this would work, if maybe she wasn't ready.

Ethan paused and gently kissed her. "Kate, do you want me to stop?"

She could feel the toll the restraint took on him. His breathing was labored and despite the cool night a thin film of sweat broke out on his back where her hands held onto him. Fearful of what was to happen, her body nevertheless responded to his close proximity, longing to be close, longing to settle the restlessness that had been ever-present since she'd first met him.

"No," she whispered, pulling him to her, urging him to continue.

He pushed into her, withdrawing then pushing again, guiding her legs apart a bit farther, finally allowing him to be completely joined to her. He held still, his mouth finding hers, and she felt a growing, clawing need begin to stir, first slowly, warming her from inside like the comfort of a burning campfire, then becoming more frenzied. She began to move, and Ethan moved with her. He filled her completely, again and again, and her body shook as she tightened and the release finally took her. Ethan's body clenched against hers, his body taut, and Kate was awash with pleasure—hers, his, the magic they created together.

As the need diminished and their bodies rested, Kate continued to hold him, suddenly aware of the tears that streaming down the sides of her face, pooling into her ears. Ethan remained atop her, wrapping his arms tighter and burying his face into her neck. Kate locked her legs around his, and together, they breathed as one.

## Chapter Eighteen

E than lay on his back while Kate slept in his arms. He dug a hand into her hair, unbraided now, and buried his nose in it. This was the best dream he'd ever had.

Totally nude against him, Ethan ran a hand down to Kate's rounded bottom and glanced at the soft cleft between her breasts, just visible above the blanket that covered the two of them.

For the first time in a long while, he felt content. Almost at peace.

He wondered how long to wait before waking her. He needed her again already.

On the heels of that thought, his body came awake.

He shouldn't have completed himself inside her, but in the final moment he hadn't been able to withdraw. Her response had been so sweet, so willing, so open, offering him more passion than any accomplished lover he'd ever had. If they had a child together, would it be such a bad circumstance? Was it wrong to want a binding between them that could never be broken?

She stirred against him. He leaned down and kissed her.

"Is it always like this?" she said against his mouth.

"No." He pushed long hair away from her face. "It's never like this."

He covered her mouth with his and indulged the taste of her, the texture of her lips, the scent of her skin. She sighed as she lay on her back, and Ethan explored her body with his hand and his mouth. In the darkness, it felt better than any of the erotic dreams he'd ever had of her. Soon, he rolled atop her, making love slowly but no less intensely than the last time.

She fit him perfectly.

---

KATE CAME AWAKE as dawn hinted on the horizon. It was too early for her, so she closed her eyes again.

"We need to get dressed and get on back to the others," Ethan said. He sat up and lightly ran a finger down her bare back as she lay turned away from him.

Kate tucked the blanket more fully beneath her chin—she didn't want to get up just yet.

"If you don't get some clothes on, Kate Kinsella, I'll be hard-pressed to keep my hands off you."

Ethan's deep voice caressed her waking dreams.

"That sounds fine to me," she mumbled, still not opening her eyes.

"You like to sleep more than any other creature I've ever met." He kissed her shoulder.

She turned her face to his. "If we're not supposed to sleep then why did God create it?" She smiled as his lips covered hers. Then he withdrew, and she made a noise of disappointment.

Rubbing her eyes, she sat up while holding the blanket to her breasts. After what they'd done all night long it certainly wasn't necessary, but in the dawning light she felt a bit shy.

Confused by which clothes were hers, she waited while Ethan

handed first her shirt then her trousers then her boots, then finally her camisole.

He repacked his gear while Kate dressed, then she combed her hair with her fingers and braided it, finally pulling on her hat.

"If we find water, we'll stop so you can get cleaned up," he said.

A little embarrassed, Kate nodded. She was sore and…well, sticky between her legs. What had she turned into during the night?

*A woman*, her mind whispered.

"Are you ready?"

She stood, a little disappointed to leave their intimate camp. "Yes."

He handed her duster to her and kissed her one more time, lingering long enough to make Kate wonder if they might be disrobing again; but then he reluctantly released her. He grabbed her hand as they walked back to camp.

She tried very hard to keep the smile off her face, but she obviously failed when Nascha saw her. "Was it really that good?" the Navajo woman asked, raising an eyebrow.

Caught off-guard, Kate answered honestly, "Yes."

"Should we be havin' hanky panky on this trip?" Harry asked, several feet away.

Kate pretended not to hear him while gathering her belongings.

"I mean, isn't there somethin' bad about relations," he continued, "in this area? You know, aren't we on sacred Indian land, or somethin'?"

"When have you ever worried about the location of relations?" Rufus asked Harry, laughing. As Ethan walked past him, Rufus slapped him on the shoulder. "I guess it don't matter that she's gonna be your sister-in-law."

"For the record," Ethan said, "she's *not* going to be my sister-in-law."

Kate slid a sideways glance in his direction as she loaded gear onto Whiskey. Ethan wasn't one to defend his actions, especially to Rufus.

"Oh." Rufus nodded his head slowly. "She's gonna be your wife." He laughed again. "I don't think Charley's gonna like this."

"There are times," Lee said from atop his horse, "when it is said the spirit lights a fire inside of a man. There is always a purpose." He moved his horse forward.

"Huh?" Harry said, confusion plain on his face.

Ethan helped Kate atop Whiskey, and she gave him the barest hint of a smile. He responded by briefly resting a hand on her thigh, giving a squeeze before he withdrew.

Rufus snickered. "Harry, it just means fellas can't stay away from fine-lookin' females."

---

It was mid-afternoon when Nascha approached Kate while they took a break near a small watering hole. It wasn't big enough to bathe in, and Kate resigned herself that by nightfall there wouldn't be anything pretty about her smell.

"Are you really such a woman?" the Navajo woman asked.

"Pardon?" Kate glanced upward as she knelt by the water to splash her face.

"To give herself to the brother of the man she is to marry."

"Oh." Kate used the end of her dark shirt to dry her face. "There's more to it than that."

"But what of the brother?" Nascha accused. "How can you treat him so?"

"Because he doesn't really love me. He loves someone else."

Nascha looked away, her face drawn and her lips pressed into a firm line.

"Why are you so upset?" Kate asked, but then realization dawned. "Are you having trouble with Scorpion?"

Nascha didn't answer immediately but slowly her face shifted into a look of bleak resignation. "It is difficult to be near him."

Kate stood and adjusted her hat. She supposed that the tall, muscular, and reserved Navajo was very handsome, to a woman who would respond to it. Heat filled her belly as she remembered how she'd responded to Ethan. The right man could change any woman's mind. If they only knew the power they had.

That was it.

"You're afraid of the way he makes you feel," Kate said.

Nascha shook her head as her eyes narrowed in clear denial. "I feel nothing for him."

Kate didn't believe her.

Nascha wrung her hands then looked to the sky. "I was promised to him. I was happy because I am much past the marriage age. But during the winter months something changed. He became different. He didn't smile, he didn't laugh. And then he did not want me. He cast me aside to marry another, a much younger maiden."

"Scorpion is married?" Kate asked, surprised.

Nascha shook her head. "No. He is to marry at the next full moon."

"If all of this bothers you so much then why did you come with us?"

The wind blew Nascha's black hair from her shoulder and she put her face into the breeze and closed her eyes. "I have visions," she whispered. "The lightning. I cannot stand by and let him die."

A chill ran down Kate's spine. "Do you mean Ethan?"

Nascha's dark eyes focused on her. "No, Scorpion. But now, I cannot be so close to him and not feel a sorrow for everything that is lost."

The wind whistled across the reddened desert. A gust caused Kate to sway, and she planted her feet firmly to the ground. A quick glance told her Ethan was still with the two Navajo warriors a few hundred yards from them, and Clive, Harry, and Rufus were bickering some distance away. "What if everything isn't lost? Have you talked to him?"

Nascha watched her, contemplating.

"Maybe he's just as confused," Kate added. She smiled and touched the woman's arm, then left her and moved toward the men.

"Everything all right?" Ethan asked, nodding toward Nascha.

"Nascha and Scorpion have unfinished business between them."

"Yeah, I've noticed. Maybe they just need their own campsite tonight." He grinned.

She returned the smile, but then became serious. "Do you think Charley will be mad? About us, I mean?"

Ethan's pensive demeanor caught her attention. "Why would you say that?" he asked. "You said he was only with you to hide his feelings for Agnes."

"Yes, but it's unlikely Clive, Harry, and Rufus will keep their mouths shut. On the surface, this all seems very untoward."

"So, you're worried about your reputation?"

"Well, yes, I suppose I am."

"How long do you plan to keep the engagement going?" he asked.

"In truth, I don't know. I need to talk to Charley first. Will he be angry at you? About us?"

Ethan hesitated. "Yeah, maybe."

"I don't want to create more problems."

"Well, you seem good at that."

"What's that supposed to mean?" she asked, feeling defensive.

He stopped and shook his head. "Sorry, that didn't come out right." His eyes locked with hers. "I don't regret what happened, and we'll deal with what comes when it comes."

Caught in Ethan's gaze, Kate knew she was in over her head.

# Chapter Nineteen

E than spotted the riding party in the distance, and before Lee returned to report back, he knew they were Navajo.

"Trouble?" Ethan asked, halting Alo. He kept the horse facing the coming riders, hiding Kate from their view.

"Maybe," Lee answered. "It is Hoskinnini."

"Charley was looking for him. I'll ride with you to meet them."

"Your woman should stay here."

Ethan turned Alo and brought the horse beside Kate. "Stay back. If there's trouble, ride with Nascha and get the hell out of here."

Kate gave a slight nod. "Be careful."

He rode with Lee and Scorpion to the approaching men. It was late afternoon, and they had the advantage of the sun at their backs. Ethan counted six men, and they all appeared capable of inflicting damage if they were so inclined.

"*Yá'át'ééh*," Lee said.

The man sitting slightly ahead of the others nodded. He was older with long black hair and a wrinkled, leathery face, giving a hint of the hard life the Navajo had endured in this area. Ethan knew some had avoided the Long Walk in '64—his pa had spoken of it to him and Charley when they were boys—and he suspected Hoskinnini had been one of many who had proved elusive to the U.S. Army and their efforts to take all Navajo to the Bosque Redondo reservation.

Lee spoke in Navajo, then said to Ethan, "I told him we come in peace and seek permission to cross the *Toh-den-nas-shai*. That is what this land is called."

The older Indian watched Lee then turned his gaze to Ethan.

"I am Hoskinnini," he said, speaking English. "A large party travel with you. What is purpose?"

"We're looking for a man called Charley Barstow," Ethan replied.

"Your kin?"

"Yes, have you seen him?"

Hoskinnini bowed his head. "He travel with Luci Tohonnie."

"Can you give his path?" Lee asked.

Hoskinnini regarded them with a shrewd gaze. "North. Is there a healer among you?"

Lee glanced behind to where the women waited with Clive, Rufus, and Harry. "Nascha is skilled."

"We invite you to camp with us tonight. Bring this Nascha to attend us."

Lee glanced at Ethan who silently agreed. Hoskinnini ruled the land they were about to enter, it wouldn't be wise to piss him off. A quick scan of the men riding with the Navajo leader didn't put him at ease. He could only hope they'd show no interest in Kate. As for Nascha, she was Scorpion's problem, and Ethan didn't doubt he would fend off any advances toward her.

He rode back to fetch his woman.

———

IT WAS WELL after nightfall when Ethan returned to the camp he had made earlier with Kate. She watched him in the flickering firelight as he sat down beside her. Lee, Scorpion, and Nascha remained with Hoskinnini and his men. Clive, Rufus, and Harry had made their own camp some distance away at Ethan's stern suggestion. Even if he hadn't wanted to be alone with Kate, he wouldn't have shared sleeping territory with the three buffoons.

"Did you learn anything more about Charley?" she asked.

Ethan placed another mesquite branch on the fire. "I've got a good idea of the general direction he's headed. Hoskinnini said Charley wanted to know the location of any copper mines, and he offered gold for the information."

"Clive's?"

"No doubt. But the chief didn't take it since he didn't know of any copper worth mining in the area."

"Do you think that's true?"

Ethan shrugged. "Maybe, maybe not. I doubt Hoskinnini wants a swarm of people in here."

"So, has Charley gone looking for it himself?"

"Apparently. Luci urged him to follow her, that she would aid him where the others had failed. At first light, we'll set out." Flickering campfires in the distance signaled the other two camps, but they were far enough away to afford him and Kate privacy.

"Ethan, can I ask you something?"

He nodded.

"Did you steal a woman from Charley like he said?"

"It wasn't the way he made it sound," Ethan replied. "After our pa disappeared, Charley up and left, leaving me no choice but to run the ranch and the finances. I didn't cut him out on purpose. One day, he showed up out of the blue with a girl named Jessica, and he meant to marry her. It all seemed fine, I s'pose, until Jessica realized that Charley didn't really have a stake in the ranch. After my pa had disappeared, everything had been in limbo for a while. I was finally able to have the local magistrate draw up papers declaring him dead, and his will, written many years before, put me in charge of everything along with the trust to run it. I don't really know why my pa did it that way. There was a time when I wasn't the most reliable son, either.

"Anyway," he continued, "Jessica got sweet on me, something I didn't encourage. I never felt anything for her more than brotherly affection, but one day, she approached me and unfortunately Charley came across us. He wouldn't believe anything I had to say, then soon after, he left. That was the last time I saw him.

"I think the business with the hex pot may be about her, not you. Charley must think I'm still with her, that I've brought her with me to find him."

"He must still be very angry then," Kate said.

"Yeah." Ethan felt resigned to the fact that the air might never be cleared between the two of them. And now he was involved with Kate, and although she and Charley hadn't really been engaged, he started to wonder if Charley wouldn't be angry about this, too.

"I knew I'd have to come after Charley in person, that he'd never come to me, so I traveled to Flagstaff. I found Mrs. Finley and she told me he'd run off and that you, his fiancée, had gone in pursuit of him. She urged me to find you because she was worried."

"That's how you came upon me?"

He nodded. "I came looking for Charley, but I discovered you instead." He found far more than he'd ever hoped. Even if he and Charley never reconciled, he could never regret meeting Kate. He smiled, his gaze locking with hers, and he could feel the hunger and desire between them, a need so compelling it drenched his senses like a thunderstorm over the desert. But uncertainty simmered just below the surface.

"Kate, I want you to know I don't take last night as a passing fancy. Maybe you could think about moving back to Trinidad."

She paused, the campfire casting shadows across her face.

"I'm sorry," he said. "It seems we Barstow men like to rush things with you."

"No, it's not that." She watched the flames sliding along the wood, snapping and popping. "It's just that my pa died there. I never thought I'd return."

"Maybe that's why you should."

The ashen look on her face eased a bit and her features softened.

Ethan moved around the fire on hands and knees and kissed her lightly. She touched his face, smiling when he fell against her as he tried to shift to a sitting position. The next kiss went deeper, and he looped his arm around her to keep her close. Her mouth opened to his, accepting what he had to offer, as starved for him as he was for her. As he eased her back, she abruptly broke the kiss and sat upright.

"They'll all see us," she said, waving her arm toward the other two fires flickering in the distance.

"I doubt they're watching." Ethan moved to kiss her again.

She pushed against his chest. He leaned further for her mouth anyway and was rewarded with brief contact.

"They'll think we're...wanton," she said, her quick breaths encouraging him.

He moved to her neck, which made her squirm and then laugh. She pushed at his chest again.

"I can put the fire out," he murmured against her ear.

"Yes, that might be best," she replied, relief apparent despite her taut voice.

He knew she meant the campfire, but he took her agreement as a sign to move forward with the seduction of her body as well. He needed her. He hoped she needed him as much. He broke contact from her just long enough to douse the flames with dirt, then he grabbed a blanket, laid it onto the ground, and pulled her into his arms, his mouth consuming hers.

She responded to him with an honesty and a desire that surprised him, and he gave himself to it. He removed her clothing, all the while tasting, kissing, caressing every inch of Kate.

Everything about her enticed him, from the curve of her breasts to the taper of her waist, and her ivory skin bared to him. He willed himself to take time to make certain she was ready for him but when she finally arched her back and beckoned him, he didn't wait. As he joined with her, his strong release shocked him with its intensity. He ran his lips from her mouth to her neck, the fingers of his right hand tangled in her hair and his left splayed beneath her buttocks. She smelled of sweat, dirt, sex, and the unique smell of Kate, a scent that made him hunger for her again. He let the desire build more slowly the second time, drinking her in, satisfying his need to know every inch of her.

When sleep called, Ethan finally relented and pulled Kate's naked body to his, covering her with another blanket. He didn't want any of their traveling party or Hoskinnini and his men to stumble upon them, but he also made no effort to convince Kate to clothe herself. She settled against him, her head resting in the crook of his shoulder.

And with no barriers between them, they finally slept.

---

AT DAWN, Kate felt Ethan awaken and shift his position. She grabbed his hand. After the night they'd shared, after his relentless assault on her body, she didn't want to be parted from him. He leaned down and kissed her.

"Hoskinnini is signaling me to come over," he said. "Stay here. I'll be right back." His mouth covered hers again and she ran her fingers along the stubble on his jawline. He broke the kiss, his lips hovering above hers. "As much as I hate to say it, you'd better get some clothes on."

She groaned, barely opening her eyes as he moved away from her.

She rolled to her back and wondered if sleep might reclaim her. It was certainly her first choice of options; but instead, she sat upright, holding the blanket to her chest to hide her nakedness. She watched Ethan walk toward the Navajo men in the distance, enjoying his broad shoulders, his steady gait, his nice hips, his...

She smiled, remembering their hours in the dark. She and Ethan had been up half the night, at least.

As the sun crested the horizon with a sharp slant of light, Kate donned her camisole, knickers, trousers, shirt, and boots. With the promised warmth of the coming day, birds began chirping, and the colors of the desert shifted from gray to vibrant reds and browns.

She was packing up camp when Ethan returned, walking with grim purpose, his face shadowed by his hat.

"Bart's gone."

"What do you mean?"

"Hoskinnini got word this morning. A band to the west picked him up."

"He's not...."

"Dead?" Ethan shook his head. "Hoskinnini doesn't think so. Two of his men are going to take me to him."

The hard lines of his face only enhanced the bleak look in his eyes, and it was clear how much the wolf meant to him.

"I'll go with you," she said.

"No. Stay here with Nascha. I'll get Bart and return as soon as I can."

Kate hesitated. "Maybe I should go for Charley." But she felt ambivalent about searching for him without Ethan.

"No. I want you here. Scorpion and Lee will protect you. Promise me, Kate, that you'll stay here." His gaze held her spellbound.

She nodded.

He took her hand, and her pulse quickened from his touch.

Wanting to move into his arms, she found herself fighting the urge. The others could see them, and while everyone knew that she'd lain with Ethan, she didn't think they should flaunt their relationship openly.

Had he really meant it last night when he'd asked her to come to Trinidad? A part of her leaped at the idea, wanting to follow Ethan anywhere. After her pa had died, and she moved with her ma and brothers and new stepfather to New Mexico, she'd felt an aching grief in her chest from leaving the last place she'd been with her pa. It had honestly never occurred to her to return until Ethan had voiced his invitation. It ignited a desire in her she hadn't known was there.

A wind blew in as the sun crested higher in the sky, and a chill ran down her spine. Were they saying goodbye?

"Ethan, are you sure I shouldn't go with you?"

"Yeah, I'm sure. I don't want you in the middle of something."

He still held her hand, so she gripped his in response. "Promise me you'll be careful."

A hint of a smile reached his eyes. "I've been waiting for all that concern you give the animals to be directed at me."

"Are you saying I dote on Fred too much?"

"I have to admit, I've been a bit jealous of the donkey."

"You do smell better."

"Well, that's something then. I'll be back as soon as I can."

He released her and mounted Alo, and with one last look at her, he was gone.

# Chapter Twenty

"You must come with me now."

Kate jumped and spun around, stunned to see Joe Tohonnie behind her. It was late afternoon and she was alone, picking her way through the cactus and shrubs, thinking of Charley and Ethan, wolves and wind. But she hadn't been as alone as she'd thought.

How had Joe crept upon her? "Where'd you come from?" Then she realized how crazy she sounded. Joe was, apparently, dead.

*I'm talking to a dead person.*

Apprehension and fear slid through her.

He grinned, a sparkle in his eyes, as his gray-black hair blew in the wind, bound at the crown by a piece of cloth. How could his hair blow in the wind? He seemed real enough. Maybe Nascha had been wrong. Maybe Joe wasn't dead.

"From my mother," he answered.

A smile tugged at Kate's mouth. His irreverence reminded her of her pa, and Ethan—two men who meant the world to her. She couldn't help but like Joe, alive or dead.

"Should I thank you for this?" she asked, resting her fingertips against the scar near her left eye, a faint bump about half an inch in length. A gust of air blew her hair around her face.

Joe nodded. "Now I need you for something I cannot do."

"I'll try." She watched him closely. He seemed so...*real*.

"Ready your supplies and horse, we must make a journey. Bring the *Diné* healer with you."

"Nascha?"

He nodded.

"I can't go right now," Kate replied. "I need to wait here for Ethan."

"No, he will not come to you if you wait."

Confused, Kate scanned her surroundings. Only Nascha was present, in the distance, tending one of the camps. "Where do you plan to take us?"

"My wife is hurt."

"Luci? Isn't she with Charley?"

Joe silently concurred.

A sense of urgency flooded Kate. "You know where they are?"

This time Joe nodded only once.

"Then Lee and Scorpion should accompany us. Ethan will be angry if we set out alone."

"There is no time. The others are gone and will not return soon."

Kate searched the campsites again. It was true the Navajo warriors had been absent most of the afternoon. Hunting, perhaps? She wasn't quite sure. She and Nascha had been passing the time in dreadful boredom and anxious worrying. Clive, Rufus, and Harry were gone too, and Kate had no idea where they'd disappeared to, either.

"You're certain we can't wait? Ethan could return by nightfall."

"Please come with me, Kay-tee of the wind."

She looked into his eyes and felt the pull of a force greater than she could imagine. She trusted Joe. It didn't make sense, but she did. There was a power forming in her, solid and fluid at the same time, and she knew Joe saw it too. It was in the way he looked at her.

What was happening?

"Trust yourself." Joe's voice carried on the wind.

And in that moment, acceptance filled her. The gaps of faith in herself from the past gained greater clarity and she could see her misguided sense of direction, her disillusionment in the world around her, in her family, in her life. But she didn't need to live with this lack any longer.

She approached Nascha, wondering how to explain. Better to not beat around the bush. "Joe Tohonnie would like us to go somewhere with him."

The surprise and shock on Nascha's face startled Kate for a moment.

"Do not speak the name of the dead," the Navajo woman said quietly, succinctly, as if she spoke to a child.

"Are you certain he's dead?"

"Yes. I was there."

Unease spread down Kate's spine. Glancing over her shoulder, she searched for Joe, but he was gone.

She swung her gaze back to Nascha, whose dark eyes held hers, steadfast and forceful. "It was before the winter came."

It was now May. That meant he'd died more than six months ago.

"If he speaks to you, it is for no good," she continued in hushed tones. "He may be a bad spirit, trying to trick you. We do not speak to the dead for that reason."

"What if he's trying to help? Surely, not all spirits are bad."

Nascha didn't respond.

"I don't think he's here to harm us," Kate continued. "What kind of man was he before he died?"

Nascha seemed to turn inward. "He was a great medicine man, very revered. There was such sadness when he left us." The woman's shoulders sagged.

"He needs us to help Luci. And Charley too. Don't you think we owe him this?"

Nascha lifted her chin. "Ethan will be angry with you."

Kate couldn't dispute that fact. "I know. But I don't think we should wait."

She watched while Nascha inwardly warred with the beliefs of her people. Finally, the Navajo woman stood. "I will do this, but please do not tell my father."

"Thank you."

They packed a portion of the gear and food, saddled Whiskey and Brandy, and set off. In the distance, Joe Tohonnie was visible atop a horse. Uncertain whether Nascha could also see the spirit leading them, Kate decided not to ask. The other woman said nothing, following Kate with an unspoken loyalty. Kate was humbled by Nascha's trust in her and hoped she wasn't making a mistake as Joe led them into the *Toh-den-nas-shai—the land of many springs*.

The red-hued desert blew its scent to her—the mustiness of yucca and the pungent juniper, the sweetness of the Navajo tea plant with its yellow flowers, the water-soaked rock indicating a recent rainstorm in the area—and Kate wondered why she hadn't noticed the crispness of the smells during the past several days. But she'd been with Ethan, always with Ethan, and he'd consumed her vision and filled her senses with only him.

Kate was awed by the land spreading out before them, open and flat, pinnacles of rock protruding from the landscape. That this was sacred land could hardly be argued. Respect filled Kate for a sense of time far greater than anything she could comprehend, held locked in the windswept buttresses and jagged summits jutting toward the heavens.

A breeze greeted them, caressing the land and soothing Kate's soul, touching an ancient heartbeat she'd had no idea existed until now. She wished Ethan was beside her.

As night descended, they came around an outcrop and saw an

elderly Indian woman lying in a heap, engulfed by a long cotton skirt. Kate dismounted and ran to her, Nascha close behind.

Kneeling beside her, Kate gently lifted the woman, feeling the frailness of her frame beneath. The woman moaned as she turned toward them.

"She's alive." Kate carefully pushed clumps of gray hair from the woman's cheeks.

"It is Luci," Nascha confirmed, examining her. "Her foot is twisted."

The old woman opened her eyes.

"We've come to help you," Kate said.

"How did you find me?" Luci asked, her voice cracking, but her dark eyes watched Kate with a level of clarity that belied her fragile state.

"It was Joe," Kate whispered.

Luci seemed to relax, and a ghost of a smile crossed her lips. "He never leaves me. Such a stubborn man."

Kate and Nascha made fast work of making the older woman comfortable and attending to her injuries.

---

THROUGH THE LONG night Luci became incoherent, and Kate and Nascha took turns sitting with her. They built a fire below the rocks and arranged her on a bedroll beside it. Nascha concluded Luci's foot was broken and set the bone then bandaged it to a piece of wood. It was a blessing Luci wasn't awake during any of this.

"So you've never seen Joe since he's passed?" Kate asked.

Nascha gave a slight shake of her head. In a low voice she added, "The dead can be up to no good."

Kate watched the magnificent sunrise overtaking the still land, clearing the cobwebs from the night. "How can you be so certain they're up to no good? Every time I've seen...*him*... he has helped." She touched the scar beside her eye.

"It is a barely noticeable wound," Nascha said.

"I think *he* was the one who healed me."

Nascha didn't reply.

"What if he's simply here to help?" Kate asked. "He led us to Luci. He still cares about her, he's still watching over her."

Nascha scrutinized her, the expression on her face unreadable. "I do not know what is happening here. Scorpion acts odd. And somehow Charley and Luci are a part of it."

"What do you mean?"

"Two nights ago, when I attended to one of the men with Hoskinnini, he told me something very strange. He say there is a place near here not to go. That there are bad spirits."

"Did he say why?"

"Just that the horses are spooked and run. That those who sleep near it are troubled by bad dreams. That fear grips them."

"I guess we should make certain we don't go there," Kate said. "Did he tell you where?"

"A little. I think I would know if I was close. He say Scorpion goes that way."

"Did you tell Scorpion what you learned?"

Nascha nodded. "But he listens to me no more." Frustration pinched the young woman's face.

Kate thought of Ethan. She had broken her promise to him by leaving camp. Would he come after her? She had to hope he would, because she had serious doubts she and Nascha could get Luci out of here on their own. And now, after hearing what Nascha had to say, she also doubted that Scorpion or Lee might help them. And definitely not Clive, Rufus, or Harry.

Their isolation suddenly hit Kate. Like ants in a grand land they sat alone—three women—and no one knew where they were, except a ghost who came and went on his own schedule.

"Will your Ethan listen to you?" Nascha asked. "Will he come to find us?"

"I hope so," Kate answered, praying it would be true.

"He looks at you with the hunger of a wolf. Do you love him?"

Kate nodded, unable to hide the truth, from Nascha or from herself.

"It is a fearful thing, to love a man so quick, so complete," Nascha stated.

"Yes."

"I understand." And Kate saw compassion and longing reflected in Nascha's gaze, her own heartbreak over Scorpion evident.

———

LUCI STIRRED JUST AFTER DAWN.

Kate made coffee while Nascha examined her and said prayers in Navajo. Luci finally sat up and took sips of the hot fluid.

"Why are you girls out here?" Luci asked, her shaky voice striking a chord deep within Kate.

The creases around Luci's thin lips smoothed as she smiled. Her hands shook, so Kate put her palms over them and felt warmth in the touch. Their eyes met and gratitude—and a feeling of love—filled the air.

"My name is Kate Kinsella, and this is Nascha."

"*Shash dine'e*," Nascha said. "I am of the Bear People Clan."

Luci's gaze shot to her. "You were with my K'aayelil at the end."

Nascha nodded.

"You weren't with Joe when he passed?" Kate asked Luci, guessing that Luci spoke English for her benefit.

"No." Luci lowered her eyes, melancholy settling over her. "He had been out traveling. How is Doba?"

"My father is well," Nascha replied.

"He is your father?" Luci's eyes widened. "That is good. So K'aayelil sent you to me?"

"He speaks only to Kate." Nascha gestured toward her.

Luci sipped her coffee then looked directly at Kate. "I believe you are promised to Charley."

Kate felt like a child caught with her hand in the cookie jar and a wave of guilt assaulted her. She simply nodded and hoped further explanation wouldn't be necessary.

"Have you come for him?" Luci asked.

"Yes, but last night we came looking for you. What happened? Where's Charley?"

"Two days ago—or three—a sandstorm came upon us," Luci replied. "We lost each other, and in my confusion, I fell and hurt my foot. I had no food or water. I waited for Charley to find me but he never came. Then, you did."

"Maybe he is hurt as well," Nascha said. "That was why he could not find you."

The image didn't sit well with Kate. "I'm sure he's fine. And as soon as we have you well and rested, we'll go and look for him."

Luci sighed. "I do not think I can ride."

Kate stared at Whiskey and Brandy, hobbled and chewing on a handful of oats from their supplies. How long would the food last? If they rationed, perhaps three to four days.

"We'll stay here," Kate said. "It's the best course of action so Ethan can find us."

"Who is Ethan?"

"He's Charley's brother. He's also searching for Charley and is with several other Navajo men. I'm confident they'll come looking for us."

"Charley spoke of his brother," Luci said, "but it was not kind. Perhaps a reunion is overdue."

"Where were you taking him?" Kate asked.

"To his heart's desire."

"A copper mine?"

Luci's gaze narrowed and a flash of shrewdness came and went, making Kate think she'd imagined it.

"It is good you've come," Luci said. "Charley will be happy to see you. He will need you."

The words confused Kate, but she let the comment pass and stood. "I'm going to scout the area. I'll be back."

---

ETHAN REINED IN ALO, scanning the ground intensely, and rubbed his jaw in frustration. He shifted in the saddle and stared at the late-afternoon sky.

*Where the hell is she?*

He'd returned well into the morning to find Kate and Nascha gone, along with Whiskey and Brandy and some of the supplies. Hoskinnini, Lee or Scorpion didn't know where they'd gone, as did none of the other Navajo men. Seems they'd all dispersed and left the women alone, including Clive, Rufus, and Harry.

The trail left by the three bumbling ruffians was easy to follow. Kate and Nascha, however, had literally disappeared. After searching for hours, Ethan could find no trace of *anything* that would lead him to the women.

"They must look for your brother," Lee said.

Ethan agreed. It was the only explanation, but it pissed him off that Kate hadn't waited. He had Bart back, after major negotiating which resulted in having to trade his Winchester rifle, something he hadn't wanted to do. The Navajo band viewed his relationship with the wolf with suspicion, referring to Bart as a skinwalker, a man disguised as a wolf bent on evil. They hadn't killed Bart because there was disagreement amongst them as to the best way to accomplish it without bringing more trouble upon them. They seemed relieved that Ethan was willing to take responsibility for the animal, but still insisted on the rifle. When he departed, they had shaken their heads in pity, certain Ethan was headed toward his own demise.

But he managed to save Bart and still had his Colt; he allowed himself a measure of relief in that. All he'd wanted to do then was return to Kate as soon as possible.

"How can two horses ride across the land as if they are nothing but wind?" Lee asked.

"We're just not looking hard enough," Ethan said.

There was just the three of them—Hoskinnini and his men had bid them farewell and safe passage through their land, eyeing Bart with the same wariness as the other Navajo. Ethan would need to keep a watchful eye on his wolf from now on, and, it would seem, his woman.

"Split up." Ethan's resolve strengthened. "We'll meet back here at sundown."

# Chapter Twenty-One

K ate, Nascha, and Luci sat huddled around the small fire, the darkness pressing against Kate. Nascha had done her best for Luci, but the elderly woman was in pain, the fatigue showing on her already-weary face. She'd eaten small amounts of dried meat and stale, flat flour cakes, which helped her strength, but Kate was worried. Her scouting mission earlier in the day had showed them to be utterly, completely alone.

"Would Joe help us again?" Kate asked quietly, not certain whether to bring up the subject.

"There is not a rhythm to K'aayelil's appearances," Luci said. "I cannot say that he would or would not."

Kate didn't want to sound rude, but curiosity won out. "You're so far away from anywhere. And then you were hurt. It's all so dangerous. Why are you making so much effort to help Charley?"

Luci smiled. "I seem old to you, and I am old. But K'aayelil had a bond with Charley's father, and we must help those we are bound to. I must finish what K'aayelil cannot."

"What do you mean by that?" Kate sensed they spoke of more than a copper mine.

"You seem very much alone, Kate," the elderly woman said. "You have always stayed apart from others."

"Maybe," Kate replied, thinking that Luci was right.

"Everyone is bound to someone." Luci paused. "And it is not Charley for you."

Kate shifted, uncomfortable with the direction the conversation had taken. Nascha remained silent.

"My pa died when I was very young, in a shooting on a stagecoach," Kate said, surprised by such an intimate admission, unsure what had compelled her to share, but a part of her wanted to speak of the incident, of the gaping hole that existed in her life without her father. "It was completely senseless."

"Have you ever tried to contact him?" Luci asked.

Kate froze, hope welling up inside.

"Have you ever tried to learn if he was happy on the other side?" Luci continued. "Do not misunderstand, I miss K'aayelil with all my heart. I miss lying beside him at night, I miss his snoring, I miss the sound of his voice and the touch of his skin. But I find comfort that we will be reunited again one day. And I find comfort that he watches over me, although he has made it difficult for me to wed again. He keeps harassing the potential mates."

Taken aback, Kate didn't know how to respond. When Luci grinned, Kate relaxed a bit.

"I am just making silly talk. Look how old I am. I will never wed again. K'aayelil was my one and only love."

"You talk as if it's the most natural thing in the world to speak to the dead."

"The world *is* natural. It is we who try to rearrange its structure to suit ourselves. The imbalance makes us unhappy." Luci glanced to Nascha. "The *Diné* have many rules about the dead, but most times we must trust our feeling in here." She brought a shaky, bony hand to her heart.

Kate drew her knees to her chest and rested her chin on them. "I miss my pa. I'm not sure that will ever leave me."

"And I miss my K'aayelil. But we must all make peace with those who have left us."

"How might I contact my pa?"

"The easiest way is in your heart. But maybe we can ask K'aayelil."

A sense of optimism flowed through Kate, and she smiled.

---

DURING THE NIGHT Kate made a decision—she would look for help in the morning. Luci was in pain and not getting better, and Kate's scouting missions during the day had yielded nothing. There was no sign of riders in the distance, no sign of men nearby. There was nothing.

It only made sense that she should go. Since Nascha had healing abilities, she should stay with Luci.

Kate needed to find Ethan.

---

JUST BEFORE DAWN, Kate awoke and prepared Whiskey for the ride. She packed very little food and water, wanting to leave most of it for Nascha and Luci.

"You are awake early."

Nascha's voice startled Kate. "You scared me." Her hand came to her chest as she tried to calm her breath.

"I am sorry. Are you leaving us?"

"Yes. It's useless waiting here for help that might never come. I've left most of the supplies. You're better equipped to care for Luci, so I will go for help."

"What if you do not return?"

Kate tied off what little gear she had on Whiskey's flank and turned to face Nascha. "You have Brandy. If I don't return in two days, then you must get Luci out of here. But I will return, I promise, whether I find help or not."

Nascha stepped forward and hugged her. Kate hesitated then wrapped her arms around the woman.

"Keep the wind at your back," Nascha said, stepping back.

Kate nodded then mounted Whiskey. She'd already tied off Brandy, knowing the female horse would rebel if her mama left her. A sense of foreboding weighed on her—she hadn't said goodbye to Luci. The old woman still slept, and it seemed heartless to wake her. But what if she never saw her again? Or Nascha?

Brandy's frustrated neighing could be heard for some time as Kate guided Whiskey away. The horse's ears were flattened, and Kate knew she was upset. *I'm sorry, girl.*

The sun broke the horizon and Kate shielded her eyes. It wasn't often she witnessed a sunrise, not with her natural tendency to sleep late, but she'd done it several times recently. She breathed in the cool, desert air and knew that, for better or worse, change was abreast. She prayed it was for the better.

---

ETHAN KNEW his patience was slipping from him like a well-oiled wagon wheel that had lost its berth.

*Where the hell is Kate?*

He walked along the valley floor, Alo trailing him, and searched for less obvious clues that might tell him her whereabouts. Scorpion and Lee were off somewhere as well, searching in vain.

Visions crossed his mind of many scenarios he didn't want to consider—snakes, Indians, mountain lions, injuries. All things that could have left Kate unable to find her way back, could have left her vulnerable to attack. An image of his pa pierced his mind. He had been as helpless then, and his pa had died because of it.

He pressed on.

He wouldn't stop until he found her.

———

KATE RODE ALL DAY, using the sun as a guide. Tired, parched, and unsure if she'd taken the right direction, she scanned the surroundings in the fading light. She'd been so careful to mark in her mind from where she'd come so that she could find her way back to Nascha and Luci, to lead help back to them, or at least find her own way to them. But now she felt disoriented. Flat desert spread out before her, but rocky outcroppings were everywhere. Prominent, jutting rock formations that were hard to miss and served as good beacons were also visible—their red-rock outlines dark monoliths against the horizon—but Kate wasn't sure now if she'd circled them or ridden past them.

Where was she?

Panic welled up and Whiskey sensed her agitation, shifting from side to side.

The colors of the desert vibrated, and Kate wondered if this was where she would die.

No! She wouldn't give up. Luci and Nascha's fate rested in her hands. She simply needed to rest.

She found an area protected by shrubs, unloaded Whiskey and settled in for the night. She collected an armful of branches, made a fire and ate a small amount of meat and flour cakes, trying to conserve the remaining supplies. Then she slept.

Kate awoke with a start. The wind blew strong. She had trouble seeing since it was still deep into the night. She held onto her blanket before it blew away. Whiskey whinnied loudly, snorting and stomping her hooves. Kate attempted to gather up her gear and get to the horse as dust swirled around her. If not for the noise the animal made, she wasn't sure she would have found her.

Kate dropped the blanket and food and grabbed Whiskey's reins, struggling to un-hobble the horse, but in Whiskey's agitation

Kate couldn't get a strong grip on the rope. She fell forward and the horse's hoof hit her in the head. Reeling from the pain, Kate pressed a hand to her forehead and covered her right eye. She wondered if she'd have a scar on that side to match the one on the left.

Wind blasted her again; she coughed and shut her eyes to keep the dust out. Blindly, she scooted on the ground to move away from Whiskey's front legs. She waved her arms until she caught the horse's rope. Holding tight she struggled to get the saddle atop Whiskey's back.

She cinched the saddle tight while attempting to keep abreast of the horse as it moved this way and that. Kate barely climbed aboard before Whiskey took off, and only then did she remember the gear she'd left on the ground.

They rode blindly, and Kate tried to get the animal to stop. Whiskey was bound to get hurt, and a lame horse would undoubtedly seal her fate. When they came upon a rocky overhang, Whiskey instinctively moved against it, offering some protection from the wind. Kate, afraid to dismount, leaned forward in gratitude and pressed her forehead to the animal's neck. They huddled for a long while, and Kate wasn't sure if she dozed or not.

She raised her head, the stillness deafening. It was still dark, but the swirling dust and relentless wind had stopped. Whiskey shifted slightly and Kate looked into the darkness. Her eyes, caked with dust and burning, could make out very little. Her dry mouth and throat begged for water, but she numbly looked down at the saddle and knew she didn't have the canteen with her. It was gone, along with the provisions.

Exhausted, she tried to think through her options. She would have to wait until daylight to assess her position. She fought back a surge of tears—*her position*. What a joke. She hadn't known her position all day. Longer than that, if the time spent with Luci and Nascha counted.

She was hopelessly lost, and with no food or water would surely die. She hung her head and hugged Whiskey. No tears came—her body couldn't afford to lose the moisture—but she felt a grief all the same.

---

ETHAN FOUND Nascha with an old Indian woman.

Scorpion moved toward the younger woman, who smiled with relief and something more evident in her gaze. "You have come at last. Kate found you. This is Luci Tohonnie."

Luci tried to lift her head. "*Yá'át'ééh*." Lee dismounted and helped her to sit upright.

"Kate never found us," Ethan said, hope dwindling to nothing in an instant.

The worry in Nascha's gaze confirmed his assessment.

"You were all together?" Ethan asked.

Nascha nodded. "She went for help. Luci has a broken foot."

"When did she go?" Lee asked.

"Two days ago, I think."

Ethan cursed. *She could be anywhere.*

"We will see to the women," Lee said. "You must go and find her."

"Come here, the one who is called Ethan." Luci waved him forward.

Ethan knelt beside her. "How did you hurt your foot?" he asked.

Luci shook her head. "That is of no concern." Her frail hand grasped his sleeve. "K'aayelil has told me of you and of your wolf. He can find her."

*Maybe.* "Do you know where Charley is?"

"We became lost to each other."

"When?"

"Many days."

He was wasting time. As much as he wanted to find his brother, he *needed* to find Kate.

He stood and said to Lee and Scorpion, "I have to find Bart."

He mounted Alo and was gone.

## Chapter Twenty-Two

Kate squinted and pulled her hat lower. It was so bright; the sun beat down with an intensity she'd never experienced. She swayed in her saddle. Whiskey moved slowly along the desert floor, kicking up puffs of rust-colored dirt.

Kate thought of water but that was all she had the strength to do—think. She hoped Whiskey might have the ability to find any moisture in this baking environment. Soon she would have to dismount, since the horse would be unable to go on much farther.

In the distance, a figure moved and Kate watched, anticipation filling her with a rush of energy. As the apparition neared, disappointment just as swiftly drained her bones of life, her body sagging. The form wasn't real. Still able to retain some grasp of her intellect, she sat atop Whiskey and waited.

It was a man. He wore a fine wool suit and a spotless, black hat with a narrow brim. He was so clean and well-kept. Kate blinked and dust coated her tongue when she tried to lick her lips.

He looked familiar. Her concern grew to amazement when her mind finally registered his identity. *Papa*.

She gasped aloud, causing Whiskey to step back and nicker in agitation.

"Katie." Her father's voice echoed across the distance, skipping on the wind to her ears, soothing her heartbreak and making her long for all the time missed. "Katie." He called to her as if she were lost.

She tried to speak but her throat tightened.

"Katie, you're as stubborn as when you were a child. You gave your mama such fits."

His voice vibrated in her ears as if he stood beside her, but he remained firmly in the distance.

"I used to tell you to tuck your tail and say your sorries, but you always did it with a stiff jaw," his voice continued. "You were so full of pride."

The heat wavered above the desert floor and Kate blinked hard. Was she dreaming? "Is this Heaven?" Her voice was barely comprehensible.

"I knew you would make your own way," he continued. "I knew you would never be satisfied with life until you had seen more of it. You get that from me. Your mama didn't much like being dragged from town to town, following the rails, but I liked the challenge of the unknown. Needed it, I guess you could say. All the new places, all the new people. It was exciting. I miss you, pumpkin."

"I miss you, too," Kate whispered, hypnotized.

"You need to go home, sweetheart."

"I know."

"Home, Kate." He faded from her.

She shook her head and tried to focus on where he'd stood, but her pa was gone. The sun was setting and a gray haze had descended, the terrain changing into cliffs and rocks rather than endless desert. Kate's heart sank—she was more lost than ever.

"You shur are persistent." Clive appeared from behind Whiskey. "You don't look so good. C'mon. If you behave, we won't tie you up."

Clive took Whiskey's reins and led the animal to a clearing

protected by boulders. Too tired and weak to protest, Kate didn't resist.

A bolt of lightning zigzagged on the horizon to her left. A longing welled up inside her for rain, blissful rain that would clean the dirt from her and quench her thirst. She turned back to the clearing and the fire that blazed at the center. Surprise was evident on Rufus and Harry's faces when they saw her. Another man sat in the shadow of the rocks, and when a second bolt of lightning struck, this one much closer, it illuminated the surrounding dark spaces, and a chill ran down her spine.

Charley was bound and gagged on the ground.

---

"WELL, I figure we got two options," Harry said, pushing his bowler hat back from his long, wavy hair. "We can torture Charley until he talks, or we can shoot whatshername in the foot and he can watch her bleed until he talks."

Rufus groaned, his lanky frame hunched over near the fire. "That's disgustin'. And it's a waste of a good bullet."

"All right, we can cut off one of her fingers." Harry nodded, clearly pleased with this new solution.

Kate glanced at Charley. They sat side by side, her arms and legs bound and a bandanna that smelled as if it'd never been washed tied around her mouth. She tried not to gag. It hadn't taken long for them to tie her up, despite what Clive had said; she'd greatly underestimated these three. And now they were going to seriously hurt her. Her stomach revolted with a wave of nausea.

Charley seemed as well as could be expected. Unfortunately, they'd been unable to exchange barely three words before Clive decided she was too much of a threat to leave loose.

Regardless of the circumstances, she was grateful to see Charley, although his gaze reflected the worry she felt.

"Wha' are you 'oing here?" he asked, his words muffled around the cloth in his mouth.

"Looking for you."

A bolt of lightning lit the sky and thunder cracked, rolling across the darkened expanse. Without warning, the wind blew hard and rain poured down in sheets.

"Get the gear," Clive shouted. Harry and Rufus ran around in confusion as the rain extinguished the campfire.

The horses pawed the ground and tugged at the reins tied to a tree.

"The horses'll bolt!" Clive waved Harry toward the animals. "Hold 'em steady."

In the confusion, Kate watched as Charley scooted closer to the gear strewn about and located a knife. He worked quickly to untie his hands. Once freed, he removed his gag and the rope around his ankles, then helped Kate.

Drenched, he grabbed her hand and they disappeared into the dark, Kate stumbling in her efforts to keep up.

They ran into the black night, punctuated by sharp flashes of light. Rain pelted Kate's face and she squinted and wiped at her eyes while trying to keep pace with Charley. Suddenly, he yanked her down behind a boulder.

"Kate, what on earth are you doing here?"

In the dark she could barely make out his features, but it was enough for her to see how much he resembled Ethan—and how much he didn't. Charley was far more high strung and emotional, while Ethan was more self-contained.

"Agnes is pregnant," she blurted out.

Charley stilled as rain washed over them in thick sheets. "What are you saying?" he asked.

"You need to go back, Charley. You need to be with her. And we need to end this ridiculous engagement between us."

"You came all this way to tell me that?"

"Yes."

"You're crazy, Kate Kinsella."

After everything that had happened, he was probably right.

"How did you find me?" he asked.

"Ethan is with me, or at least he was."

Charley leaned back to look at her. "You've been with Ethan? I knew he was trailing me, but I didn't know you were with him."

"If you knew he was behind you, why didn't you wait?"

"I've told you how it was. I don't wanna see him."

"He wants to reconcile with you, Charley."

"You mean he wants me to forgive him. That's convenient."

Something nagged at Kate. "If you didn't know I was with Ethan, then why did you have T'odonah place a hex on both of us?"

"You know about that? I didn't really mean anything by it, I was just pissed that Ethan was following. A Navajo rider spotted him with a woman. I really thought it was Jessica. The hex was meant for her, not you."

"But you put a piece of one of my weavings in the pot."

"Did I? I can't even remember now. Jessica was a woman Ethan stole from me."

"I know."

"You do?"

"He told me. And you were wrong. He didn't steal her from you. He's not with her."

Charley paused and watched her, then laughed sarcastically. "You believe him?"

Yes, she did. Didn't she?

"I can still find the copper," Charley said. "We just need to ditch Clive, Harry, and Rufus."

"Charley, we need to go home."

"But I'm close, I can feel it. I'd planned on finding it, then bringing it back to Agnes. And the baby now, I guess." He appeared dumbfounded. "You can help me, and I'll give you a share for your efforts."

Kate thought of Nascha and Luci. By now the two women would have headed south and, hopefully, to safety. Ethan was probably out there somewhere, searching. Surely, he would find them.

"All right," she said. "I'll go with you."

## Chapter Twenty-Three

Bart led Ethan directly to Clive, Rufus, and Harry. The men stood in their battered camp, tired, wet and looking defeated. The sun shone bright this morning, but Ethan wasn't feeling very cordial. He drew his gun.

"What the hell happened?" he asked.

Harry jumped, his shoulder-length hair clinging limply around his face. Rufus spun his gaunt frame around. Clive was the only one who held his ground, resting hands on his hips, his pot belly moving up and down with each breath. He methodically spit tobacco on the ground.

"It figures," Clive said. "Charley's been nothin' but a pain in the ass. And so are you."

"Where's Kate?"

Bart appeared beside Ethan and Alo. The three men immediately focused their attention on him, and Harry and Rufus took three steps backward. Ethan still marveled that Alo wasn't skittish around the wolf.

"What is that?" Harry whispered.

"It's a wolf, you fool," Rufus replied.

"Oh no," Harry whimpered. "I don't wanna be ripped apart."

"Where's Kate?" Ethan asked again.

"She's gone," Harry said, caving quickly. "We had her, and Charley, but there was a terrible storm last night and they escaped." Harry's breaths came in rapid succession.

Clive rolled his eyes and glared at Harry. "Would it pain you at all to keep your claptrap shut for once?"

"He won't attack, will he?" Harry flicked his eyes from Bart to Ethan.

Bart stood unmoving, his grayish-white ears standing erect, his back rigid with the black hind hairs standing upright. Bart sensed the danger but didn't move forward. Ethan honestly wasn't sure he could stop the wolf if the animal decided to attack. Bart wasn't his pet—he didn't obey commands. And yet, the animal had been a faithful friend during a time when Ethan wasn't sure he deserved one.

"Depends." No sense letting those three know that. "Explain to me what's going on."

Clive paused then shook his head. "This was a hair-brained scheme if there ever was one." A look of disgust crossed his face. "Charley and I had this deal, you see."

Rufus frowned. "What're you talkin' about?"

"He knew you were comin' after him," Clive said to Ethan, "cuz he got your message in Flagstaff that you were on your way, so he had a plan."

"If you're in cahoots with him then why'd we tie him up?" Harry demanded.

Clive let out a weary sigh. "Harry, there's no way in hell you'll understand this, so don't even bother tryin'."

For the first time Ethan could remember, Harry was rendered speechless.

"We was supposed to take the girl from you," Clive said.

"Why?" Ethan asked.

"Charley said you deserved to lose her. He said you deserved a lot of things. Only thing was, he kept sayin' her name was Jane or Jezebelle or somethin' like that."

"Jessica. Why did he think she was with me?"

"When he heard you were coming to Flagstaff, he said she'd be with you. He left town right quick, but damn if all our plans didn't go up in a puff of smoke when that other dame took our donkey and the gold. When we finally caught up to Charley a few days ago, he was suddenly backing out of our deal, so I decided to tie him up. He owes me some money, and more than just the other half of the gold he took from us. He owes me for taking the woman, even if she was the wrong one. Except she's his fiancée. Ain't she the right one, then? Does he know you've made time with her?"

Unease stirred on the outskirts of Ethan's mind. What if Charley really had feelings for Kate? What if she'd been confused by his relationship with Agnes? It wouldn't have been the first time Charley had twisted the truth when it came to women and his own selfish motives.

Ethan had made a major muck of things with Jessica, and now he'd done the same thing—only worse—with Kate, Charley's fiancée. He'd never made love to Jessica, had never burned for her, needed her, breathed the air around her as if he would die without it.

But he'd done this with Kate.

Being without her had hollowed out his heart, leaving him desperate to remain sane. He would have to choose Charley or Kate. And either choice would break his heart because he didn't want to lose his relationship with his brother. But he'd fallen hard and fast for Kate Kinsella and couldn't imagine a life without her.

"Where have they gone?" Ethan's voice was thick.

"They took that horse, Whiskey, but their tracks are gone. The rain washed 'em out." Clive glanced at Bart. "I wasn't gonna hurt Charley. I just want what's due me."

"And us," Rufus whined. "Did you double-cross us, Clive?"

"No," Clive said with more patience than Ethan would've given him credit for. "But you've got a pea for a brain. I was lookin' out for you."

"I thought we shared everythin'. This isn't right. You ought to tell us everythin'."

"What are you gonna do with that wolf?" Clive asked Ethan.

"He'll help me track Charley. And this is the last time I'll say this—stay away from Kate."

"Sure." Harry agreed quickly and Rufus nodded his head.

"Me and Charley have a score to settle," Clive said, determination in his eyes. "And I mean to settle it, one way or another. You take that girl and leave. I don't care now."

Ethan wished it was that simple. But he had to consider the other alternative. "If Kate stays with him, you leave 'em both alone. I'll settle your account. You have my word on it."

"How do I know what your word is worth?" Clive asked, taking two steps toward Ethan and Alo.

Bart stepped forward, a low growl vibrating in his throat. Ethan silently praised the animal's instincts. He wished he could say the same about himself and his brother's women. "You don't. I'm telling you. That's all you need to know."

Clive stared at him then slowly nodded.

Ethan turned Alo and headed into the desert, Bart at his side.

---

"Do you know where you're going?" Kate asked Charley.

It was late afternoon and they were taking a break, Whiskey standing several feet away.

Charley considered her question. "Kinda."

"A copper mine?" Exhaustion washed over Kate. "Is it really worth being out here? We could be lost. What if we don't find the mine, or even our way out?"

She contemplated what little gear and food Charley had stashed before Clive, Rufus, and Harry had nabbed him. The result depressed her: three canteens of water, three cans of beans, one small cook pot, a bag of coffee grinds only one quarter full, and a thankfully larger bag of oats. Whiskey would eat, for now.

She wondered how they'd get those cans of beans open and began searching the pile for a knife. An ax would be nice, she thought. The idea of hitting Charley upside the head with it felt much too satisfying.

"You've got more gumption than I realized, Kate, coming all the way here." He grinned. "I might just have to marry you after all."

Kate looked into Charley's green eyes, so like Ethan's. But he wasn't Ethan, and the contrast between the two men came into sharp focus. Charley was inconsiderate, foolhardy, and selfish. Ethan was none of those things. "And what about Agnes?" she spit out. "I've come all this way to bring you back to her and you don't seem concerned about her at all."

Charley frowned. "I'm concerned, but honestly, are you certain the baby she carries is mine?"

Kate was speechless. She had dragged herself across half the territory of Arizona to bring him back to a woman she assumed he was hopelessly in love with. But she'd been wrong. It was an infatuation, and with some distance between them, Charley had already begun to recover from his feelings. Anger welled up inside her.

"Would you tell me what happened with Jessica?" she asked, finding her voice again.

Charley shrugged. "I met her while in Denver. She was sweet and pretty, worked in her pa's mercantile. We hit it off and decided to get married. Her pa didn't like it, so we ran off, and I brought her back to my folk's ranch in Trinidad. My pa was dead, so Ethan had the run of things." Charley shook his head. "I really should've known, I guess, not to trust him. I won't make that mistake again."

The parallel between his relationship with Jessica and then Agnes didn't escape her. She was beginning to think Agnes would be better off without him. But then, there was the baby.

"There's really not too much else to tell," he continued. "I caught them together."

"Ethan said it wasn't what you thought."

"Do you think he'd tell you the truth? Jessica was young and easily impressed by what he could offer. He knew he could outdo me in that respect. I didn't have the ranch, I didn't have control of the money, the stupid trust. And now, he dangles that out to me like it's supposed to make it all right. When I heard he was trailing me with a woman, I knew it had to be her."

"But it wasn't," Kate interrupted.

"No. Maybe she's holed up at the ranch, waiting for him."

The thought shocked Kate. What if it were true? What if Ethan had lied to her all along? She shook off the feeling, not wanting to believe it. It couldn't be true, not after what she and Ethan had shared. But she realized what a short time she'd known him. How well did a woman know a man who'd wanted nothing more than to bed her? But it wasn't like that between them. Was it?

Kate swayed from her confused thoughts.

"Who're you?" Charley asked.

She spun around and saw Joe Tohonnie.

"Joe," she said.

"You know him?" Charley asked.

Kate nodded. "Is Luci safe?"

"Yes," Joe replied and smiled. "And now I am here to help you."

"Are you talking about Luci Tohonnie?" Charley asked.

"She is my wife. And she was trying to help you, but since she can no longer complete her mission, I will do it for her."

"You know where the copper is?" Charley's voice was skeptical.

"I know what you seek, and I know where it is. And it is past due that you find it."

Relief washed over Kate.

"Can we trust him?" Charley murmured.

"Yes." She looked back at Charley. "I think we should follow him."

"There's something odd about him."

"You'll get used to it."

## Chapter Twenty-Four

They walked into the night—Joe, then Kate, and then Charley leading Whiskey, all of them moving at a steady gait. A sense of urgency pressed on Kate.

She wondered about the visit she'd had with her pa. Luci had told her to contact him, to learn if he was at peace on the other side. Had she managed to call her pa to her? More importantly, could she do it again?

Joe continued through the night and the following day, finally stopping so she and Charley could sleep. Exhausted, she'd fallen to the ground only to realize later that she'd used a flat rock as a pillow. Her legs and back ached, and her mind was numb; she had no energy to think of anything beyond putting one foot in front of the other. Ethan hung in the shadows of her thoughts, hovering beyond her perception in a fog that made her question whether he was real or not.

And not for the first time, she stifled the urge to weep.

But thankfully during that one lengthy rest stop, there had been a water hole. It had appeared clean enough, so they were all able to quench their thirst, including Whiskey, and replenish the canteens.

Joe headed down a rocky incline as the sun began to set.

Kate stopped, tugging on her hat and glancing at her filthy clothing. How far had they come? The terrain had changed; they were no longer on flat desert land but now traversed a boulder-strewn canyon.

Charley handed Whiskey's lead to Kate then passed her to head downhill.

"This is crazy," Kate uttered under her breath.

"He knows, doesn't he?" Charley asked over his shoulder.

"Knows what?"

"Where the copper is." The gleam in Charley's eyes worried her. He was obsessed.

"I don't know, Charley," she said helplessly. "And I'm too tired to care anymore."

He halted and turned to her. "I trusted Luci. You trust him." He pointed his thumb behind him at the retreating figure of Joe.

Kate frowned. *Why didn't Joe just fly, for God sake?* He wasn't bound by the constraints of this world. Irrational laughter bubbled in her chest since it didn't seem odd that she was following a dead man into the vast unknown. It didn't seem odd that she'd spoken with her pa, dead and gone from her life all these years.

"C'mon, Kate," Charley urged, running ahead. "We're almost there. I can feel it."

She watched him move downhill as if it were a dream. Her feet slid in the dirt and she braced herself to help Whiskey, but if the horse were to fall, she would hardly be able to stop the large animal. Turning sideways, she slowly inched her way downward, praying that Whiskey would be able to find her own footing. Kate's legs quivered and the muscles in her thighs rebelled.

Whiskey neighed loudly and tried to jerk free. Trying to soothe the horse, fear gripped Kate. With no way to turn around they could only move forward. Taking tiny steps, she inched her way downward in tiny increments, giving painstaking attention to the ground before her, but it became more nondescript as the light faded. Murmuring under her breath, she sought to reassure

Whiskey as well as herself. It felt as if they were descending a mountain.

But they weren't at the top of a mountain; they were on flat ground that dropped away into a canyon. She supposed the location of a copper mine wouldn't be easy to get to, but how would they get out? *Be careful what you wish for.* Her mama's voice hovered in her mind. *You might get it, and then some.*

Had she wished for this? Hadn't she always wanted more out of life? Hadn't she always wanted adventure? This certainly qualified. So did meeting Ethan. *Loving him is an adventure. And I do love him.*

She struggled to get downhill and catch up to Joe and Charley. When she finally reached the bottom, she breathed a sigh of relief and hugged Whiskey around the neck. She soon realized they were alone.

"Hello?" she yelled. "Charley?"

She listened and heard nothing except her own breathing, and Whiskey shifting her feet.

A gust of wind blasted them as the distant howl of an animal pierced the silence. Whiskey froze, ears upright and alert, and Kate shivered. *A wolf? Bart, perhaps?*

Longing filled her, and she desperately wanted to see Ethan again. Holding Whiskey's reins, she moved around a sharp bend and nearly ran into Charley.

"Easy," he said, grabbing hold of her.

"I didn't know where you were."

Joe turned back to face them, and he nearly glowed white from head to toe. It was dark now, but a full moon illuminated the area. Kate's heartbeat went into double-time.

"We are here," Joe said.

"The entrance to the mine?" Charley asked, releasing Kate.

"No. We are here for what you truly seek."

"I don't understand."

"I knew your father," Joe said. "And it is this final favor I do his sons."

"You knew my pa?"

Joe nodded. "When he died, his body was never recovered. And it has divided Calder Barstow's sons ever since." Joe stepped aside. "I have brought you to your father, Charley."

A pile of bones lay beyond in the dirt. "Joe, what are you doing?" she asked in a frantic whisper.

"This is what each of them seeks," he replied.

"You're telling me that's my pa?" Charley demanded.

"Yes. If it helps, Calder's spirit no longer lingers here. He has not stayed in this place and time, and neither should you."

"It was Ethan's fault, not mine. What's done is done. All I'm trying to do is make my own way in the world. I've moved past my pa's death, and I sure as hell don't give a damn what Ethan does."

"I'm sorry to hear that."

Kate's heart jumped to her throat at the sound of the voice that was so familiar, so dear.

Charley turned around but Kate kept her gaze on Joe and the bones, frozen in place. She wanted to run into Ethan's arms, but something kept her rooted to where she stood.

"Ethan." Charley laughed but there was no humor in it. "About time you caught up."

"You certainly didn't make it easy. Kate? Are you well?"

Charley fixed her with a glare. Kate didn't miss the control Charley was trying to exert over her, but it was misplaced. They might be engaged but it wasn't *real*. She spun around and went to Ethan, embracing him, melting into his arms.

"Thank God you found us," she said into his neck, inhaling the scent of him, filled with sweat and grime, but she didn't care. It was Ethan, and she loved him.

"It wasn't easy," he replied, his arms encompassing her, holding her tight against him.

"Seems now we can have a proper burial for pa, thanks to Joe, here," Charley said. "Hey, where'd he go?"

Kate reluctantly withdrew from Ethan and glanced around, but Joe was gone. He disappeared as if he'd never been, as was usual for him.

"What's going on?" Ethan asked.

"Joe Tohonnie led us here," Kate said. "Those bones over there are your father's." She nodded toward the pile.

Ethan stared in the direction of the remains, and Kate slipped her hand into his.

"Does this location ring a bell, Ethan?" Charley's voice dripped with sarcasm.

"I honestly don't remember. It was so long ago and coming in here at night makes it worse."

"How did you find us?" Kate asked.

"Bart."

"Who's Bart?" Charley asked.

"Ethan's wolf."

"Yeah, sure." Charley moved to stand beside the bones. "He's here because he's always known the location."

"I never did," Ethan replied. "I don't know why you won't believe me, Charley."

"Because pa was gone," he yelled, "and it had to be your fault. Pa wouldn't have left us willingly. He was a good hunter and tracker—he never would have *just fallen*. It's the stupidest thing that could've ever happened, and a Barstow wouldn't be so stupid." Charley sank to his knees and hung his head.

His grief filled the night air and made Kate's throat tighten. As Ethan went to stand beside Charley and the bones of their father, a wet nose nuzzled her hand, and she stroked Bart's neck. He was so tall his head came almost to her chest, but she didn't fear him.

Bart came with her as she backed away into the darkness until she could no longer see Ethan and Charley, affording them the privacy she knew they needed. The wolf would keep her safe.

ETHAN STARED at the remains of his pa with a heavy heart. He'd always known his father was dead but now he had the truth of it. Perhaps Joe Tohonnie might have led them to any pile of bones, which Ethan doubted, but an inspection of the remnants of clothing left no doubt. Ethan knelt and unhooked the silver belt buckle. BARSTOW was marked in the center. It had been his pa's.

"His body could've been thrown down here," Charley said.

"Yeah, it could have." Ethan scanned the bushes beyond the remains. It was difficult in the dark to see, but he had a hunch. His pa's horse had also never been found; could the animal's remains be here as well? It would explain how his pa had fallen over a cliff.

Ethan pulled his gun as he moved toward the shrubs in case he disturbed a snake or any other dangerous creature and found bones scattered on the ground. "I'll be damned," he murmured. He retrieved a piece and turned back to Charley. "I think I know what happened."

Charley waited.

He held up the evidence. "What does this look like to you?"

"That's a bear claw."

"A bear must have attacked him, and then they plummeted over the side." Ethan glanced upward to view the cliff, a dark outline in the night sky. It had to be a few hundred feet or more.

Charley stood and took the claw bones from Ethan. "This is bullshit. Why would a bear be out here, in the desert? It doesn't make any sense."

"Maybe the animal was lost. He would likely have been deranged from thirst and hunger. It was all just a damned tragedy." Ethan sank down on a nearby rock. Tracking Charley and Kate had been a relentless pursuit, and now that he'd found them, exhaustion overwhelmed him. At long last, he knew the truth of his pa's death. He wondered where Kate had gone, but trusted she was nearby.

Charley threw the claw bones to the ground. "You think this cleans the slate. Well, it doesn't. And what the hell is going on with you and Kate?"

"She told me the truth, Charley."

"When? Before or after you bedded her?"

"Before. I'm not as much of an ass as you think I am."

"Well, it didn't stop you with Jessica."

"Nothing ever happened with her. Why can't you just let it go? I'm really sorry she got attached to me. I didn't do anything to encourage her but be nice, because I thought she was going to be my sister-in-law."

"Is that the same courtesy you've shown to Kate?"

"Jesus, Charley, she told me about Agnes. Isn't she the one you love?"

"What if I told you I loved *Kate*. What then? Would you still take her from me? You have no respect for anything, Ethan."

It was a blow Ethan hadn't expected. He took off his hat and ran a hand through his hair, leaning his forehead on his palm. "Shit. I'd never willingly hurt you, Charley. But what the hell are doing with Kate anyway, stringing her along with Agnes?"

"And *you're* not stringing her along?" Charley accused. "Were you planning to marry her? How do I know Jessica's not living on the Barstow ranch as we speak?"

"She's not, she never did." But it was clear Charley thought she had. No wonder he rebuffed Ethan all these years.

Did he want to marry Kate? It was a distinct possibility. Of course it was. He was crazy about her. But had he inadvertently come between Charley and something his brother wanted with her? What if Kate wanted it too? Maybe Charley was right about him.

Ethan stood. "I'm going to look for Kate. You're welcome to come."

Charley moved away, muttering obscenities under his breath.

Ethan didn't have to go far before he found her curled up on the ground with Bart. She slept soundly so he didn't disturb her; instead, he sat beside her and stroked Bart's head as he contemplated the situation. He wanted to reconcile with Charley, but he was beginning to think it might never be possible. He didn't want to lose Kate; every cell in his body rebelled at the thought of being parted from her. But if he had come between her and Charley in any way, he needed to rectify that. It was suddenly, startlingly clear: he only wanted what was best for her. It filled him with joy but broke him at the same time.

Leaning over, he kissed her lips lightly. "I love you," he whispered, then lay beside her and let sleep take him.

---

KATE AWOKE on the ground alone, the sun high in the sky. Tired and sore, she went in search of Ethan and Charley, beginning with the location of Calder Barstow's bones. Ethan was there, sitting beside them and keeping vigil. When he saw her, he smiled.

"I didn't want to wake you," he said. "I'm guessing you hadn't slept in a while."

"Where's Charley?"

"I don't know. But I didn't want to leave you."

"I'm glad. I'm sorry I didn't stay put like you asked me, but Luci was hurt."

"I know. I have a little food. Are you hungry? It's rabbit."

She took the meat and sat beside him. Despite his friendliness and genuine smile at seeing her, she still felt as if she intruded. She wanted to kiss him, to hold him, and wished he would make the gesture so she would know it was all right. But he didn't.

"Are you sure it's your pa's remains?" she asked. She tore a small piece of meat with her teeth and chewed.

He nodded. "I found a buckle that belonged to him. I think he was attacked by a bear."

"That's terrible. I'm so sorry."

"Not a great way to end a life, but then, do any of us have a say when and how the end will come?"

Kate paused her eating and thought of her own pa. "No, I suppose not."

"Can I ask you something?"

"Yes."

"Do you have any feelings for Charley?"

"What kind of feelings?"

"Romantic ones."

Surprised, Kate didn't know what to say. "Well, I suppose in the very beginning I found him interesting in that way. He does look a lot like you." She nudged him, trying to lighten the mood but it didn't breach the distance between them. "Why are you asking me this?"

"Just wondering."

"Are you concerned that you and I have been together? That we shouldn't be because Charley and I are engaged?"

"Maybe."

"Where is he? I'll end the engagement right now."

"You mean you haven't already?"

"Well, I told him we needed to, but then we didn't talk about it again. I always intended to, Ethan. You must know how strongly I feel for you." Panic welled up in her chest. Was he leaving her?

He looked at her and tears filled her eyes.

"I love you, Ethan," she whispered.

He put an arm around her and kissed her. She savored the touch, so hungry for him, wanting the contact more than the food he'd given her. Abruptly, he stopped.

"I don't want to make things more complicated," he said. "I don't want to make your life more complicated."

More panic. "I'm not sure what you mean. Do you love me? Do you think you *could* love me?"

Ethan wouldn't look at her. "Yeah," he replied.

"But...." she prompted.

"But if I'm the obstacle...."

"For what?"

"For you and Charley to be together."

"We're not together. I told you that. He loves Agnes. She's having his baby."

"What if he doesn't love her? What if he loves you?"

"That's absurd. He doesn't love me." The panic flooded her chest. "And it doesn't matter, because I love *you*." She sensed she wasn't getting her point across and it made her feel as if she were sliding down a slippery slope, much like the one Calder Barstow must have fallen down, the one that had claimed his life. To lose Ethan was to lose her life.

She looked away, feeling hopeless. Nothing she said seemed to convince Ethan of anything, least of all that she loved him.

"I've not loved a man before, except for my pa," she said, setting the rabbit aside. Her appetite had vanished. "You're the first."

"Kate." Ethan grabbed her hand, drawing her gaze back to him. "I don't want you to regret this."

"Do you regret this?" she asked pointedly.

He leaned his forehead against hers. "No."

"Then we'll work this out. I'll talk to Charley, and I'll explain everything. I came to you, remember? I wanted to be with *you*, Ethan."

His mouth crushed hers and despite the grime of the past days she cherished the contact and savored his touch. Nothing mattered. Her arms embraced him as the kiss deepened and his hands pulled her to him.

"I've missed you," he breathed into her mouth.

"Not as much as I've missed you." She kissed his face and his chin then buried her face into his neck. He brought her closer and her body responded, the pleasure from the contact sliding through her. Her hands fumbled with his shirt, trying to find a way to his skin.

"Kate." Ethan pulled back. "We can't. Not here." But he kissed her again, his hunger flaming her own.

"Then where? I want you."

He stood and pulled her beside him, glancing all around the area, his shallow breathing matching her own. Grabbing her hand, he led her through a thicket of shrubs and trees to a small alcove that provided shade against the cliff face and some semblance of privacy. It was good enough for Kate, and apparently for Ethan, too, since he pulled her into the shady area, pressed her against the rock, and kissed her until she gasped for breath. His hands grasped her buttocks, then moved to her breasts. She was on fire, desperation compelling her to remove the clothes between them.

Ethan pulled her shirt ends free then opened two buttons before pushing the garment down her shoulders to bare her breasts. Before she could release her arms, his mouth went to work, sucking and nipping first one breast then the other, his hands squeezing. She closed her eyes, hardly able to stand it, then he kissed her, long, deep, and hard, and his hands yanked the trousers down from her hips. Her boots created an impediment they couldn't get past, so Ethan had to stop his relentless assault on her to untie her shoes and pull them from her feet.

She laughed, nervous and excited, and pushed her pants down her legs, tossing them aside. Ethan dropped his trousers and lifted her legs to wrap around him. She gripped his shoulders as he slid into her.

And then Kate was lost. Ethan took her against the rock, dragging wave after wave from her climax. She clung to him, shaking, completely overwhelmed as his hands held her tight, and all either of them could do was try to catch their breath.

"I love you, Kate." Ethan buried his face into her neck.

Overcome by the release of emotion between them, Kate held fast to him, the tension from earlier draining away. Her cheeks stung from rubbing against the stubble on his face, but she didn't care. She couldn't imagine ever being parted from him.

## Chapter Twenty-Five

Ethan gathered the remains of his pa and moved the bones to a shallow grave he had dug nearby. It was early morning and Kate still slept near the alcove where he'd taken her the previous afternoon. He'd moved Whiskey and Alo nearby and unloaded all the gear so as to sort through what supplies remained. There was enough food and water, for now, but they couldn't abide in this place indefinitely.

To Ethan's surprise, Bart had stayed close. Even now, the wolf was curled up beside Kate.

She was clearly exhausted, as was Ethan, but he'd loved her once more during the night. Maybe it was the fear of searching for her the past few days, worrying that something might have happened, or maybe it was the fear that she harbored feelings for Charley, but either way, he'd been unable to hold back from her, to claim her as his own, to show her how he felt and that she belonged with him, and not with Charley.

He hadn't seen Charley since yesterday. He should look for him, and he would, but first he needed to do something with his pa's remains. He was glad for the diversion of the physical labor; it let him give Kate a rest, because God knew he ached to have her again. It also helped him work out his frustration about his brother. If Charley really wanted Kate, then he'd have to get through Ethan, a thought he didn't want to consider. He doubted their relationship, what little there was of it, could withstand it.

He didn't have a shovel so had to use a sharp rock, and then finally, his hands. He paused and looked at what was left of the bear. Remnants of dust-covered fur clung to the nearby shrubs. Cal Barstow's spirit was intertwined with the bear, even in death. Ethan collected the animal's remains and placed them in the grave with his pa's bones then covered the hole with dirt. He patted the ground, wiping sweat from his forehead with his arm, and sat back on his heels.

He stood and walked to the head of the grave, where a gravestone should be placed, but he had none. Maybe it was for the best. His pa had loved this area, and now he could finally find peace. Ethan remained silent for a time, unsure what to say.

"I haven't always been the man I wished to be, and I hope you can forgive me for not being able to save you the day this happened." Tears burned Ethan's eyes. "I've missed you a lot. I'll try to do better with Charley. I'll try to make you proud. With hope, you're in Heaven with ma. Give her a hug for me."

Ethan leaned forward, scooped a handful of dirt, and let it fall through his fingers onto the burial site. "Farewell, Pa."

---

KATE AWOKE on Ethan's bedroll, alone, and with a glance at the rock where he'd taken her, her body responded with a longing for him. She stood and dusted off her clothes, tucking her shirt and making certain all the buttons were secure, then she ran fingers through her hair and braided it. She found Ethan standing beside a fresh grave.

"Did you bury your father by yourself?" she asked.

He nodded.

"You should have woken me. I could've helped."

The look he gave her told her his skepticism.

She smiled. "I would've gotten up for you. All you have to do is ask."

"I know," he replied. "I wasn't sure what I was doing until I started. It was easier just to finish it myself."

"At least, now you know for certain what happened."

"We should leave soon," he said. "There's no reason to stay."

"Where's Charley?"

"Hell if I know. I haven't seen him since yesterday morning."

"We should at least look for him."

"We've been doing nothing *but* looking for him." Ethan's frustration was evident in his exasperated tone. "I'm not sure why I've been trying so hard with him. It seems it's all been for nothing."

Kate understood Ethan's feelings, but couldn't help correcting him on one point. "It hasn't all been for nothing, Ethan," she said quietly. "You finally know where your pa has been all this time." She hesitated, wondering if she was overstepping, but finally added, "And *we* found each other."

Ethan moved to her, removed his hat and leaned in for a kiss. Her mouth met his and she didn't hide her response to his touch.

"I stand corrected," Ethan murmured against her mouth. "It's all been worth it."

---

By NIGHTFALL, Ethan had tracked Charley's trail into a narrow slot canyon, the red cliffs rising at least thirty feet above them. He signaled Alo to stop, feeling uncertain.

"What's wrong?" Kate asked from behind.

Whiskey neighed and flicked her head, agitating Alo. The two of them had been dancing around one another since meeting two days ago. While Ethan could appreciate the potential attraction between the stallion and the mare, he really couldn't give them any time to pursue it.

"Why would Charley come here?" he murmured.

"We can't just abandon him," Kate replied, but the resignation in her voice matched Ethan's. He was getting close to the point when he might do just that.

He moved Alo forward and the horse nearly ran into Joe Tohonnie. The sudden stop brought another round of skittishness from Whiskey.

"What the hell, Joe!" Ethan tried to manage Alo so that Kate could calm her horse, but both animals were none too happy about the Indian's presence.

"Well then, it is time for you to come with me." The Indian turned and walked farther into the canyon.

Ethan hesitated. As Joe moved away the outline of his body could barely be seen. Was Ethan imagining him?

"Kate?" he said, swinging Alo around to face her.

"I know. I see him too."

Her conflicted expression matched his own.

"Should we follow?" he asked.

"We've no reason not to trust him."

Ethan pulled the gun from his holster. "Stay close." He let Alo pick his way into the enfolding darkness.

For a time, it felt as if they wound through a maze, the sandy trail slowing the horses. The moon shone above, not quite full, lighting the way. Ethan had lost sight of Joe, but it didn't seem to matter. They could only move forward unless they turned back. Ethan was about to suggest just that when slight movement ahead caused him to halt the horses.

Ethan thought he could see the dark outline of a figure. It appeared to be sitting near a tree with long, leafless branches rising from the ground like a spider.

Out of nowhere Scorpion appeared, startling Ethan, and he

reflexively raised his gun. The Navajo man didn't speak, and Ethan didn't lower his weapon.

"How did you find us?" Kate asked.

Scorpion didn't answer but continued to stare from his position beside Alo. Slowly, Ethan dropped his gun but something about the other man didn't seem right.

"At last, you've come," Scorpion said. He turned and walked away.

"What's going on?" Kate asked, confusion and fear lacing her words.

Something was wrong, and Ethan didn't like it. "We should leave." He guided Alo around so they could backtrack the way they'd come, but the horses became agitated again and Kate struggled to control Whiskey. Ethan tried to reach out and grab the mare's reins but couldn't. He finally dismounted and Alo immediately bolted into the night.

"Get off!" he yelled before Whiskey threw Kate.

She complied and slid to the ground with a thud.

Ethan spent several minutes soothing the mare with his voice until the animal quieted.

"You must stay," Joe said.

Ethan didn't look at the apparition. "You keep startling the horses," he said. "Could you please stop?"

"No," Joe answered. "I need your help. Tie off the animal and come."

A man's agonizing scream pierced the air.

"That's Charley." Kate took off running.

"Kate! No!" Ethan quickly wrapped Whiskey's reins on the brittle branches of a bush and bolted after her.

She halted at the figure against the tree. "Charley?"

Ethan raised his gun again and scanned the surroundings.

"Please help me." Charley's voice cracked.

Kate fell to her knees beside him.

Charley was tied to the tree, his hands bound behind him and his feet roped off.

"Who did this to you?" Ethan asked.

"That one," he mumbled, barely able to lift his head, "the one you call Scorpion."

A heaviness hung in the air as though many eyes watched from the crevices and shadows that surrounded them. Ethan assessed the danger and his options. He wanted Kate out of here, but he didn't want to leave Charley if he was hurt. And Scorpion was somewhere, but Ethan couldn't pinpoint his location.

"Ethan, do you have a knife?" Kate whispered from her crouched position. "We need to cut him free."

He agreed. Unfortunately, his knife was with Alo, running somewhere in the wilderness.

With a prickly unease tingling down the back of his neck, he chanced a glance at Kate and his brother.

And then, everything went dark.

---

THE FIRST THING Ethan noticed was the throbbing pain behind his eyes as he abruptly came awake. His hands were tied behind him, his feet bound. He sat not far from Charley, imprisoned in the same way as his brother. He scanned the area but couldn't see Kate anywhere.

Scorpion approached from a dark entrance to Ethan's left. It must be a cave.

"Where's Kate?" Ethan asked.

"She is not dead, if that is what you fear." Scorpion carried a large wooden bowl and set it on the ground. "It is not she I tried to guide here."

"You've been trying to guide us?" Ethan asked.

"No, your brother. It was I who sent two *Diné* to summon him with a story of my own making."

"Why?"

"Because of your father." Scorpion sat on the ground and began scooping piles of something on the ground and putting it into the bowl.

Ethan strained his eyes in the darkness and alarm coursed through him when he saw pieces of scorpions and some type of meat, likely animal flesh. Were he and Charley to be forced to eat this unappetizing meal? He strained against the ropes around his wrists, but they were drawn tightly together. He tested his leg muscles and tried to free his feet, but they were just as securely bound.

Where was Kate?

"What did my pa do to you?" Ethan asked. It must be serious. Scorpion had gone to great lengths to lead them to a remote place among the desolate valleys inhabited by the Navajo. But hadn't Luci and Joe led them?

Scorpion used a smooth-ended rock to grind the mixture in the bowl he held. "Your father and K'aayelil."

"What about them?"

"I need to undo a trickery they did, and for that I need Charley, or you. When I lost the trail of Charley, I thought it was luck to find you." Scorpion raised his gaze to Ethan. "I knew I could bring you here." He went back to his gooey mixture and shook his head. "But your wolf protects you. It is a problem. Your wolf is maybe a *yee naaldlooshii*. But I cannot tell."

"What's that?"

"A skinwalker, a shapeshifter."

Dread slid around Ethan, slowly tightening its grip.

They were in trouble.

He struggled again with the rope around his wrists. He wouldn't let Scorpion kill Kate, or Charley.

"But no matter now," Scorpion continued. "You are here. You will speak to K'aayelil. You will find how to undo the binding."

"What're you talking about?"

"I do not think your father told you of the night he and K'aayelil were here, many years ago."

Ethan twisted his wrists again. There was a little slack, very little. He kept working at it.

"They thought they had come in contact with a *chindi*."

"What's that?"

"An evil spirit. But they were wrong, it was not evil. But they bound the spirit to this place. I am here to set it free."

"Why would you want to do that?" A shiver of unrest snaked down Ethan's spine.

Scorpion looked at him, quiet in the darkness surrounding them. Then he stood and walked away with his bowl of whatever it was he was concocting. Ethan was beginning to think the spirit in question, whether it was real or not, was perhaps not as innocent as Scorpion implied.

## Chapter Twenty-Six

There was movement all around her. Kate could feel many people in the darkness, shuffling along the dry creek bed, others standing near the shrubs. As she glanced in all directions, confused, panic began to overcome her. Frightened by the presence of so many and shocked they had appeared as if out of nowhere, she searched her surroundings for a way to escape. A black spot in the rock caught her eye. A cave. Not feeling certain about this at all, she moved toward it nevertheless, more afraid to stay where she was. She backed into the cave trying to watch behind and ahead at the same time, stepping carefully, worried she would trip on some unseen obstacle.

A glow began to build as she went deeper into the cave. Her heart pounded, and a part of her screamed to turn around and leave the enclosed space, but she willed herself to go farther. The light grew and as she rounded a bend she stopped, stunned.

The...*thing*...before her lifted its head and looked into her eyes, paralyzing her. A small creature, humanoid in shape but not human, watched her with a glittering tenacity. Its arms were too long, its legs folded beside it as it squatted on a rocky ledge.

*You have come to free me,* it said, but its mouth didn't move.

Kate opened her eyes, the dark night surrounding her, and awareness flooded her. She'd been dreaming. Thank goodness. But then her predicament became apparent.

She was alone, lying on her side on the ground, her hands cinched behind her and her feet tied off. As her mind cleared, she remembered that it had been Scorpion who had done it. He had jumped them, somehow overpowered Ethan, and had knocked her to the ground. The right side of her skull throbbed, likely where he had hit her.

She struggled to sit upright but couldn't, then strained her neck to see if Ethan and Charley were near but saw no sign of them.

"I knew this would be difficult."

Kate jerked her head over her shoulder. Joe! She was glad to see him and angry at the same time. It would seem he'd brought them nothing but trouble.

"You better help me," she demanded.

"Yes. But you must promise to do something for me in return."

Frustrated, she wanted to scream but refrained, uncertain of where her captor might be. "You sure have a lot of gumption, Joe," she ground out softly, her voice lethal.

"You must help me kill Scorpion."

"What? Is that what this has been about all along? You want Scorpion killed?"

"No!" Nascha suddenly materialized.

Joe was gone. *Of course he was!*

"Nascha, untie me," Kate pleaded.

The woman rushed to Kate's side, sinking to the ground on her knees. "You cannot kill him," she commanded, her face close to Kate's, her eyes frantic and wild.

"Can you untie me?" Kate asked, exasperated by the Navajo saga of which she now found herself involved.

"You must promise me, Kate. You must promise that you will not harm Scorpion."

*Why did everyone demand promises?*

"I have no idea what's going on," Kate said. "I think Scorpion has Ethan and Charley. We have to try and help."

"Please." Nascha didn't move.

"Nascha, I have no intention of killing Scorpion, but I think he's dangerous. We're wasting time. Untie me, dammit."

The other woman hesitated but appeared to compose herself, then stepped over Kate's body and began to work at the bindings. Finally, Kate's hands were free. She set to work on her ankles, but they wouldn't budge.

"Do you have a knife?" Kate asked.

Nascha's look said she did, but it was clear she didn't trust Kate.

"You can cut the ropes," Kate said. "I promise I won't touch the knife."

Nascha pulled a small blade from behind and set to work sawing at the rope around Kate's feet. When at last she was free, she stood and flexed her legs.

"What does Scorpion want with Ethan and Charley?" Kate asked.

"I am not certain. But following him here has confirmed my suspicions."

"And what would those be?"

"Many months ago, when Scorpion had returned after being gone, he was different. He was not the same with me." Nascha glanced all around them in a nervous gesture and stepped closer to Kate. In a low voice, she added, "I cannot say the word, what I believe him to be, for saying it could summon it. He is not right, and we must get it out of him."

"Get what out of him?" Kate whispered, feeling vulnerable and exposed in the dark.

"The evil spirit."

Kate's dream came to mind and she shivered. In this place, feeling as if eyes watched them from the bushes, fear began to build. "Do you think Scorpion will hurt Ethan?"

"I do not know."

"Do you know how to expel an evil spirit?"

"I know enough to try."

"Have you done it before?"

"No."

*Just great.*

---

ETHAN FELT Joe Tohonnie before he saw him, a shadow a few feet away.

"What's going on, Joe?" he asked.

Charley's head snapped up. "What happened to the copper mine?"

Joe ignored him and spoke to Ethan. "I will tell you why you are here. It was the year before your father died. He had come to this place like he had many times before. He had always felt drawn to the land. There is an energy that is special. I often told him he had the heart of a *Diné*, that he was a Navajo in spirit. But there are many other spirits here as well, and one must take care. Calder Barstow did not always believe in the warnings I gave him. We were in this place, enjoying our time together and on our way to see Luci, when he became agitated."

"Why?" Ethan asked.

"Calder became possessed."

"You're saying my pa was possessed by an evil spirit?"

Charley made a sound of contempt.

Joe moved closer and Ethan could see his face now. He appeared damn real, unless Ethan was so lost in the shadows that he couldn't distinguish the boundaries between the real and the unreal any longer.

"Yes," Joe replied.

"How did you know this?"

"The man that was your father was still there, but he became more and more unbalanced. I have dealt with such things before. I knew he was filled with a vermin."

"What happened?"

"I knew I had to cast out the entity, which I did. Then I used Calder's blood to bind the spirit to this place."

"But it's escaped?" Ethan asked.

"It would seem a part of it has. That piece has entered Scorpion, and now it wishes to free all of it."

"Why does it need Charley and me?"

"It needs Calder's blood to free itself. That blood flows through your veins, and through Charley's."

"Scorpion said he needs you to undo the spell."

Joe hesitated. "Perhaps. But if we destroy him, I can help you restore the entity completely to this place."

Ethan didn't like the turn of the conversation. "Is that necessary?"

Joe nodded.

"Why did that bear kill my pa? Did it have something to do with this?"

Joe paused before speaking. "Perhaps. I was not with Calder when he died. I cannot know why he would return to this place. Maybe he was curious."

Grief pushed at Ethan. He'd journeyed here all those years ago with his pa but hadn't understood why they had come. He wished he had. Maybe he could have helped; maybe he could have prevented his pa's death...somehow.

Charley shook his head. "So, there never was anything valuable out here? I came all this way for nothing?"

"Not for nothing," Joe replied. His gaze held Charley's, who stilled under the scrutiny, finally sighing as he accepted the strange circumstances in which they now found themselves.

"Can you get free?" Ethan asked his brother.

"No. I've tried."

"Yeah, I can't either."

"Then what are we gonna do?"

"I'm not sure." Ethan twisted his wrists again but had no luck once again in loosening the knots.

He was about to ask Joe for help, but they were once again alone.

---

KATE AND NASCHA hid deep in a thicket and deep in the shadows. They heard the muted sounds of conversation drifted to them, and Kate thought it might be Ethan and Charley. Twice, they noticed Scorpion in the distance, moving along the dry creek bed.

"Can we sneak behind him and hit him with something?" Kate whispered. "A rock or a stick?"

Nascha adamantly shook her head, glaring at Kate. "Would you strike Ethan in such a way?" she demanded in a furious, hushed tone.

Kate's stomach flipped. No, she could never bring herself to hurt Ethan. Nascha's concern was understandable, but with that option gone, Kate wondered what else they could do. Scorpion was too big for either of them, or both, to wrestle him to the ground and tie him up. If she could find Ethan and Charley, then maybe they could help. She signaled for Nascha to follow her.

Kate moved slowly, as much from the darkness as not wanting to alert Scorpion to their presence. Of course, he would no doubt realize soon enough that she'd disappeared from where he had left her. They didn't have much time.

Fortunately, the soft ground—a thick, fine sand—masked the sound of their movement as they crept to the right, Kate instinctively hoping this direction would lead to Ethan. If she and Nascha couldn't do something to help *now*, Kate feared by morning it would be too late.

Although the rock-against-the-head scenario was a bad one, her mind kept coming back to it. Would she have the courage to do it? With hope, it wouldn't permanently injure Scorpion, and instead would just knock him out. But if she tried this plan, she wouldn't have Nascha's cooperation, let alone her help. It would have to be done swiftly and with enough force to make certain he was unconscious before Nascha was even wise to it.

What other options did she have?

Male voices halted her and Nascha's progress, and Kate tried to see through the shrubs from their hiding place. The muffled sounds soon gave way to a bickering that Kate knew all too well.

Clive, Harry, and Rufus.

Now what? If she alerted them, they'd likely not only give away their presence but hers and Nascha's too. Too risky. On the other hand, they could use their help.

What was wrong with her? Those three had proven time and again they weren't reliable or trustworthy, and possibly dangerous to boot. But she was fast becoming desperate.

"I told you I saw somethin' around here earlier," Harry said.

"We should be quiet," Rufus said, his low voice still loud enough to reach Kate's ears. "It's too damn spooky here at night. We should make camp and figure somethin' out tomorrow."

"I think you might be right," Clive said. "We'll set up right over here."

Kate couldn't believe it. The three buffoons were making camp right next to Scorpion. It seemed unlikely any of them would make it through the night at this rate.

Nascha nudged her, an incredulous expression on the woman's face, and all Kate could do was shrug.

Nascha leaned close and whispered, "We have to tell them."

Kate shook her head. Nascha didn't know about their recent criminal activity of abducting Charley and then Kate, and Kate didn't really have the time to explain it all to her.

Nascha nudged her again.

Reluctantly, Kate began moving when activity to the left caused her to crouch again quickly, bumping into Nascha as she pushed back to their hiding spot. A tall figure approached the three men. Scorpion.

Harry and Rufus looked startled by the Navajo man's sudden appearance but not Clive. Kate frowned. They could barely hear what was said.

"...are you doin' here?" Harry asked. "Do you know where the mine is?"

"We're here like you said," Clive said to Scorpion, who nodded.

"Like who said?" Harry's surprise carried his voice back to Kate. She crept closer to listen.

"Are we gonna get a cut or what?" Clive asked, looking at Scorpion.

"As we agreed," Scorpion answered. "But first a task. There is a cave near. You must remove what is blocking it inside."

"Why?" Clive asked.

"The mine is inside," Scorpion said.

Clive hesitated. "All right," he said finally. "We'll do it in the mornin'."

"No. This night."

Harry and Rufus, who had stood motionless during the conversation, shook their heads and backed away.

"There could be critters," Rufus said.

"Yep, bad ones," Harry added.

"Clear the cave." And with that statement, Scorpion turned and walked away.

Clive swore, then said, "We better get to it."

"Are you kiddin'?" Harry asked, exasperated.

"We need him for the mine," Clive replied. "Just stop complainin' and let's get it done."

"How're we gonna find the damn cave?" Rufus asked.

"C'mon." Clive started walking away. "It's gotta be over here somewhere."

The three of them disappeared into the darkness.

"What now?" Nascha whispered.

"We need to find Ethan."

With great care, they crept through the brush and toward the direction Scorpion had recently departed.

---

SCORPION RETURNED with his bowl of goo and the shadow of a large knife in his hand. He set the bowl aside and approached Charley, who had dozed, and grabbed him, causing him to jerk awake. As Charley yelled, Scorpion dragged him along the ground near to Ethan and held the knife to Charley's neck.

"Call Joe," Scorpion said.

"I've never been able to summon him at will," Ethan replied, anger rising in him.

"Try." He pressed the blade to Charley's throat. Charley sputtered and tried in vain to struggle against the much larger Navajo man.

Ethan took a deep breath. "Joe? Joe, are you there?"

Nothing.

"Joe, can you show yourself?" Ethan asked into the darkness, feeling foolish and desperate.

Still nothing.

Scorpion cut open the front of Charley's shirt.

"Wait!" Ethan yelled. "He comes when he wants to!"

Scorpion unexpectedly released Charley. "He is weak." The Indian closed in on Ethan, and in one swift motion he retrieved the bowl and cut deeply into Ethan's right forearm. From behind Scorpion braced an arm around Ethan's chest and with incredible strength immobilized him, draining blood from his throbbing arm into the bowl.

A tremor shook the ground. Ethan heard men scream and then a woman's cry. Scorpion grabbed the bowl and fled.

"Charley, are you all right?"

"Yeah."

Someone was behind him.

"Kate!" Relief flooded him. "How'd you find us? How'd you get free?"

"Never mind." She fell against him as the tremor continued but began working a knife on the ropes binding his hands. "We don't have much time. My God, what happened to your arm?"

"It'll be fine," he replied.

With a deafening silence, the ground stopped moving.

Kate freed his hands, and he took the knife from her to cut the cords around his ankles, blood dripping everywhere. He removed his shirt and Kate helped him wrap his arm to stop the bleeding, then he went to Charley and cut him free.

Kate signaled for both of them to follow her. They ran several yards, dry brush and tree limbs scratching their skin and snagging their clothing, when Kate stopped abruptly. Nascha was with Scorpion, speaking quickly and with obvious desperation. She was clearly in danger. As they approached, Ethan pulled Kate behind him.

Nascha flicked her gaze to them but remained focused on Scorpion, who watched her like a mountain lion stalking a fawn.

"In the name that is holy and sacred, you are to be banished from this soul," Nascha intoned under her breath. "We break the spell with the help of the Great Spirit. We call on the help of Bear and the wind itself." She began backing up as Scorpion moved toward her.

A soft glow spilled from a nearby cave, and the sound of men reached Ethan's ears. He readied himself to jump Scorpion before the man could hurt Nascha.

Joe appeared then, standing beside Nascha, and also began chanting in Navajo. Scorpion stopped.

As Nascha and Joe continued their mantra, Scorpion appeared spellbound. Clive exited the cave, moving faster than Ethan would have thought the man capable, and Ethan scrambled to intercept, but Clive got to Nascha first and tackled her to the ground, a scream escaping her throat. Ethan pulled at Clive, kicking the man to get him off the Navajo woman.

When Ethan managed to wrap an arm around Clive's neck, he leveraged hard, choking him. At last, Clive relinquished his hold on Nascha, but during the scuffle Scorpion had grabbed Charley, shoving Kate in the process. She had landed on Scorpion's mysterious bowl filled with animal pieces and Ethan's blood, spilling the contents.

Another tremor struck. Ethan struggled with Clive, holding tight, and finally, the man went limp. Hoping he hadn't killed him, Ethan did a quick pulse check. Still alive. For now. Ethan rose to his feet and searched for Kate, but she was gone, as were Scorpion and Charley.

Joe materialized before him. "You must stop him."

Irritated by the obstacle, Ethan said in frustration, "Scorpion wants *you*. Where the hell have you been?"

"He wants to release the *chindi*. That cannot happen."

"Then help me stop him!"

"There is one way. The wind is the answer."

# Chapter Twenty-Seven

Kate ran into the cave and stopped. A make-shift torch burned in one corner, a pile of wood and small twigs nestled into a niche in the rock. She paused, becoming aware of the red, slimy concoction covering her shirt. Repulsed, she flicked pieces of scorpions and fleshy raw meat from her, registering that the crimson stain now covering her shirt was likely blood.

Unsettled, she scanned her surroundings. A rocky debris field lay strewn several feet into the cave, likely caused by the tremor. There was enough space to crawl through, so she moved to the opening, compelled by a curiosity she couldn't explain. Crouching down, she shuffled on hands and knees to the other side. It was darker now, the light from the fire a faint glow.

As she waited for her eyes to adjust, she sensed movement on the ground. Roaches? When she stooped over to see better, revulsion slammed into her. Scorpions, tan and colorless, crawled around her. With frantic movements, she kicked and stomped her feet.

*Get away! Get away from me!*

All of a sudden, heat washed over her and she became motionless, arms hanging at her side, trying to catch her breath.

Her vision changed and the walls of the cave became crystal clear, the red rock alive before her, every crack, every angle, every shadow visible. The scorpions fled, scurrying to the back of the cave and up the walls.

Confused, she looked at her hands—small, delicate, thin-boned, and dirty. She moved toward the cave opening, and a sharp pain sliced through her side and she doubled over, gasping.

With longing, she approached the opening again.

*Have to get to it.*

As she cleared the debris field, Harry, Rufus, Charley, Scorpion, Nascha, and Ethan formed a half-circle that blocked her from the entrance. They watched her with fear and apprehension in their eyes, as if she'd grown another head or had suddenly contaminated the air they breathed.

*What's happened?*

Kate didn't feel well. She pushed to her feet but swayed from dizziness.

Joe Tohonnie appeared to her right, chanting a low drumbeat of words she couldn't understand. It disturbed her, the intonation of his voice scraping at her insides.

"Stop!" she yelled.

But Joe continued.

The desire to flee became stronger.

Her gaze swung to Ethan's, his eyes filled with determination but also a hint of worry.

"Let me go," she said quietly. "Let me leave."

"What's going on, Kate?" he asked in a low voice.

She flinched from a piercing pain in her temple. Her hand rubbed at her forehead, trying to make it stop.

*He is responsible for killing your father.*

Where had that voice come from?

*That one. The one you love. He killed your father.*

She took a step back, shaking her head back and forth. A scene began to fill her mind, one she was unable to stop.

*Ethan rode a horse at full speed along a dusty road, coming upon a stage racing along swiftly. He pulled his rifle and fired, the staccato of gunshots inside the stage tapping out a deadly rhythm. Kate's pa! A man inside the stage had shot him, along with another man and a woman. Why? He hadn't needed to kill them, had he? Ethan hadn't shot her pa, but he'd pressed on the stage, causing the man inside to murder the innocent bystanders in anger.*

The imagery ended.

Kate met Ethan's gaze. Tears filled her eyes. "You caused my pa to be killed," she whispered.

"What?" His face drained of color.

"The stage you chased. You made the man—his name was Bains—inside so angry he shot everyone. One of those people was my pa."

Recognition registered on his face.

Hopelessness rose in Kate's chest. He *was* the brutal man Charley had said he was. Kate had refused to believe it, but it was true. If Ethan hadn't chased down that stage, then maybe her pa would've been spared. How could this be? How could she love a man who'd been a part of the death of her beloved father?

"Let me pass," she said, her voice gaining authority again.

Joe had never stopped his infernal chanting and she swung her gaze to him. "Enough!" she roared, feeling as if ants consumed her body.

*I have to leave!*

"What's wrong with her?" Rufus asked.

"She is possessed of the *chindi*," Scorpion replied.

Nascha, standing beside the tall Navajo man, turned to him. "And what of you?"

He shook his head. "It is no more inside me."

Nascha looked relieved.

Still, no one would move, no one would allow Kate to leave.

"Kate, I had no idea how many people were on that stage," Ethan began, "and I didn't know one of them was your pa. I didn't even know you then. Bains had worked at our ranch. He killed our cook and raped his wife. My pa and I and Charley found out where he was headed so we didn't wait for the law but took off ourselves. I was headstrong and stupid, I know it now. I'm so sorry. If I could go back and change what happened, I would. Please believe me, Kate. I'd never willingly hurt you." The anguish was clear on his face, his voice hoarse as he pleaded with her. "God knows how much I love you."

Kate wavered, feeling a connection so strong and so deep she almost fell to her knees from the force of it.

*No, he doesn't love you.*

Confused, Kate focused on her pa and the vast loss she had felt when he was murdered. There was no replacing that, there was no putting a bandage on it and hoping it would go away. There was no forgiveness for such a cruel and heinous act.

"Let me pass, I say." She enunciated each word, wondering even as she spoke why her speech had changed. "If you don't, I shall be forced to take drastic measures."

Ethan's face blanched and a muscle in his cheek flexed.

She'd had enough of him. She shifted her focus to Harry and Rufus.

"You two are capable of guiding your own minds," she said, wondering at the force that seemed to flow through her. It made her feel impatient and frustrated.

"She scares me," Rufus muttered. "Maybe we should let her go."

Harry glanced at Joe, who continued to chant, standing with eyes half-closed in a trance. "Maybe we should bury her in the cave," he said.

"Like hell we will." Ethan's voice held no compromise. He took a step toward her, but she stopped him with a stern glare.

"Nascha, can you help?" Ethan asked, not taking his eyes from Kate.

The Navajo woman didn't respond, uncertainty playing across her face. This pleased Kate for some reason.

"Let me pass, Nascha," Kate said. "You have your Scorpion back. Leave now. Return to your life."

"Kate is my friend," Nascha responded. "You can't have her."

Kate looked to the ground before her. Frustration welled up and still that damn Joe kept chanting. "Shut up!" she screamed. "Just shut up!" As she moved toward him, he opened his eyes, bridging a connection to her in his gaze.

*No.* She shook her head slightly. *No, no, no, no.*

She knew the weakness in the group and swung the force of her will to it. Harry and Rufus stumbled backward; she didn't wait. Sprinting forward, she rushed through the gap.

"No!" Ethan yelled. "Grab her!"

But she was too fast and eluded his hands. She ran into the darkness, dodging trees and boulders and shrubs. Her vision was excellent, and her lungs filled with air as she worked this young body. She would be free at last, after all this time. She scrambled over rocks, ignoring the bruised knees and the scrapes on her hands.

All of a sudden, she slammed forward to the ground. Stunned, she spit dirt from her mouth and tried to catch the breath that had been knocked from her. Slowly she pushed herself up, arms shaking. What had she run into? The stars twinkled in a canopy above, and the red landscape glowed in an eerie haze. Nothing was amiss. As she proceeded to continue, yellow eyes and a low growl impeded her path.

Bart?

Breaths came rapidly as her heartbeat kicked up a notch. She didn't fear Bart. Not really. He'd come to accept her, in a way, over the past weeks.

"Easy," she murmured. "It's just me, Bart. It's Kate."

She stepped forward but stopped when he further bared his teeth, a menacing rumble emanating from deep in his belly.

She glanced from side to side, seeking an escape; he stood

nearly to her shoulders and she had no doubt he would tear her to pieces before she could accomplish that feat.

Bart advanced and she was forced to back up. Anxiety mixed with panic and she began to build momentum to push him away, as she'd done with Harry and Rufus. But Bart wasn't weak, not in spirit or intention, and she found the way blocked. She continued to press, her energy building, pulsing with the irritation of her botched getaway. He was a formidable animal, and she could feel his intense loyalty to the humans. To one human. Too late, she realized why. Ethan grabbed her just as she turned to run, trapping her, pinning her arms to her sides.

"No!" she screamed and struggled against his bare chest.

"Kate, stop it!" he yelled. "I'm gonna help you!"

"Let me go!"

He twisted her around, then pushed her to the ground. She fought and cried like a wounded animal about to die.

*You won't take me. You can't take me.*

Ethan wound a rope tightly around her wrists behind her back.

"Take her quickly back to the cave." It was that damned Joe Tohonnie. Kate decided she would vanquish him in the afterlife.

Ethan pulled her to stand, pinching her shoulder blades. She winced from the sharp pain.

"I'm sorry for this, Kate," Ethan said, dragging her along.

She fell to her knees and he yanked her back up.

"I hate you," she spat.

"I think you have every right," he replied, not slowing down, "but I love you and I'll do everything I damn well can to protect you."

"Well, I don't love you." A part of her mind wondered at the spiteful nature oozing from her. Had she always been this awful? Is that why her mama hadn't known what to do with her? And yet she couldn't stop the vitriol coming from her mouth.

"Your pa thought he caused your ma's death," she said. How

did she know that? But she did. "It tore him up inside. He could hardly look at you and Charley without feeling disgust."

Ethan stopped and looked at her. "Why are you saying these things?"

The pain she caused him was so clear on his face, he practically dripped with it. She should stop, but a part of her didn't care. "He loved Charley more than you."

His cheek flexed. She wondered if he would hit her. Yes, he should hit her. That idea was very good.

Joe appeared again. "You must not speak to it," he advised.

Kate flicked a gaze to the Navajo. That's when she understood. "You blocked my escape," she said.

"There was a boundary in place to stop you," he replied.

*How?* He was smart. Smarter than she had ever realized all those years ago.

"Go now," Joe instructed to Ethan.

Ethan continued to drag her along.

They came to the cave again. The others were there, scattered around the entrance, and Bart too, having followed them. Everyone stood, looking worried when they saw the wolf.

"You gonna bury her in the cave now?" Harry asked, keeping his distance.

"No," Ethan answered. "Nascha, Charley, help me." He gestured for them to follow.

Once inside the cave, he pushed her to the ground but didn't release her. Her legs were free, she could run again and he knew it.

*I won't let you trap me again.* Her mind searched for possibilities.

"You must do exactly as I say," Joe said from behind her. "Draw blood from her hand."

She looked into Ethan's eyes and saw the hesitation, the doubt.

"Don't hurt me," she whispered.

He shuttered his gaze, moved behind her, and spread her right hand open. She winced from the pain of the knife slicing through her palm.

She rolled to the side and kicked him in the face. He fell back and she kicked again, hitting his chest as he crashed into the wall. She struggled to stand and run when Nascha shoved her hard to the ground. Kate used her legs again as Nascha fought to contain her. They struggled, screaming and grunting, until Ethan dragged her up hard, and she shrieked from the pain in her arms. Then Scorpion and Charley were there, and she couldn't move.

"Take the blood and make a cross over the cave entrance," Joe said.

Ethan did this.

Kate shuddered. A wave of nausea accosted her.

Scorpion and Charley held her on each side while Nascha sat on her legs. Ethan placed her head on his lap, holding her head firmly. She looked into his eyes, feeling herself sliding away, lost and hopeless, sad and angry.

Joe began chanting again, in a language that made no sense.

Pressure mounted behind her eyes, and she gagged as something moved up her chest. Her eyes rolled back, and she remembered nothing more.

# Chapter Twenty-Eight

E than sat beside Kate, wrapped in a blanket about thirty feet from the entrance of the cave, a cave that was no more. He, Charley, Scorpion and even Clive, Harry, and Rufus had spent the entire morning packing the rocks and boulders back into the entrance, effectively sealing it once again.

Kate had remained unconscious the entire time. Ethan worried over her, but Nascha had kept vigil.

Lee was also mending nearby. Scorpion had ambushed him the previous day and restrained him. Thankfully, Scorpion recalled the incident, and soon recovered his friend.

Clive, Harry, and Rufus argued for some time with Scorpion and Charley about the supposed mine and treasure and riches that had been promised them. It took some doing to convince them they'd been duped, since Charley had been duped, and Scorpion hadn't been in his right mind. He appeared in his right mind now, or so Ethan thought, although he didn't really know the man well enough to know for certain. But after what had happened during the night, Ethan was hopeful that the *presence*, or whatever it was, was contained once again. Scorpion had been contaminated it seemed when, several months ago, he'd been in this area, had slept for two nights near the cave and taken a rock he'd fancied with him. It had been enough to get a hold over him.

Ethan still couldn't wrap his mind around any of it. He wasn't certain he believed in bad spirits that could possess others. But apparently a demon, a *chindi*, had inhabited his pa all those years ago. Maybe, maybe not. Ethan didn't know. What he did know was that his pa had died at the hands of a terrible accident, an ill-timed encounter with an aggressive rogue bear. At least he and Charley could finally put their pa to rest.

"How is she?" Charley asked, approaching from his discussion with Clive.

"The same," Ethan replied. All of this had brought him Kate, a treasure he could never have imagined. And now, through his own actions, he was losing her. The knot in his stomach and the pressure in his chest told him how much he dreaded it.

"How's your arm?" Charley asked.

Ethan hardly noticed. Nascha had cleaned and rewrapped the wound in the same blood-crusted shirt from the previous night. Having recovered Alo, he'd found another shirt in the meager supplies and slipped it on. The sun would beat down on them soon enough.

"Fine," he replied, content to have a giant scar one day. It was the least of the pain he'd endured.

"Did you know it was her pa on that stage?"

Ethan shook his head. "How on earth could I have known that?"

"Yeah, I suppose not. You really care about her that much?"

*Yes,* but instead he said, "Will you take her back to Flagstaff?"

"Why?"

"She won't want to stay with me now, and I can't say as I blame her."

"You gonna give up that easily? I always pegged you as more tenacious than that."

"I think you're talking about yourself, Charley." He rested his gaze on Kate. "I love her. I won't coerce her into staying with me, forcing her to relive what happened to her pa every time she looks at me. Just promise me one thing."

"What?"

"You guard her like she's your sister."

Charley snorted. "I almost married her."

"If it would make her happy, then you should."

Charley stared him, shock registering on his face. "Guess I was wrong about you." He gazed up at the sky. "Guess I was wrong about a lot of things."

Ethan suspected this was as much of an apology that he would get from Charley.

"You're always welcome at the ranch," Ethan said.

Charley nodded.

After all this time, after the weeks of searching, Ethan was satisfied that he had done all he could to repair his relationship with his brother.

"We certainly have a knack for picking the wrong women," Charley said.

"This is where I'll disagree with you." Crossing paths with Kate would never, in Ethan's mind, be the wrong choice for him. If only he could go back and change what had happened. If only he hadn't been so stubborn and angry back in his youth, had stopped to consider there might be others in that stage, then maybe the outcome could've been different. God knew the remorse he had felt later when he'd learned of the deaths that had occurred. So he'd left the ranch and found solace in the company of a rough group of men, doing questionable things in an effort for justice. He had found Bains and killed him. It was a side of himself he wasn't proud of, a part he'd tried hard to put in the past. That he would fall in love with the daughter of one of those victims seemed like a cruel joke.

He kissed Kate's cheek and smoothed her hair gently with his hand. "Be safe, Kate."

As he departed, riding Whiskey and Brandy trailing close, Bart appeared. The wolf stared at Kate's slumbering form and for a moment Ethan thought the animal might leave him and stay with a new master, but with Nascha and Charley nearby, Bart decided not to approach. Turning, he trotted after Ethan.

A wind blew from the east as they climbed out of the canyon, and dozens of clouds dotted the late-day sky, casting shadow after shadow on the red-hued land.

It had a beauty to it, of that there was no doubt.

*May Pa rest in peace in this place.*

And may Kate find the happiness that he was ultimately unable to give her.

With a heavy heart, he headed home.

# Chapter Twenty-Nine

K ate stopped and stared at her weaving. She had wanted to
honor her pa by creating a blanket with his likeness, but
she'd never been good at faces. So she had decided to put Fred the
donkey into the design. But now, it would seem the creature
looking back at her was something else.

Bart.

Her fingers played idly with the loose strings. She set aside her
weaving comb and wondered how to proceed. Ethan came to
mind, as he did daily, hourly. It was an ache she had no balm to
ease.

She missed him beyond comprehension. At the same time, she
couldn't reconcile his actions in the death of her pa. She despaired
over ever seeing him again while also mourning her pa and the
agony of loving the one thing that had been a part in his death.

Ethan had left her by the cave. When she'd awoken, he was
gone. Charley had explained it all to her, but it still felt like the air
had been drained from her lungs. Thankfully, there had been many
things since to occupy her time. The return trek with Charley had

brought her back to Guy, Popay, and Mashi. Charley had Alo and they'd returned him to Masito. Seeing the children had been bittersweet, reminding her of the time they had spent together, time with Ethan. She promised to visit again since they were despondent over having to return to the boarding school at Keams Canyon, and that she would write to them each week.

There had been endless negotiations with Clive, Harry, and Rufus, mostly over the animals. It seemed that Ethan had privately settled Charley's debt with the three hooligans, as well as Charley's debt with herself, but Clive couldn't abide losing some of the horses or Fred. It took some doing, but Kate had prevailed and both Pick and Fred were now in her possession, stabled at the nearby livery in town. Clive, his brother Harry, and cousin Rufus had decided to make their way to Creede, Colorado. She'd felt a surprising twinge of sadness at their departure. As annoying, as worrisome as they had been, they were a part of the adventure with Ethan.

There had been no more visits from Joe, but thankfully, Luci had returned to her people and was recovering. Kate felt a stab of jealousy that Scorpion and Nascha appeared to be headed toward a happily-ever-after. She had wanted that with Ethan, but now it was gone, nothing more than a memory.

Some nights she dreamt of him, of his touch, his scent, his essence—of everything he had been to her. She would wake wanting, her body humming with desire, and she would roll to her side and cry, feeling lost and desperate for the ache to leave. Surely, it would subside eventually. She just needed to suffer until it did.

There were also the more unsettling dreams of...she couldn't name it but felt certain it was when she'd been in possession by something not of this world. Charley had filled her in, but she had to admit she couldn't recall most of it. But sometimes, deep in the night, when her mind was at rest and the shadows came forward, her dreams would remind her of the longing to be free, the longing to flee. But wasn't this from somewhere deep inside herself? Hadn't she always wanted to escape, from her family, from the simple life they represented, from the memories of her childhood with her pa?

She would awake unsettled and trace the scar on the palm of her right hand. Blood had been taken from her; at times the wound throbbed and ached. Had a piece of her remained in the land of the *Diné*? And if it did, was it there willingly? Or should she rescue herself?

Sometimes she thought to go to Ethan, demand he explain why he would simply walk away from her and everything they had shared, demand why he could have been such a single-minded and ruthless man in his youth, demand that he stop making her ache for him. Demand that he return her pa to her.

She resumed her weaving. She sat in her room at Mrs. Finley's boarding house, the loom and piles of yarn occupying one corner while a bed, nightstand, and bureau were pushed into the opposite corner. She liked having space when she worked.

It was late in the night and she couldn't sleep once again, an oil lamp glowing nearby. It was when she had done most of her weaving of late. Her days had been spent keeping busy with chores and errands for Mrs. Finley, cooking and cleaning, whatever needed to be done. The busier she was, the less time she had to think of Ethan and of her pa.

She gave in and began weaving a likeness of Bart, wondering how he was. When she had awakened at the cave, Ethan was gone and after a time she realized Bart was, as well. When was the last time she'd seen the animal? She couldn't recall. According to Nascha, the wolf had been present at her...*depossession*. Is that what it was called? She had no idea. But she couldn't deny it gave her some comfort to know that Bart had been there, watching the shadows that no one else could. If she were being totally honest, then she had to admit she found comfort in knowing that Ethan had been by her side, as well.

She turned her thoughts to the coming day. She had written to her mama, telling her she wanted to come for a visit. Her mama had replied, saying to stay put. She and Jim, Kate's stepfather, were planning a trip to Flagstaff. And today was the day they were to arrive.

Kate almost wept thinking of it.

She missed her mama. She imagined if she could just lay her head in her mama's lap all her cares and worries would vanish.

---

LATER THAT DAY, Kate took Mrs. Finley's horse and buggy to the train depot, Pick doing the driving. She tied off the mare and stroked the horse's nose. Pick snorted and nuzzled Kate, which made her smile. The horse seemed glad to be home after their grand adventure north.

*And it was an adventure.*

A wave of longing swept through Kate, for the wide-open spaces of the land of the Navajo, for the breathtaking red rock, for the look in Ethan's eyes when he touched her, for the feel of his arms around her—

"Kate!"

She turned to see Charley striding toward her. She had seen very little of him upon their return, since there hadn't been much to say. She had heard from Mrs. Finley that Agnes hadn't been pregnant, that her folks had gotten fed up with her behavior, and they had sent her to San Francisco to live with a cousin.

"It's been a while," he said, once he caught up to her. "How are you?"

She plastered her best smile onto her face, not unlike the one she had given Ethan months ago in the woods upon their first meeting. "I'm fine. I really thought you might have gone to San Francisco to find Agnes."

"Yeah, I thought about it. She and I've exchanged a letter or two. I don't think it's gonna work out with us." He paused. "I guess you heard about the baby."

Kate nodded. "I'm sorry for that." But she really wasn't. Charley didn't have the capacity to settle down, and Agnes had shown more flare for drama than Kate had at first realized about her friend. She had been rather relieved to be free of both of them since her return to Flagstaff.

"You might be happy to know that the hex has been removed," he said. "I heard from Nascha that once the business with Scorpion was cleared up, her father didn't have any trouble getting rid of it."

"That's reassuring to know," Kate replied, although she had scarcely given it a second thought. That hex had hardly been weighing on her mind, what with everything else at the forefront of her thoughts. And his name was Ethan.

"What brings you to the station?" he asked, glancing at the large stone building.

"My mama is due to arrive at noon."

"That's great news. I'm sure you'll be happy to see her."

Kate smiled again, a forced and courteous response. Charley resembled Ethan just enough to make her heart twist.

"He asks about you," Charley said, "all the time, I might add."

Feeling her throat tighten, she nodded and looked to her feet, hidden in the folds of her dark skirt. "It's good the two of you talk now. Family is important."

"Kate, I know I've said a lot of things against him in the past, and the past can't always be reconciled, even if we want such a thing. But I think Ethan really wishes he could change what he did."

Kate gazed into Charley's eyes, green and familiar and so achingly reminiscent of a similar set of blue ones, and smiled again, this time with a heartfelt surge of fondness for him. She had always liked Charley, had always found him funny and easy to be with. But he reminded her too much of Ethan, and for that, she needed to keep her distance.

"Well, I do wish him the best," she forced herself to say. "Please let him know that I'm fine."

The distant sound of a whistle signaled the impending arrival of the train.

"I'd best go now," she said.

Charley stepped back. "I'll be seein' you around."

She waved and made her way into the train depot and then the platform, trying to keep her thoughts on what lay ahead instead of what lay behind her.

When her mama disembarked, Kate ran to her, threw herself into her arms, and cried.

---

As she sat with her mama in the parlor of Mrs. Finley's boarding house, Kate couldn't help but feel as if some of the weight of the past few months had been lifted from her. It was late in the evening. After her breakdown at the train station, she'd managed to pull herself together so that the three of them could have dinner and visit.

Jim Dawson, her stepfather for the last ten years, insisted they all eat a good meal—pheasant, beans, cornmeal mush, sourdough bread, and peach cobbler for dessert—before retiring to his room, giving Kate and her mama some time alone. Kate was acutely aware that she had never acknowledged what a good man Jim was, how he cared for her ma, how he had treated Kate with kindness this evening.

"You're lucky to have Jim, Mama," she said, sitting on the sofa beside her mother.

"Yes. I know you haven't always accepted him into our life."

"I know. I'm sorry for it."

"It's alright, Kate. I know you're a good girl. I know your heart has always been in the right place." She brought a hand to Kate's cheek. "Where in the world did you get this scar?" She ran a fingertip along the bump of flesh near Kate's eye where Guy had hit her with the rock, a lifetime ago.

A wave of longing coursed through Kate again, for the Hopi children, for Bart, for Ethan. "I have so much to tell you." Tears spilled down her cheeks, her ability to hold it in check suddenly gone.

For the next hour, Kate shared the story, all of it, of her pretend engagement to Charley, her foolhardy plan to pursue him north, her acquaintance with Ethan, the encounter with the children, then the Navajos, even the unexplainable presence of Joe Tohonnie. She told of Clive, Harry, and Rufus, and didn't hold back describing the shooting on the banks of the Little Colorado River and her multiple abductions. When her mama seemed able to handle that news—her only agitation apparent in the furrowing of her brow and the clasping of Kate's hand—Kate knew she needed to say all of it. So, out came the disclosure of her love affair with Ethan, although she glossed over the more intimate details. Kate needed to confess, and she needed a witness. Thankfully, her mama didn't faint.

Finally, she shared the end—the strange doings with Scorpion and his possession, her own behavior when the spirit entered her. Her mama's surprised, gaping expression was the only response she shared, staying silent so Kate could finish.

Then she uttered the words she dreaded, sharing the truth of Ethan's involvement in her papa's death. Her mama's husband.

Kate sobbed and laid her head into her mama's lap.

"Shhh, Kate," she crooned, stroking Kate's hair. "It'll be alright, child."

"I'm so sorry, Mama."

"Whatever for?"

"For loving the man who caused Papa's death." There, she'd said it. That sentiment filled her with so much guilt that she could hardly stomach it.

"From what you've said, there's no clear evidence he did cause Frederick's death. Good Lord, Kate, you've been carrying a burden, haven't you?"

"You must hate me."

"Of course I don't. You're my dear sweet Kate. I could never hate you. And from what you've said, Ethan Barstow sounds like a man who's done his best to right himself. He certainly looked after you. Although I must ask, you're not with child, are you?"

Kate shook her head. "No."

"Well, maybe your pa looked after you on that one. I can't tell you what to do, but it's clear you love this Ethan very much."

"I wish I didn't," she mumbled, clutching her mama's skirts.

"Even if you choose to walk away, it would do you well to forgive him."

"How? Sometimes I miss Pa so much."

"I miss him, too."

Kate sat up and wiped the tears from her face. "How do you cope with it?"

"Well, I have you and Owen and Petey. You all are the best parts of your pa. He lives on through you, and it gives me strength. And Jim understands. That helps a great deal. He lost his wife, if you remember, so we both know there's a part of ourselves that will be forever with them." Her mama smiled. "But life must go on. Your pa wouldn't want it any other way. You were the absolute light of his life. He wouldn't want you to suffer so because of him."

She pushed a bunch of hair behind Kate's ear.

"Do you know what he used to say about you?" her mama continued.

Kate shook her head.

"He used to say you were too smart for your own good. Your tendency to wander would drive me to distraction, but he would say we must let you be you. He said you were in search of something."

"Of what?"

Her mama shrugged. "I think only you can answer that. But you were so special to your pa. Perhaps Mister Barstow saw that as well. I suspect there will be few men in your life who can anchor you. I learned a long time ago that I would never be able to hold you. Your pa even said that you moved like the wind."

The last bit startled Kate. It was the same thing Joe Tohonnie had said to her numerous times.

"You look utterly exhausted," her mama said. "I think you should sleep. As long as you need, Jim and I will be here."

Kate hugged her mother. "Thank you, Mama. I love you so much."

"And I love you, sweetheart."

---

FIVE DAYS later her mama and Jim boarded a stage bound for Grand Canyon. They had invited her to come along, but Kate declined. The days spent with her mama, and with Jim, had gone quickly but had uplifted her spirits so much. She no longer felt adrift in an endless sky of stars.

Before their departure, Jim had given her money folded inside a sheet of paper. She hadn't known what to say. The gesture warmed her heart, and she gave him a hug, something she'd never done in all the time he had been in their lives.

"Thought you could use it," he said. "You take care of yourself. If you ever need anything, you let me know."

"Thank you, Jim."

During the next few days, as she tried to settle back into a routine while missing her mama, Kate ruminated over what she wanted to do, what she needed to do. On the fourth day, she returned to the train station. With the money Jim had given her, she purchased a ticket.

To Trinidad.

# Chapter Thirty

*October 1893*

E than threw another log into the brick fireplace, a blaze igniting. It was damned cold tonight as the wind howled outside the window. He returned to his desk to continue working on the ledger for Barstow Enterprises, shuffling through the bills sitting in a pile. Charges for feed, lumber for the barn repair, and farrier fees stared back.

He rubbed his eyes and sat back in the leather-padded chair.

Bart raised his head from the floor where he lay near the entryway, ears alert like two perfect triangles atop his head.

"Just me boy," Ethan said. "Sorry to disturb you."

Ever since he returned to Trinidad about three months ago, Bart had moved in. It was the damnedest thing, but Ethan hadn't resisted the animal's desire to be closer to him. In truth, Ethan was glad for the company. It wasn't that he was alone—there were the ranch hands, the foreman, Tom Augustus, and his wife, Mary, who cooked and cleaned for Ethan, and the men in the bunkhouse—but Bart seemed to sense that Ethan needed more than just company. His presence was a balm for a very large wound, one that resulted from day after endless day of living without Kate. Truth be told, if it weren't for Mary, Ethan was certain he would've starved himself; Bart wasn't suffering either, having added some pounds to his already lean frame. Eating hadn't been high on Ethan's list of activities to accomplish of late. The older woman's stern and methodical demeanor gave him no room to wiggle out of her directives, but every now and again he saw the look of concern in her eyes. She worried over him.

He worried over himself.

He had left Kate because it had been the right thing to do. He'd been in contact with Charley numerous times since then and had inquired after her. He didn't care what Charley thought. His brother's recent rekindling of contact was something not to be taken lightly it was true, but Ethan had to know if Kate was alright.

She was. Charley had told him such.

That was good. That's what he wanted to hear.

No. He wanted to hear that she was asking after *him*. But Charley never conveyed such interest from her.

So that was it. His relationship with Kate Kinsella was over. He should be able to move on. Why hadn't he then?

Bart flattened his ears, looking annoyed.

The whistling wind caused the big house to creak.

A knock on the door made Bart rise quickly and stand sentry in the foyer. Ethan wondered if the tap was imagined and remained seated, waiting to see if another came. Probably just one of the ranch hands with some concern about the weather and the horses.

A second knock. Ethan stood and walked to the entryway, Bart backing up but still on full alert. The animal's watchfulness caught Ethan's attention; the wolf had been agitated all evening.

Ethan opened the door, then took a step back in surprise.

There stood Kate, bundled up in a tan-colored duster, a scarf wrapped around her neck, her nose red and her hair in disarray.

"What're you doing here?" he asked, shocked.

"Is it alright that I came?" she asked, wrapping her arms around herself.

"Come inside," he replied quickly, moving aside so she could enter, stunned that she was here, with him, in his house, right now.

As she moved past, he shut the door and Bart lunged at her. She let out a surprised scream and caught herself from falling as the beast planted two large front paws on each of her shoulders and began licking her face.

Ethan stared, trying to steady himself. His mind was blank except for one thought.

*Apparently, Bart missed her as much as I did.*

"Oh Bart," she said between licks, "I'm happy to see you too." She laughed and tried to turn her face, but the wolf was persistent.

Ethan caught himself. "Bart, get down." He pushed the wolf back to all fours. "Sorry about that."

"I'm glad to see him too. I thought he didn't like being indoors."

"Yeah, well...." Ethan looked into her eyes, still reeling that she was here. "He decided to move in once we returned." The last part was a mere mutter. Ethan couldn't remember what he said.

"How are you?" she asked.

"Fine."

She glanced around, clearly uncomfortable, the silence dragging on.

"I'm sorry, Ethan, maybe this was a bad idea," she said, her words in a rush. "I thought, well, I guess I didn't really think it through—"

"Why are you here?" he cut in. "Why didn't you tell me you were coming? I would've met you at the train depot. You didn't have to ride out here all alone in the dark and in this weather."

She paused. "I wasn't sure if I was going to come. I wasn't sure if you wanted me to come." Distress pinched her features. "I...I wanted to see you, but if you don't want me here, I'll go."

She started to walk back to the front door. Ethan stepped in front of her, hardly believing she had traveled all this way, that she wanted to see him. She stopped but kept her gaze on his chest.

"I want you here, Kate," he said. "I've always wanted you here."

Her eyes lifted to his. He saw worry and...hope?

"But after what happened, with your pa," he added, "I didn't think you wanted to see me again."

Tears filled her eyes. "It's been difficult for me, I'll admit, but I've been quite lost without you. So I came here to tell you that I forgive you for what happened," she whispered.

Ethan could feel the effort those words had cost her, could see the conflicting emotions on her face.

"Kate." He wanted to touch her but held himself back. "I'd give anything to have you stay here with me, till the end of our days, but I won't make you choose between your duty to your pa's memory and me."

He loved her, and with that love was a desire far beyond himself and his own selfish motives. He wanted her to be happy, even if that happiness was without him.

She didn't respond.

"You're freezing," he said. Now he did touch her, guiding her toward the blazing fire in the sitting room where he had been doing mundane ranch tasks just minutes before.

"My horse." She turned abruptly and bumped into him.

"I'll take care of it," he said. "Stay here and get warm."

He moved quickly to the door, grabbed his coat, and went into the dark cold where Kate's horse was tied at the bottom of the porch.

"C'mon girl," Ethan said, grabbing hold of the reins. He guided the animal to the barn off to the right and made fast work of getting her into an empty stall, removing the saddle, quickly brushing her and making sure she had water and fresh hay. The other horses, agitated by the wind, watched his movements.

*Kate's here.*

The thought turned over and over in his mind. A ray of hope shot through him. Maybe they had a chance.

He finished with the animal, checked the others briefly, then returned to the house. Kate, having removed her coat, sat on the sofa in a dark blue, thick wool walking dress with a string of pearl buttons down the bodice. Bart was curled up beside her.

She turned her head and smiled. "He's so sweet," she said softly, scratching his neck.

Ethan hung up his coat and moved toward the fireplace. "It's amazing how quickly he adapted to the life of a kept creature."

"How are you?" she asked. "You look thin."

Ethan leaned a hand on the mantel. "I suppose I've lost some weight. I guess that happens when you don't eat." He looked at her. "I've missed you like hell."

He saw the brief flash of surprise on her face. "You have?"

"How have you been, Kate? How have you really been?"

"Confused."

Bart raised his head when she stopped scratching. "Sorry," she said, and resumed her ministrations. Bart laid his head back down and let out a contented sigh.

How easy he had converted from a wild animal to a domesticated house cat, Ethan thought. Was it really that easy to reorient one's perspective? Could Kate?

"If I could change that day, Kate, I would. If I could tell my younger self to not act on every instinct, I would. But I can't, and I'm so sorry. You'll never know how sorry I am."

"My mama came to visit a few weeks back, and I told her about you. I told her about everything."

"What'd she say?"

"She said my pa would've wanted me to be happy, that surely from his perch in Heaven he has forgiven all that happened down here."

"She's made peace with it?"

Kate nodded.

"I'll do anything to make it up to you, Kate."

She stared down at Bart as he slept beside her and smiled. "Can we name our first son after my pa?" She glanced up, an expectant glow in her eyes.

"I'll give you anything I can," he replied quietly. "And if that's a proposal, then I accept."

She laughed, startling Bart. Ethan moved to the sofa and shooed the animal away. He held her face with his hands and kissed her with a building hunger and happiness that was more intense than the arousal of his body. He thought he'd lost her, had thought he could bear it only to realize as the days dragged from one to the next that he was slowly dying without her. But he knew he had no right to go to her, to appease the gaping hole she had left with her absence. So, he'd resigned himself to a shadow of a life.

She met his hunger with her own, clinging to him, melting into his embrace as if they had always fit together.

He made love to her on the rug in front of the fireplace, holding her tight and consuming every inch of her, taking none of it for granted, caressing every curve, loving every crevice of her physical self. Later, he carried her to his bedroom, laid her on his bed, and covered her nakedness with heavy blankets and himself.

Holding her close as she fell asleep, he buried his lips into her hair. "I love you."

She burrowed closer. "And I love you."

And in the darkness, she chased the shadows from his soul.

# Epilogue

Freddy and Cal ran out of the house and across the dusty expanse toward the corral. Kate followed behind, determination increasing her pace.

"You boys had better get back here," she said sternly. At six and five years old, they were often in trouble these days.

They rounded a corner and were caught by Ethan.

"Whoa, where you both goin'?"

"Nowhere," Cal squealed.

"Let go, Pa!" Freddy demanded.

Kate caught up and stood before them, arms folded across her chest. "Those little rascals ate two peach pies that I'd just finished baking. There's pie *everywhere*."

"Boys," Ethan's tone was firm, but Kate knew she was the taskmaster. "You owe your ma an apology."

The boys turned, with Ethan behind them, and faced Kate.

"Sorry, Ma," they mumbled.

"But he said it was alright," Freddy said.

"Who said it was alright?" Kate asked, catching Ethan's eye, his concern matching her own.

"An old Indian. He said his name was Joe."

Kate's gaze flew back to Ethan.

"He said he knew you," Freddy continued, "and he knew Grandpa Cal, too. He said he'd look after us."

"And then what happened?" Kate asked quietly.

Freddy shrugged, a smaller version of Ethan. "He said eat the pies. They were good. Then he disappeared. Why haven't we seen him before?"

Ethan's eyes softened, a look she often saw when he was with her, or of late, when he held little Emily in his arms. Speaking of which, their daughter would be waking from her nap soon and be looking for a meal. Kate's breasts felt fuller just thinking of her, all sweetness and wonderful baby smells. She loved her boys, adored them to pieces, but she hadn't realized how much she wanted a daughter until she'd given birth five months ago. She was the apple of everyone's eye.

"Your punishment for misbehaving is cleaning out the horse stalls," Ethan said to the boys. Their shoulders slumped. "Just the last four at the end."

"You old softie," she murmured to her husband as she walked over to the boys. She pulled a damp towel from her apron and wiped sticky pie first from Freddy's face then Cal's. While the older one took it stoically, Cal squirmed and grunted as she wiped most of the evidence from his cheeks. At the first opportunity, he pulled away from her.

"Bet I can do my two stalls faster than you," Cal said to his brother.

Freddy punched him in the arm and the two took off running.

Kate shook her head and turned back to Ethan. "Do you think it was Joe Tohonnie?" she asked.

They hadn't seen Joe since that fateful night when something had crawled inside Kate, the same night Ethan had left her. Like she had every day after traveling to Trinidad to face Ethan and the grief of losing her pa, she silently acknowledged how grateful she was for the life she had, how grateful she was for the beautiful and sometimes exasperating children she had, and most especially how grateful she was for Ethan. Whatever mistakes he had made in his younger days, he more than made up for them now. He loved her with a steadiness that still left her confounded and with an intensity that left her breathless. That amazed her too, how she could love him so much. But she didn't worry over it. Their gift was each day, and she did her best not to waste a one.

Ethan stepped closer and wrapped an arm around her. "What do you think?"

She smiled. "Of course it was him. How could it not be?"

He kissed her, playful and quick, and then long and serious.

She pushed back. "Alright now, we've both got chores to finish. And Emmy will be awake any minute."

"Then later." He nuzzled her neck.

She laughed and spun away. And that's when she saw them, standing about a hundred yards away on a nearby hill. Joe, and her pa, and another man who looked so much like Ethan that she knew it had to be Calder Barstow.

"Ethan." She barely breathed his name.

He came up behind her. "I see them."

"All is well," Joe said, but made no effort to come closer.

Tears ran down Kate's face, and Ethan hugged her from behind.

Bart appeared beside them, clearly watching the three apparitions, and Kate gently laid a hand on the wolf's neck.

A light wind bore down on them, lifting Kate's spirits. Her pa was at peace, and Calder as well. Leaning back, Ethan's strength surrounded her. She had found her home.

---

If you enjoyed *Into The Land Of Shadows*, would you consider posting a review? I'd be most grateful. ~ Kristy

---

IF YOU LIKE westerns with paranormal elements, check out *The Crow Brothers Collection*, a set of three short stories. It's Hallowtide in the Old West. Join three bounty hunters fighting dark magic and the women destined to love them. (kmccaffrey.com/thc-crow-and-the-coyote/)

---

SIGN-UP FOR KRISTY's newsletter to receive her latest book news at kmccaffrey.com/subscribe.

***Don't miss the Wings of the West series***

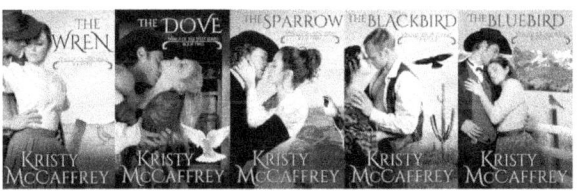

Honorable men and courageous women. Experience the grit, the hope, and the romance of the Old West.

"Ms. McCaffrey writes from the heart…" ~ The Romance Studio

THE WREN – Captured by Comanche as a child, Molly Hart was assumed dead. Ten years later, Texas Ranger Matt Ryan finds a woman with the same blue eyes.

THE DOVE – Reunited with Logan Ryan on the steps of the White Dove Saloon, Claire Waters hides under the guise of a fancy girl…and lets the ex-deputy believe the worst.

THE SPARROW – Within Grand Canyon, raging rapids and ancient spirits sweep Texas Ranger Nathan Blackmore and Emma Hart into a wild adventure.

THE BLACKBIRD – Haunted by a deadly attack, Tess Carlisle turns to bounty hunter Cale Walker to find her missing *padre*. But in the land of the Apache, can he free her heart?

THE BLUEBIRD – Molly Rose Simms arrives in Colorado to meet her brother, but instead finds herself searching for the mythical Bluebird mining claim with a man known as The Jackal.

Learn more about each book at kmccaffrey.com/books

# About the Author

Kristy McCaffrey has been writing since she was very young, but it wasn't until she was a stay-at-home mom that she considered becoming published. A fascination with science led her to earn two mechanical engineering degrees—she did her undergraduate work at Arizona State University and her graduate studies at the University of Pittsburgh—but storytelling has always been her passion. She writes both contemporary tales and award-winning historical western romances.

An Arizona native, Kristy and her husband reside in the desert where they frequently remove (rescue) rattlesnakes from their property and try to coax their American bulldog, Jeb, to go for walks (he's moody and lazy). She also spends her time reading and researching her next book and playing with her three grandchildren.

"It is good to have an end to journey toward; but it is the journey that matters, in the end." ~ Ernest Hemingway

Connect with Kristy
  Website: kmccaffrey.com
  Newsletter: kmccaffrey.com/subscribe
  Facebook: facebook.com/AuthorKristyMcCaffrey
  Instagram: instagram.com/kristymccaffreybooks
  BookBub: bookbub.com/authors/kristy-mccaffrey
  TikTok: tiktok.com/@kristymccaffrey

www.ingramcontent.com/pod-product-compliance
Lightning Source LLC
Chambersburg PA
CBHW070858180626
46817CB00003B/816